Dedicated to:
Bootsie, Cupie, Bear, Hoover, Libby and Bud.
The dogs that have enriched my life
And made it better... Thank You!

Contents

Murder on Hilda
- Slippery Slopes -

Space Detective
A Skip Brown Adventure

Pj Belanger

Cover Art by RB

Murder on Hilda
- Slippery Slopes–

Space Detective
A Skip Brown Adventure

Copyright 2014
BRP Publishing

ISBN 978-0-9916415-5-0

BRP PUBLISHING
Email: pj@pjbelanger.com
Web: http://www.pjbelanger.com

PROLOG

I felt myself tumble. The snow wave hit me as I tried to run away from it. I was suddenly being tossed around like a small rag doll. It mattered little to the snow barrage that I was a large 215lb., 6ft. 1in. man. It tossed me around with such force that I couldn't catch my breath. Time lost its meaning as I was pushed violently forward. When it stopped, I was completely covered, trapped in white silence. I was buried alive in the avalanche.

I tried to remember what I had been taught about surviving such a disaster. First make yourself an air pocket before the snow settles. My arms were spread to the side of me. I slowly brought my arms close to me and inched them up to my face. I dug as big an air pocket in front of my head as I could, stopping only when the snow started caving in.

They had told us at the ski resort that you have just a fifty-fifty chance of digging in the right direction. The avalanche could have turned my body upside down. Panic was rising up into my throat, acid bile was coming up into my mouth. Despite wiggling my fingers, my little blue pills remained out of reach. I didn't need an epileptic seizure just now.

I remembered what my therapist, Dr. Lily, had taught me of taking the time to just relax, to set my mind in a calming mode. I tried not to breathe too deeply. I didn't want to use up my air pocket too fast. My ears caught the sound of the snow starting to crack. No longer silent, the unstable snow layers now tormented me with loud shifting groans.

Did Hill get caught it in too, I wondered? What about Fred, did he make it? They were my only hope. How were they going to find me? *Stop torturing yourself*, I thought. *Keep it positive.* Right! *They will find me, they are still alive! Think productive thoughts.* I could feel my heartbeat was rapidly pulsing in my chest. My brain again tried to calm down.

Well, time to dig upward and pray. I turned my arms and pushed my hands up above my head. I wondered why I wasn't cold, but I wasn't. *Come on, dig*! My mind bent to the task. It seemed forever, my arms were getting tired. I wasn't making much headway and my air pocket was starting to disappear.

I thought of my family, of my detectives, of my big Hiberian dogs. Would they miss me? *Stop thinking*, I yelled at myself to keep digging. I had to rest for a minute. It didn't help that I had little sleep the night before. I was mentally and physically exhausted.

I shook myself psychologically. What good would despair do? *Keep digging*, I yelled into my mushed up brain. *You've been in worse situations.* But of course I hadn't. My body was really in a pickle now. I tried to move my feet but it only caused me to sink lower, so I stopped.

A drop of water fell on my nose, followed by another drop. Water dripped downhill. My head was going in the right direction. Euphoria gave me some renewed energy as I pushed my hand upwards.

More water was dripping on me. A whole bunch of water was flooding my face. I started seeing sunlight. Suddenly, a huge hand reached down and started pulling me up. My jacket and mittens were drenched as the snow was melting around me. I went to yell but the water flooded my mouth making me gag. The hand, however, kept pulling me; the snow falling around me. The sun! The blessed sun hit my eyes! I knew I was crying as I was pulled to freedom. It was the best tears I've ever spent!

MAPS

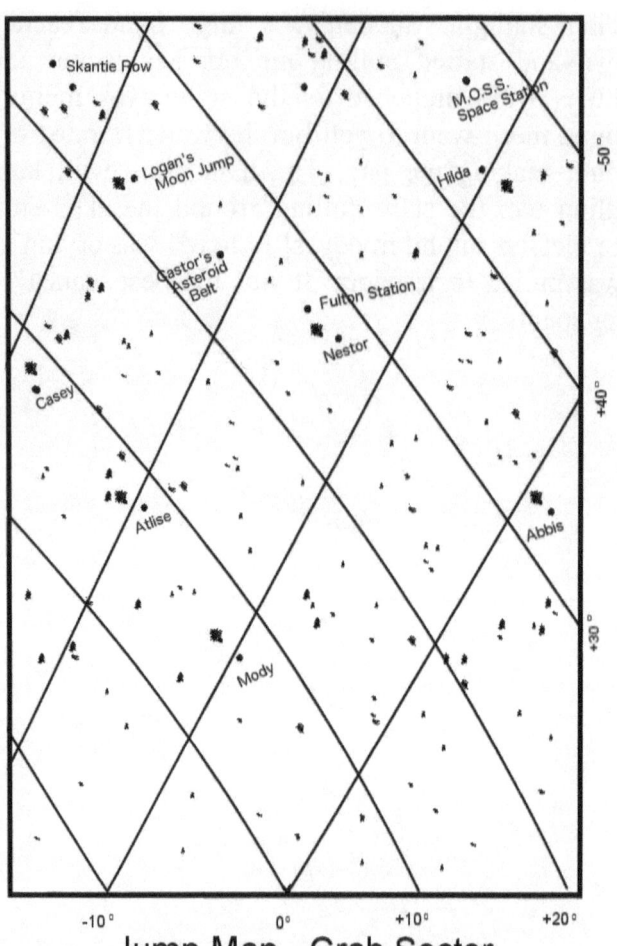

Jump Map - Crab Sector

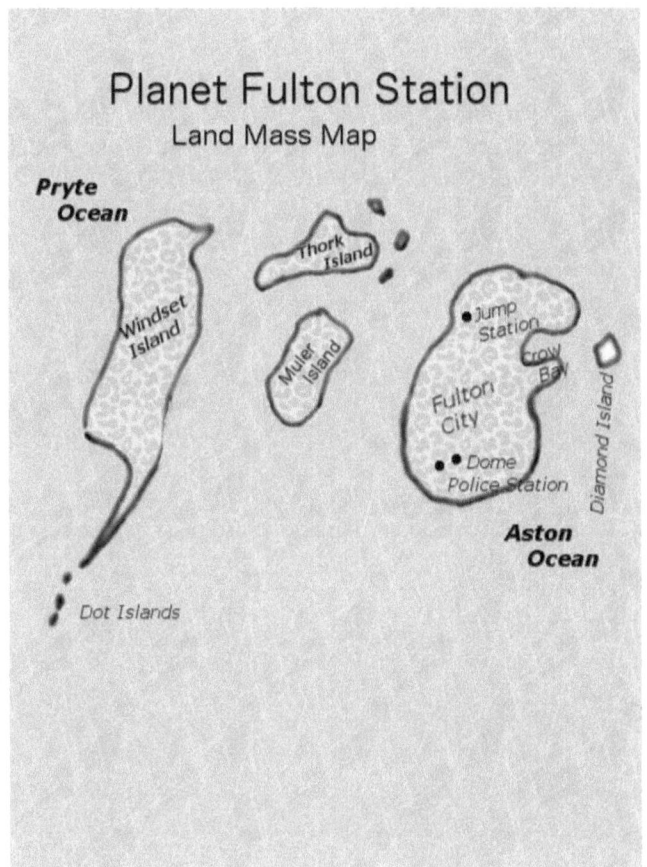

Chapter One

I awoke to two large tongues licking my face. "Come on, guys!" I tried to push them away but they were persistent. *No rest for the wicked*, I thought. The dogs, being large Hiberian hounds, took up most of my bed; they weren't easily ignored considering each weighed close to 190lbs. I grabbed Bear's floppy ears and playfully shook his head. Hoover, not wanting to be ignored, dug his cold nose into my armpit making me jump up.

"I'm awake!" I swung my feet over the side of the bed. I reached over to my nightstand pushing the button on my remote to open the window shades. As the blinds slid open, I could see dawn was just coming up. I glimpsed part of Crow Bay, but only in dark outlines as the sun's rays hadn't fully reached high enough for details. My clock was still dimmed. I touched the top and 05:02 became brightly lit.

"Damn, what are you getting me up this early for?" The dogs usually lay quietly at the foot of my bed until my alarm goes off at 06:30. They are allowed on my bed only to wake me up. Let's face it, we could not all fit, even on a queen sized bed.

I heard what must be Killa banging around some pots and pans in the kitchen. Considering the tiny woman never made noise, she was trying to get me up too! What was my old nursemaid, who was now my apartment complex's superintendent, doing in my apartment so early?

I grabbed my old terrycloth bathrobe, stubbing my toe on my unfinished closet. *Damn*!

One of these days I'd have to finish my apartment. I just didn't have the time to convert the whole top floor. I had managed to build a kitchen, den, half of my bedroom and a nice big bathroom by the stairs going up to the roof. Still, mostly it looked like the warehouse it once was. I'd spent most of my money on completing the other sixteen apartments below me. Fixing this building into viable apartments had cost me double because I'd made them accessible to the disabled.

Hoover bumped against my legs. He wanted his breakfast! My bet was that Killa had sent the dogs in to wake me.

The kitchen lights stung my eyes. "What the hell, Killa?" I muttered, shielding my eyes from the bright lights.

"It is time to get up, Skipper." My old nursemaid, who helped raise me and my brother when my parents died, still thinks of me as a little kid despite the fact that I'm thirty one years old.

Then it hit me, today was Hilda day. I was taking my first vacation in four years. Killa and I were meeting my brother Ray and his family for a skiing holiday. "Our Jump isn't until this afternoon. We have plenty of time," I moaned loudly.

"You haven't even packed yet." The excitement in her voice told me how much this vacation meant to her. Killa, being a Ligithian (from the planet Ligithia in the Orion Sector) was only 4 ft. 2 in. tall, but she was a powerhouse of energy. When she got excited, like now, her eyes were a dark purple, her pure white hair fizzed as if she was receiving an electrical charge, and her small pointed ears twitched. Right now they were jerking quite rapidly.

"I'm not taking much. I don't own any *keeping warm* clothes. I'll have to buy some when we get to the ski resort." Considering our planet, Fulton Station, is one hell of a hot planet with temperatures usually over one hundred degrees, there was no need for cold climate clothes. Our planet was constructed quickly. It was the first planet the engineers put in the Crab sector with the idea that it was to be used only as a base for further sector construction. Thus, the Bassodian engineers spent little time on constructing the planet and planned only the small land mass which became the few clusters of islands we now inhabit. It was originally a place to store equipment and house the construction workers but a little consideration on climate control would have been nice.

Fulton Station was later abandoned, but rediscovered when a location for the new Crab Nebula sector government was needed. So here we are, with each of our sector planets sending two Senators and one Parley (judge) to govern at the Dome. I could see the top of our big government structure from my apartment's large windows that faced Fulton City. Its ornate golden dome ceiling stood out above the other more "quaint" brick buildings including right across the street - my own place of employment - the police department.

At work I wore the lightest suit clothes I could manage to get away with. I am the Chief of Police for the whole Crab Sector. My fifth floor office is located in the yellow brick Police Station building which is a sore blister on the landscape, especially next to our new Dome building. Although the Dome is a new beautifully designed building with a central fountain, manicured lawns, etc., etc., our police station, which is right across the street, is a left over storehouse. Our building, which dates from the planet's beginning, has a wimpy air conditioning system. We depended on old-fashioned power fans; fans in every place we can fit them and lots of deodorant for the stains under our armpits.

"I got some toys and clothes for the baby," Killa pointed over by my elevator. Six suitcases filled my foyer.

"I don't think baby Jim needs too much," I ventured trying not to hurt her feelings but of course, I failed. Her eyes went darker, her hair wilder and the ears twitched faster.

"This is the first time we see him!" she sputtered. "Who knows when we will see him again?"

"Considering he's only two standard federation months old..." I started to say, but she interrupted me.

"I should have been at his birth. I was at yours and Ray's," she teared up. My headache got worse. I slipped a blue pill into my mouth just in case. *This was going to be a stressful day*, flooded into my brain, and an epileptic episode would not help. I felt myself go into "calm mode" just as my therapist had been teaching me. Thank you, Dr. Lily Issam - best damn doctor in the known universe.

I didn't get to reply to Killa as the elevator was coming up. It was Lt. Hill. No matter how many times I tell her to ring, she ignores me and comes right up anyway! She had looked over my shoulder when I put in my security code. Damn nosey woman!

The dogs bounded over to the elevator. Somehow they always knew when it was her. It must be those damn bones she brings for them. She has spoiled my hounds rotten!

Sure enough, Hill came out of the elevator and stoically went down on one knee, grabbing both dogs in hugs. Next she reached into her bag and out came the big bones. They clamped down on the large treats, their jowls puffing out as they ran to a corner to chew on them.

"Hill, stop bringing them bones. And I don't care that you get them from the vet. You're spoiling them. Tonight they won't eat their dry food!"

She just smirked at me, "Well, you won't have to worry now, will you? I'll be feeding them and you'll be on your way to a fabulous Hilda vacation."

Hill was staying at my apartment while we were away. She worked for me; the small intellectually superior woman (so she says) was my newest detective. She had become friends with Killa and had offered to stay at my fifth floor apartment watching the dogs.

"I'll go get the rest of my boxes," she announced. "I left Stanley with Artchie at the front desk."

"You brought your female cat?" I pointed my finger at her, "Are you crazy? The dogs will tear her apart!"

"Really, Skipper," Killa put her two cents in, "what was Judy going to do, leave the poor thing alone?"

"But the dogs…" I tried to make my point but I could tell from the look on their faces it was a lost cause. I shrugged. "I'm taking a shower. I just have to go in to work for one last check."

"I don't think that will be necessary, Chief," Hill remarked as she returned to the elevator. "I'm sure Captain Issam will do just fine."

"When did you take charge of the department, Hill?" I stood there in my bathrobe, hands on my hips challenging her audacity. The woman could be so pushy.

She didn't answer me as the elevator took her back down to the ground floor. I headed toward my bathroom. It was the one room I had really splurged on. I keep adding on to its luxurious features. My shower was huge with multiple showerheads and a drying-off blower. The bathroom was air conditioned and filtered with the smell of a spring morning. I pressed the stereo button and the room flooded with music. The toilet and sinks were in an adjacent section and off to the side was a separate dressing room with a washer and dryer. All my suits were hung up on one side, with my formal "Chief of Police" uniform at the end. I only wore the uniform on special occasions - good thing, it was heavy and hot.

I let the scorching water just soak in. I'd had temperature voice recognition control software added - "Hotter" I said and the water became warmer. The bathroom was just perfect. I had every one of the six jets spraying. The shampoo squirted into my hand and I scrubbed it into my hair.

Suddenly I heard a lot of commotion and yelling in the outer room. "Off!" I yelled; the shower abruptly stopped. Grabbing my bathrobe, I rushed out. The apartment was in total chaos. The dogs were running around barking, knocking everything over. My heavy dining table flew in the air along with four chairs as the two large Hiberian hounds darted between the legs. I heard them dash into my den. Lamps were crashing.

I tripped on my way into the study; dripping water everywhere and trying to hold my bathrobe closed. Something black went rushing past me followed by the dogs. I fell backwards on my keister, sliding back out to the foyer.

"Heel!" my loud voice giving the command I'd learned at doggie class but of course it did not stop them. I'm the only one who learned it. I got up as gracefully as my dignity allowed. I had sent the dogs to obedience school. Waste of money. They were still running around chasing a black blur of fur, completely ignoring my command. More furniture flew as the dogs raced after the black fuzz ball. They careened around the unfinished part of the apartment, barking loudly.

Hill and Killa stood near the windows, uselessly watching the ruckus. "Grab your damn cat, I'll grab the dogs," I yelled over to my lieutenant. I tied my bathrobe and tried grabbing Hoover. I got him by the fur on his neck. Neither dog wore a collar inside. We both skidded to a halt. Killa had grabbed Bear and amazingly he sat without pulling her anywhere. The dogs were always careful with my small Ligithian, perhaps realizing how tiny and vulnerable she was.

Hill tried grabbing Stanley, but it was useless. The cat finally jumped up on the top of my refrigerator and glared down at us all. I let go of Hoover and he ran over to the refrigerator but the cat was just out of range. He started barking and trying to get up my fridge but this time I yelled loudly for him to stop and he did. Both dogs sat at the front of the refrigerator with heads turned upward - glowering and growling at the cat.

I looked up at Hill's cat. It was huge for a feline. "Where the hell did you get that black monster?" I glanced up at bright yellow angry eyes. It looked like a frigging demon.

"Stanley is quite loveable," Hill stood next to me.

"The cat can't stay here. The dogs will kill it!" my voice sizzled at her stupidity. My Hiberian hounds were bred for killing boars. Surely, her cat would feel their hunting instincts.

It was Killa that answered me, "Really Skip, cats can take care of themselves. They'll be great friends in a little while. Just leave them alone."

"I think you'd better rinse your hair out," Hill pointed to my sticky soapy wet hair. "It'll frizz on you if you don't get that shampoo out soon."

I glared at her. Turning back to the bathroom, I tried to ignore all of the hissing as I slipped into the bathroom past the puddle I left on the floor. I loudly slammed the door shut.

When I came out, all dried and dressed, my lieutenant had left for the office. Killa was busy rearranging her boxes after they had been scattered all over the apartment by the dogs. All the furniture had been put back in place. The cat still sat at the top of the refrigerator with the dogs faithfully watching it from below. Killa had put a bowl of water near the hissing feline.

"Give it up guys," I told them and got only a "**Woof**" in stereo.

"They'll get tired of it shortly," my old nursemaid remarked. "You'll see."

She was putting their canine breakfasts out and sure enough they abandoned their watch to eat. The cat, however, meowed loudly looking at them chowing down. Killa placed a bowl of cat food on top of the refrigerator. The damn cat purred so loudly I could hear it from my bedroom.

It was past 09:00, late for me, when I finally parked my compact Ant hovercraft in my parking spot at the office and walked the underground tunnel to the police station. The temperature outside was already over a hundred degrees. The fans were roaring. Captain Issam had taken the time to turn on the two huge fans I had in my small office.

As I have pointed out, the Fulton Police Station was across the street from the Dome, our Government complex. The ultra-modern governing building contained a huge circular drive headed right up to the entrance with a beautiful water fountain in front. It was an all up-to-the-minute building with central air, beautiful offices, modern bathrooms, an ultra-fancy gym, cafeteria, etc. Jealous? Yeah!

Our police station was housed in an old storage facility across the street. We had air conditioning but it rarely worked. The building's

AC system sputtered along. The city fathers were tight on the purse strings. Thus we lived with permanent stains on our shirt's underarms, especially my twenty detectives that were housed up on the fifth floor where the heat seemed to congregate.

Most of my other Fulton police were either on foot patrol or hoverpatrol. They wore ultra-thin uniforms that breathed. I would have loved to have bought them AC suits, but again the tight purse strings.

My Dome police, of course, did have the best. Heaven forbid our government representatives have to look at outdated hovers and old computer tabs. My dome police had new AC uniforms changed every year - bright and shiny. Don't get me started!

My first meeting was with my detectives. They were all scheduled for the week that I would be gone. Twelve of them would be off planet. None were going to Hilda. Hilda was cold. Criminals preferred the warmth. I hoped it stayed like that, at least this week.

Captain Issam, who just happened to be my therapist's husband, would probably have them more organized than I usually did. Carl Issam is a Castorian. He was from the sector's small asteroid belt; Castor is the smallest planet we have. The asteroid belt may grow them small, he is only 5 ft. 4in. tall, however Castor grows their inhabitants' brains big. His IQ was off the charts. Carl could also whip my butt; he has reached the tenth level of Federation Martial Arts.

Issam is also my friend. He and his doctor wife know about my epileptic seizures. His wife is one of my doctors. She has been teaching me calming techniques and it has cut my use of the "little blue pills" in half. Carl is losing a battle with his hair line, blaming that on his two teenage daughters. He tries desperately to get me on his Castor vegetarian, black tea diet but even he has given up on me as a useless junk food addict.

My second meeting was with my sergeants of the regular police force. Issam would be watching them too. The Dome was out of session so our population was cut by 20,000 as the politicians and their staffs skipped off-planet quickly. With them gone, it made it a lot easier to watch the capital, Fulton City. The "fat cats" were away, so crime was automatically down. No one with money was left to rob.

After my last meeting, Captain Issam and I went next door to "Danny's Café". It was another eyesore leftover storage building but at least their air conditioning worked. Sasha and her husband Boris were manning the counter. There is no "Danny" but there sure are good muffins and dark rich java. To me, there is nothing more enjoyable than a good cup of java. My Uncle Jack, who raised us after my parents had died, introduced me to the taste of the dark java bean when I was only eleven years old; been hooked ever since.

We took our corner seat. Issam shook his head. "What! No muffin?"

"I can't, our Jump is this afternoon. I haven't eaten anything since yesterday morning and that was only some broth," I told him. I did not take spatial travel well. As a kid my parents had tried everything to keep me from throwing up on family trips. It was no use. Even with nothing in my stomach, I'd have the dry heaves.

"The only good part of all this is I don't have to eat the crap Hill has got Killa feeding me. They are trying to feed me those god-awful salads and soy products. Just think what the planet Mody would do if we stopped importing their meat products? Good grief, we'd ruin their entire planetary economy. The planet would go into a depression!"

"So you ruin your health instead." Carl looked at me over his newspaper. It was a real newspaper too! Sasha and Boris were from the Sol sector and actually printed out a real newspaper. They thought it a personal touch from their original homeland. Personally, I preferred my tabloid. It told me what unfamiliar words meant, let me check whatever news I wanted, and I still had access to the office. I suppose brainy Issam doesn't need the dictionary.

"Are you all packed?" his words floated over the newspaper.

"Yeah, don't have much, have to buy cold weather clothes there," I informed him.

He put his paper down. "Go to Belchers." He touched his cellbutton on his collar activating his tabloid. He then put the screen to keyboard typing size and punched some keys. An ad for "Belchers" came up. *Snowsuits, gloves, boots, knitted hats, and ski equipment are our specialties* graced the holographic screen. Soft swishing type music drifted over the café's table with the lively jingle *"Shop with us, we'll have you on the slopes. Shop with us, you'll look great on those skis."*

Supermodels posed in their latest fashions. I'm sure I will look just like them.

"Yeah and they'll clean out my wallet too!" I snickered. "Nothing is getting me on those slopes. I'm a great landscape watcher!"

"You'll ski." He lowered his newspaper. "You are not a *sit down watcher*, anything but!"

He is wrong. There are plenty of other things to do, like catching up on my reading. I couldn't remember the last time I took up a good novel.

I checked out the rest of my messages. Most were from others wishing me a good holiday, even my boss Consulate Borger telling me to have a good time. I said goodbye to Issam, wished him good luck this week and headed back to the garage. I was just getting into my hover Ant when Hill came around the corner. "Hey Chief, wait, I need a ride, my hover is in the garage."

"Where do I drop you off?" I asked squeezing myself into the small vehicle.

She looked at me like I was an imbecile, "Your place! I'm taking you and Killa to the Jump."

"You know Hill, for being an ambassador's daughter, sometimes you lack common sense," I told her. "There is no way we are all going to fit into this hover. I'm worried Killa's luggage won't even fit."

"That is a low blow, Chief!" she glowered at me. "You promised we would not mention my father, you promised!"

I felt my face get red, I had promised. "Sorry, it slipped out!" Hill's father was one of the most influential politicians in the Humanoid Federation. He was the Consulate Assembly Governor General,

Thern Pinote. The general had been adamant that his daughter, his only daughter left after her sister's death, was to follow in the Pinote family tradition and be a diplomat. Her four brothers were all in the Governor General's entourage. The Governor and I had butted heads recently when we were on the Medical Operation Space Station, known generally as MOSS. He finally agreed to let Hill follow her own path and enter law enforcement.

Instead of firing her for lying to me, I promised instead to never mention her high pedigree. My lieutenant wanted to be thought of as just another off-sector (from Orion) police academy graduate. She'd also graduated from Orion's law school and the academy with top honors. It was why I'd hired her and, as a new graduate, she had come cheap. As I've pointed out, we have budgetary concerns. She was all I could afford.

"You have my apology, I won't do it again," I told her. This now put me trying to make up to her and left me driving contritely to my apartment. Damn woman!

We pulled into the underground garage. Artchie's van was parked in my spot! Then it hit me - Hill was driving us to the Jump Terminal in the van. It was a large vehicle that could house Artchie's motorized wheel chair, so there would be plenty of room. Leave it to Hill to plan ahead.

My turbocycle was parked in my other spot. I made a mental note to hide the key. Hill had a fascination with my expensive cycle. I would not put it past her to take it out for a "spin". I could hear her now, "I just had to make sure it didn't get rusty."

Artchie was behind the counter. His wheelchair motorized up so he could stand and look over the high counter. "Hi Chief, Ms. Hill." He was a graduate student at Fulton University majoring in government. He fills in as superintendent when Killa needs him.

"All set?" I inquired. "Anything goes wrong tell Lieutenant Hill or call me direct. Know where we are staying?"

"Yes, sir." He was so polite, his soldiering training coming to the fore. He had lost the use of his legs in the Cathian War. Now he was trying to get a law degree and work at the Dome. He brought out his tab sheet. "You're staying at the Sunrise Snow Retreat. You have number 14 chateau. I have all the numbers and of course both your cell and Killa's cell numbers."

"Remember there is no time call delay getting to us. We should be pretty easy to access. Our skiing lodge is located right outside of Giles, the main capital of Hilda. The capital has really grown up. So they have modern facilities including a dedicated news Jump line and a fast speed cell Jump line."

"Yep, all set", he told me. "I'll help the lieutenant with the dogs. I'll check on them during the day and bring them down here every once in a while."

"Just remember to be careful of Mrs. Hippnow. She hates the dogs. I don't need her putting in a complaint to the Housing Authority."

"That old bag," his normally young happy face was frowning. "Let's raise her rent, maybe she'll move out. She complains about everything.

Yesterday, Hippnow complained that their roof hot tub should be warmer. On Fulton? Give me a break!"

"Just be nice to her, she's quite old and has trouble walking," I reminded him.

"She's faking it!" he told me.

I headed toward the elevators, dragging Hill with me. My rookie lieutenant, perhaps because of her family background, was nosey and wanted to help everyone. Sure enough, in the elevator, she addressed the subject of old Mrs. Hippnow.

"Maybe I can help her. Sounds like a case of loneliness." Her hand went thoughtfully to her forehead.

"Do not get involved! You are here to help Artchie and the dogs!" I gave her one of my sternest looks. Of course, it did no good, she just continued on.

"Well, I know someone in OPD that might be able to help her," she continued. "Artchie could introduce me."

"Trust me the *Old Peoples Depression* agency cannot help Mrs. Hippnow. Stay out of it!" Thank goodness the elevator opened and the dogs took her mind off Hippnow.

Everything was ready to go; all the boxes and luggage were stacked by the elevator. Killa, obviously excited, had all our tickets and instructions on how to get to the resort. We really didn't need any instructions as Ray was arriving from his home on Nestor shortly after us and we'd wait at the Jump station for him. "I hope the baby likes everything we got him."

By "we" she meant her and Hill as I'd done none of the shopping. "He's only a little over two months old, he's not going to know." I didn't want her to worry.

"Stop being such a spoiler, Chief." Hill eyed me with displeasure. "Let Killa be excited. I'm sure Julie will love everything."

"Where's your cat?" I asked. I had looked at the refrigerator but the yellow eyed demon wasn't there.

"Stanley is sleeping on your bed," Hill nonchalantly told me.

"On my bed!" I crossed over to my bedroom's doorway. Sure enough there was this big ball of fur lying on my pillow. "He'll get fur all over my bed," I moaned. I didn't' even let the dogs sleep on the bed.

I looked over at Hoover and Bear, eyeing them with annoyance. "You cowards, are you going to let a stupid pussycat sleep on my bed?"

Their ears went up as if trying to understand me. I then noticed both dogs had scratches on their big noses. "Did your cat do that?" I pointed at the dogs, catching Hill's attention.

"Oh, my goodness. Stanley, did you do that?" she yelled over to the bedroom.

"Don't worry Skipper, they have made up. I put some anointment on their wounds and brushed Stanley's fur back to normal," Killa said as she checked her pocketbook one last time.

"Oh no, did they hurt her?" Hill asked, going into the bedroom and picking up the black fur monster. The cat's yellow eyes seemed to look right at me, daring me to dislodge her.

"He can't be that hurt, I can hear him purring all the way from the bedroom," I yelled over to Hill.

Both Hill and Killa said, "*Her*, Stanley's a her."

"Stanley is trouble." I got a *woof* from the dogs as they agreed with me.

We trucked everything down to the van. I said goodbye to the dogs and wished them luck. They rubbed against me whining. They knew the signs of me leaving. They then laid down chewing on the bones Hill had gotten them. Their new strategy was to ignore the cat. Somehow I didn't think Stanley liked being ignored.

Hill drove us to the Jump station, chatting away, "I hope you have a good time. Relax Chief, The Sunrise Snow Resort has some of the best ski slopes on the whole planet."

"I'm not skiing," I adamantly remarked. "I'm reading."

Hill looked annoyed at me. I had to remind her to keep her eyes on the road. Killa, as usual, had to side with my lieutenant, "Of course he's going to ski. Ray will teach him." I just shook my head. I was getting used to having two against one. On Hilda I was going to find myself a corner and hide! My former nursemaid couldn't contain herself, "I'll take care of the baby. Then Julie can join you. I believe she skis wonderfully."

Great, everyone skied but me - I could already feel the pressure. Again I told myself, *find a book on my tabloid and read by a roaring fire.* Hopefully I'd be nursing a hot brandy - Yeah!

We found a porter, really two porters since we had so much luggage. I laughed as I rolled my one piece of carryon suitcase behind me. I hoped baby James Brown was ready for the Killa onslaught.

Hill started to take her leave of us. She hugged Killa. "Have fun with little James," she told the Ligithian. "Have a good time, Chief." She awkwardly hugged me too. "Please don't worry about anything. I'll take good care of the dogs and I'll help Capt. Issam keep the department organized and functional."

My heart sped up, "Don't worry about helping Issam," I tried to keep my voice from getting loud and panicky, "just worry about the dogs and help Artchie." Good god, I could see the department now - all their desks in a neat row, regulation meetings every few hours. My whole body shook and I popped a blue pill in my mouth. "Please, Hill… Hill!"

I didn't get to say anything else as she'd already jumped in the large hover vehicle and was starting to pull away. "Hill…" I shouted but she was out of range. I swear I saw her smile in the rear view mirror. Damn woman!

I angrily stomped into the terminal. My newest detective was not good for my blood pressure. All the station's security enforcers knew me, obviously, as I was their boss, and so we were rushed right through the security check. Our boarding passes had us scheduled to go out of Port 17. We had about an hour wait time. Killa sat quietly; I could tell she was excited. Her feet didn't even touch the floor; she swung them back and forth like a little kid. Her eyes had turned dark purple. She wore a good sized hat hiding her fizzing hair and twitching ears. The thought of seeing her grandson (make no doubt of it, that's what she thought of him as) filled her with delight.

"You know, Skipper, you are awfully hard on Judy." She looked over at me, disapproval on her face. "She's still recovering from being shot in the head. Her hair is just growing back. You should not yell at her."

"I thought I was doing pretty well. I let her demon stay at my place!" To be honest, I'd really made an effort. I knew what it was like to have a brain injury, at least my lieutenant's injury wound wasn't permanent. "She can be a little too pushy, a little too nosey."

"It is not her, it is you. You should not compare all women to Charlene."

Charlene! Why was Killa bringing up my first wife? For god's sake I'd been seventeen when I had married. Back then I was a young famous rookie racer on Nestor. After my accident my wife served me divorce papers on the Medical Operation Space Station (MOSS) the day they took off the bandages from my eyes. She'd also taken most of my racing money, leaving me just enough to go to law school and buy my apartment building. "Now you are talking nonsense!"

"You are bitter and won't let any woman get close to you."

"Of course I'm bitter, she took everything I had. She just married me because I was rich and famous! When I couldn't race anymore, I was useless to her. Charlene's divorcing her second husband by the way." I smiled thinking of Hank Sims, how Charlene was dumping him because he had lost his ride sponsors. She was a predictably selfish, overly beautiful woman, who lived through her husbands' egos. When her spouse no longer kept her in the racing winner's circle, he was disposable garbage.

"I am right Skipper. I feel your bitterness." She placed her small fingers on my arm, "You must let it go."

"I have." Though even to myself I didn't sound convincing. "Besides, Hill isn't someone I'm interested in. For goodness sake she works for me! It's not allowed, not proper!"

Killa didn't say anything but rolled her purple eyes as if to say "unconvinced."

I shook my head, grabbing onto a news tab that had been left on the next seat, ignoring her as I opened up the front page. Hot weather was predicted. Now that was news! Must be a slow day. The top news headline was about the big drug bust. The news article had gotten most of the facts right. It didn't mention Fred Stoshingburg's name but my detective had uncovered a huge drug ring right in Senator Inglet's office. We couldn't tie the Senator directly but we got all his aides. Inglet was one of the senators from the planet Skantie Row.

That planet was famous for its bordellos and gambling casinos. Most importantly it was where all the drug families were headquartered. Most of the Crab Sector drugs were funneled through them. It was a real pain-in-my-ass planet and being the farthest out, hard to keep an eye on.

Fred who was a big guy, 6ft. 6in. tall, 275lbs, was relentless in his pursuit of nailing them. He'd been instrumental in most of the arrests these last couple of years. Of course rookie Hill last year had gone to Skantie Row in pursuit of her sister's killer. I had gone after her when someone made me aware of why she had volunteered to investigate a Skantie Row murder. We had almost gotten ourselves killed but we also got the Blithie family's drug records. It ended up with many of them going to jail. We were lucky to come out of there alive. Not a healthy planet for cops.

I was so concentrating on the news story, they had me quoted as saying we were going to *throw the book at the druggers*, that I missed the speakers calling our Jump. Killa had to pull me out of the chair to get in line. I took my seat and swallowed another spatial disorient pill, knowing damn well that it wasn't going to do one bit of good. And I was right! Ten minutes into the trip I was throwing my guts up!

Chapter Two

My head was thumping as Killa and I got off the Jump platform and headed to retrieve all her luggage. I grabbed a trolley. There were so many boxes and luggage bags, I wouldn't have been surprised if the trolley had sunk to the ground but no, packed to its gills, it floated after me. We headed up into the terminal which was nicely designed. You could tell that Hilda was a tourist planet. Plush cushioned chairs adorned the lounges. Tastefully done stores lined the passageways. Fancily done restaurants dotted the hallways. Well-dressed vacationers with expensive ski equipment mingled among the shops and terminal crowds.

What really made me stop was the huge floor-to-ceiling windows showing a spectacular view of the snowy landscape of the planet. Snow! Lots of it!

Maybe because Fulton Station was dry, hot and nondescript, this white wonderland took my breath away. It always did, even when I came here on business and not for a holiday.

"We should meet them." Killa excitedly pranced next to me. "They'll be coming in on platform four."

"No, we told Julie we'd meet them in the main lobby." I knew it was useless to try and calm her down. Ligithians are highly sensitive and highly excitable. Killa was no different, and very typical. Since she'd fled the slave planet of Ligithia with my mother over thirty years ago, we were her family.

Since my parents died when I was eleven and Ray was five, she'd been our substitute mom.

A cure to set the Ligithians free from their slavers, the Laositian Highbloods, had recently been introduced to the planet Ligithia. Killa had gone home with my grandfather, Ambassador Alphonso Medicinis, to help get the slavers and highbloods to accept the new world order. She'd come back home, however, realizing her life really belonged with us. I used to be her bonder, but now that she was cured of the blood bond, it was just a bond of family.

"Do you think the baby will like the old train set of Ray's?" the little woman asked as she clutched her pocketbook.

"I'm sure he will." I sat next to her. I touched my collar-attached cellbutton bringing up my tabloid screen. I browsed the online bookstore looking for a good novel. Might as well start my reading! I hadn't bought a book in a long time. I finally settled on a good bestselling crime mystery. I downloaded it, imagining myself sitting in front of a fireplace with a big log burning, sipping a brandy. I could feel myself falling asleep with my tabloid on my lap. Yes!

"Skip, what are you doing?" Killa leaned over trying to peek at my screen.

"I'm downloading a book to read," I informed her. "I plan to catch up on all my reading." And I meant it. I couldn't remember the last time I had just relaxed.

"That's good," she said looking down the long terminal hallways as if Ray and his family would be early. Jumps are never early. "It will be a good thing to do at night, you'll be tired after skiing all day."

"I'm not skiing!" I tried to keep my impatience with the subject out of my voice but I failed miserably.

"You can be so obstinate." My old nursemaid took on that lecturing tone that I knew so well from my younger days. "Sometimes you are your own worst enemy. I remember your mother trying to get you to try skiing when we came here on holiday. You had the same bad attitude. It took your father dragging you along to get you out on the slopes. That is why Hilda exists. You need the exercise."

I had forgotten our family trips here. I was probably all of ten years old when we spent a couple of weeks here. Ray, even as young as he was at the time, had taken right away to the slopes. I had just wanted to build snow castles. I was never one for sports until my Uncle Jack got me into auto racing. My father, at my mother's insistence, had forced me to try skiing. Then when that didn't work he tried snowboarding. When that didn't work he tried sledding. Then I had tried snow shoeing, then snowmobiling. I had ended up building snow castles, which were quite good if I remembered right.

Killa had emotionally exhausted herself so much that the little Ligithian fell sound asleep sitting in her chair. When I saw Ray coming, I gently nudged her. She awoke with a start but her eyes popped open when I told that her baby Jim had arrived. She jumped down, walking as fast as her little legs could carry her.

Julie was pushing a baby carriage, Ray was right behind her with their luggage cart, and behind him was their cousin/housekeeper, Marty Howard, who I had met when I was on Nestor. She always wore black with an overall severe look; tight black bun, pale face with dark brown eyes and thin as a rail.

"Killa," Ray shouted, hugging the small woman in his arms. Killa hugged him but quickly went to the baby carriage only to find it empty.

"Jim is with Marty," Julie said, giving Killa a quick hug and taking her to Marty who was right behind her. Sure enough, the baby, all bundled up was being held by their housekeeper. Killa looked so downhearted that Julie quickly grabbed the bundle and brought the baby over to the little Ligithian. I noticed the frown on Marty's face when Julie had pulled the baby away.

"Oh, Jimmy," Killa cooed, taking the baby in her arms. Ligithians have a natural bond with people as they were born with the urge to "serve" and others feel it immediately. The baby was no different, as Ray's son smiled, settling against Killa in total contentment.

Marty came to stand next to Julie and said, "Oh he must have gas, babies only smile if their stomachs hurt."

Killa looked up and frowned. Before it got out of hand I interjected, "Hello Marty, glad to see you again, this is Jim's grandmother, Killa Brown."

I saw Marty's eyes go wide but to her credit she just nodded and said, "Nice to meet you and it's nice to see you again, Chief Brown."

"Just call me Skip, we are all family here." I looked at Ray who was smiling from ear to ear. He found this all amusing, I could tell. My brother never took anything seriously except for his car racing and Julie. He wore his feelings on his sleeve. He could never lie to me, I saw through him every time. But then again, he chided me for being too serious. Of the two of us, he was by far the more athletic and now the slimmer one.

Julie came to the rescue, taking the baby from Killa and putting Jim in his stroller. "We'd better get over to the resort. Jim needs a nap."

We all got into a long bus-type hover that Julie had the foresight to see we would need. The back was packed with our luggage but the three layers of seats gave us plenty of room. Ray and I sat up front, Killa and the baby sat in the second seat, while Julie and Marty were in the back. Marty kept leaning over checking on the baby, while Killa fussed over him. This was going to be a long vacation if they kept it up. I could see the signs of Ligithian anger, as my old nursemaid's hair was standing on end, her ears were twitching and her eyes were deep purple.

Ray looked at me, he also knew the signs well; we'd seen them as children. "Better do something," he smiled as if I was the family enforcer.

It was Julie, however, that interceded by leaning over the back seat forcing Marty back. "So Killa, what do you think of Jim? Who do you think he looks like?"

I saw my former bondee relax, her eyes now were light lavender and sparkling. "I think he looks just like Ray did. He's so beautiful." Her hand went to the car-seated baby, "I wish I could have been there at his birth."

Of course, Marty could not keep quiet, "You know, Julie had the same features. He has the Bollie's eyes," she made reference to Julie's maiden name.

"Really?" I interjected, "I think it's a little early to say who little Jim looks like."

"To tell the truth," my brother just had to have his fun, "I think he looks just like you, Skip. The pouting mouth, the angry temper when he's hungry…"

"Funny," I snickered at him but at least it got them laughing in the back seats.

"Wow, look at all the snow," Julie commented. "We don't have a planet over in the Sol Sector just dedicated to snow sports. We have several with areas, like New Venus, that has a couple of mountains with resorts and the planet, Gates Way, has a few mountainous resorts but nothing that approaches Hilda." Julie's whole family was from the Sol sector. Ray had met her when he was racing in the sector and had been autographing racing memorabilia in her father's store.

"Sol is an old sector, most of the engineering was done by humans," I told her. "The Crab is new, comparably, and has the fingerprints of those damn lizards. The Bassodians customized each planet and considering they now do 85% of the engineering, we get what they want us to get."

I remembered my history lesson - when the future inhabitants started setting planets for the

Crab Nebula sector, they had to rely on the Bassodians to place and engineer the planets. Even "hot as hell" Fulton was setup for constructing the other planets by the damn lizards. Hilda, for instance, was bought by the Hildan Company just for building ski resorts. It has a small land mass and controlled immigration has kept the population down and the environment beautiful. "If you look at each planet in the Crab, they were engineered for a purpose," I told Julie. "Of course, some failed, like Abbis which was supposed to be a manufacturing hub. Too many people flocked to it and now it's over-populated, poor and full of crime! I don't even want to get into Skantie Row, that hell hole."

"That's not fair," my brother joked, "Skantie is doing exactly what the mob families wanted it for - gambling, bordellos and drugs!"

"Yeah," was all I said. The outer planet was a thorn in my side. Even though we sent most of the Blithie family to jail, the drug Supfline still flowed from that planet. The damn planet kept Fred Stoshingburg, my drug enforcer, busy tracking the drug dealers all over the Crab sector.

We drove through the capital city of Giles, named after the first president of the Hildan Company. It was just plain charming, set in the biggest valley Hilda had. I usually spent my time in Giles at their amiable modern police station. Chalet-type buildings, no skyscrapers were allowed, only buildings up to five stories could be built. I would have enjoyed the city more if it wasn't so damn cold!

We took the main highway, which looked like an old fashioned brick road but was three lanes wide each way. The hover glided easily over the well taken care of super roadway. The road led right away from the city to the mountains where all the resorts lay in the picturesque valleys with towering mountains surrounding them. We were staying at the biggest and most expensive resort, Sunrise Snow Resort. We followed the signs that led us to the main building.

"This is absolutely gorgeous," Julie remarked, her neck straining to take in all the scenery including the myriad of snow covered mountains that completely surrounded the resort.

"Yeah, got a great deal on our chateau," Ray commented, "the manager is a big racing fan."

As we pulled up to the resort, Julie came out of the third seat to dress little Jim in a heavy ski outfit. Only his bright blue eyes seemed to peak out of his hood. Of course, Marty had offered to dress him with Killa telling Julie she had gotten the perfect snow outfit. Julie just smiled, grabbing the baby before anyone else could. It was going to be a long week for my sister-in-law.

Of course, no one was paying attention to me as I shivered away. The cold hit me as I walked from the car to the huge stained-glass main lodge doors. I gladly felt the warmth as the doorway slid silently open.

"Let's register, then we'll tackle the baggage," Ray said. There was a multitude of bellhops all eagerly waiting. I noticed they were dressed in brightly colored outfits. I'd seen one of them touch his pocket regulator as he headed outside - the suits were temp controlled giving them warmth from the cold outside. Nice, I'd like to have my foot patrol officers have them but instead of bringing heat they would bring air conditioning. Fat chance, even my Dome officers didn't get these newly styled uniforms.

The interior was highlighted by huge, lit stone fireplaces with large bison heads adorning each. Comfy chairs lay in semi-circles with cushiony rugs to let tired skiing feet relax. Not many people were there but I imagined, it not yet being the middle of the day, most were on the slopes. We left Julie supervising the two women who were both trying to fawn over the baby, and headed over to the front desk.

"Good day, Mr. Brown," the front clerk started typing on her cellregister. "Oh, I should say *Misters*," she laughed. I saw her press the manager's button. I'm always alert to what people are doing on their tabloids, part of my job I guess.

"You are all set. You are in Chateau No. 14." She waved to a bellhop, "Help the Brown family get settled."

Before the bellhop could grab our luggage, a man came out of the back, "Ray Brown?" he asked. He was dressed in a dark brown suit that somehow fit into the atmosphere of the lobby.

"That would be me," Ray answered.

"What a pleasure to meet you, congratulations on winning the Championship!" he exploded with enthusiasm. Before Ray could answer him, the man's attention went to me, "Are you Skip Brown, the famous Rookie of all time?"

"That was a long time ago," I answered him, he was too slick for me, "I prefer Sector Police Chief Brown."

"Oh, of course, but you'll have to forgive this overzealous racing fan!" he came from around the counter. "Our resort manager is even a bigger fan!"

Ray, being the current racer and always putting fans first, shook his hand. "Glad to hear it. Beautiful place you have here."

The lobby manager went over to the women, "Mrs. Brown, a pleasure to meet you. Maybe while you are here you could tell me what makes Ray Brown's car so special?"

Julie had the baby in her arms, a good excuse not to shake hands but she also was Ray's mechanic and crew chief and was also conscious of his fans. "Nice to meet you, Mr.?"

"Paul Bell," he answered.

"Well Paul, it is Ray *the driver* that makes his number 15 Golden Attenson's car special!" Julie left no doubt she was her husband's biggest fan.

He laughed, "No doubt!" He snapped his fingers and a rather tall middle aged bellhop came strolling over. "Mario will help you with your luggage, your number 14 Chateau is just down the path from here."

"Thank you," Julie was the one who answered and took charge of getting everyone together.

But it was Marty that interjected, "The baby needs to be fed!"

"You won't need to return to your car, just give Mario the keys. We have a heated *sleigh* to take you to your chateau," Paul informed us as he waved us to a side entrance.

Sure enough a hovercraft in the shape of a "sleigh" did indeed await us.

It was quite something; plush heated soft seats with blankets. The upper part of the hover could be opened but it was now an all glass top. The outside looked like Santa's sleigh; I was waiting for Old Saint Nick to appear. Instead the driver was dressed like a damn elf.

Ray, who sat next to the driver, held his stomach and said "HO, HO, HO". The elf either didn't get it or was so used to being teased that he completely ignored my brother. He'd probably heard it a hundred times.

"Look, Jim!" Marty who had grabbed the baby, was holding him on her lap. "Look at the cute elf!"

Killa, taking a seat next to me, just looked downhearted as the hover headed down towards the chateaus. We didn't ride for more than a few minutes. We were in the first chateau. Our van was parked out back and the bellboy was already unloading everything. The sleigh hover went in front and we all piled out of the overly ostentatious vehicle.

We went up the two steps through a portico that had several porch chairs with racks for skis and the side of the porch ended in a ramp, easy to access to the ski slopes! I could already feel the pressure to participate.

Inside was a full kitchen, modern and attractive slate counter tops with every convenience, including a place on the wall for ordering out. I walked over and tapped the icon for a menu - jeesh it had everything! I also noticed no prices. I suppose those that came here didn't worry about prices!

There was a full dining room to the side. Our luggage was all stacked neatly in the large living room. I saw Ray giving the bellhop his tip and the man left through the back entrance. The fireplace took up an entire wall. I sighed looking at the plush furniture - perfect for settling in for a good read.

It was Julie's comment that brought me back from daydreaming, "It has only three bedrooms. Didn't you tell them four?" She looked over at my brother, who just shrugged, a typical Ray reaction.

"I can sleep on the couch," I offered, "looks comfy." Heavens we didn't need Killa and Marty sleeping together in the same room.

Julie got her cell out and called the front desk. At first, the front desk was clueless but my sister-in-law can be quite persistent, it is what makes her a great Crew Chief. "Okay," she smiled, "all set. The chateau next to us has four bedrooms and the guests just cancelled. They are switching us to that chateau. God that desk clerk was ditsy."

Of course, we had to lug all our luggage next door as the bell boy (although he was middle aged) had already left and Julie didn't want to deal with the ditsy clerk. It was just like this one, except it had one more bedroom. Julie had Ray and I carry the baby's crib, which had been placed in the middle bedroom, to the new chateau.

"Having a kid changes everything!" Ray moaned as we struggled to get the baby's bed up the ramp.

We all got settled. The day of travel left everyone tired. We ordered a late lunch or early supper, whichever one wanted to call it. The meal was delicious. Even Killa, who tends to pick at her food, ate a good portion. The baby was sleeping and I lost count how many times Marty and Killa went in to look at him. Julie just shook her head. "What am I going to do?" she pleaded to Ray and I.

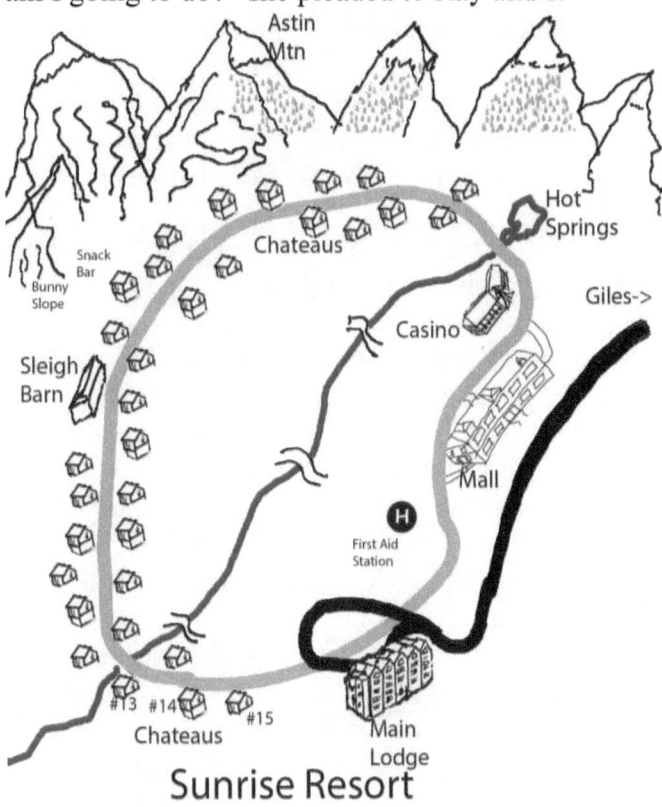

Sunrise Resort

Ray said, "They'll work it out." I just shook my head. I was feeling contented as I sat in one of the deep cozy chairs in front of a roaring fire. Although, I was a little disappointed that it was a radiant fire, a cleverly designed wood burning hologram. Still, I curled up with my book and was just about to ask someone to get me a brandy when Killa had to rattle the illusion.

"Ray, your brother needs a coat and some skiing outfits. You should make him go shopping." Killa pointed to me as if Ray didn't know who I was.

"I heard they have some great ski shops." Julie sat across from me. "I need some equipment myself, my stuff is pretty old from before we were married."

"Well, you and Ray go shopping," I looked up from my tab. I had just started Chapter two in my book. "I'll stay here with the baby and Killa, you go get Jimmy some clothes too." I looked expectantly at Julie, hopeful she'd take the hint.

"No, no," Killa had better ideas, "you all go, I can take care of the baby."

"He hardly knows you," Marty interjected, "he can't wake up to a stranger!"

"Marty!" Julie yelled at her, "You'll hurt Killa's feelings. That is her grandson."

"I didn't mean it, I was just thinking of the baby!" Julie's cousin was about to cry, surprisingly it was Killa that saved the day.

"It's okay, she's probably right." Killa continued, "I'll go with you, Skip will only get the wrong size if I'm not there."

Now I had to go, damn. If it kept Killa from feeling bad about taking care of the baby, I'd go. Damn! I noticed Ray was snickering.

We ended up taking Jim with us. We called for a "sleigh" and we went over to the resort's mall that lay at the bottom of their biggest ski slope. Killa and Marty didn't say much, each sitting on opposite sides. Julie kept hold of Jim until we all got out. She then handed him to me. I must admit I did enjoy holding the small bundle until Ray got the stroller all set up.

Marty and Julie headed off toward the other end of the mall with the baby, while Ray, Killa and I trounced off toward the ski shops. The minute I walked into the store, my nerves went on high alert and a blue pill headed into my mouth. I didn't need an episode on my vacation. The place smelled expensive. The patrons looked expensive.

"Welcome to Belchers," a mealy mouthed sales clerk smiled. He reminded me of the ad Carl Issam had shown me about the ski shop; just like a model. "Hi, I'm Kalen," the clerk who looked like he went right to either the slopes or the gym after work. Of course his tight ski outfit showed every muscled bicep he owned. Or maybe he went to his hairdresser, as each of his blonde curls of hair seemed impeccably placed. "What can we do for you?"

You could do possibly nothing for me. Well maybe lend me your perfect body along with probably your perfect ski slope skills, I thought.

Ray, however, was all ears. "We need to be outfitted, especially my brother here who needs everything including a regular winter jacket and boots.

The clerk revved himself up to high gear, I'm sure dollars signs flashed in his head!

"Suit him first," I emphatically pointed at my brother. Perhaps no one would notice me slip out to the ice cream parlor that I could see across the way. Unfortunately, as if she knew, Killa came and took my arm pretending to lean on it! Yeah right. Oh well.

Ray is a thirty two inch waist, trim and fit. He has to be slim and trim to race. It takes a lot of physical strength and agility to drive his number 15 Golden Bird. I was not the least surprised to find him get a ski outfit in his orange/gold colors. He came out of the dressing area looking very similar to his racing outfit. The clerk went over and pressed a button on Ray's front pocket. The whole skiing outfit began clinging to him, making him a sleek aerodynamic skier. I must admit I was impressed.

Next were his ski boots. Of course, they matched his golden outfit. He slipped his feet into the boots, the clerk pressed the button on the top of the boot and voila, the shoes snapped shut. He pointed out this was also a safety feature for getting out of the boot quickly. You unlocked the mechanism from your suit so no accidental pressing. I was impressed again!

His helmet had cellbuttons so he could be in touch on the slopes, including an emergency touch or a *news* touch for weather and slope conditions. Impressed again!

Then he quoted Ray the price - *NOT IMPRESSED*!

Killa and Ray pointed to me. "I think I'll pass. I just need a coat and some regular boots," I tried to soften the refusal with a smile. It got me nowhere.

"I'll treat you," Ray offered. "We'll call it a Yultide/Birthday gift."

"We have used equipment," the smartass clerk interjected.

Of course, that got my ire up. "No! It's not the price." I saw Killa going to say something and I beat her to it. I didn't need her telling everyone of my budgetary problems. "I'll get the same outfit!" I made it sound just as enthusiastic as possible.

"Oh, great!" The clerk pounced on the offer. "Let's go out back. What color?"

"Baby blue," Ray got his two cents in first, "it was the color of his *Blue Horizon* car."

"No, I don't think so." I tried to interject but I was overruled.

"Oh, yes Skipper," Killa jumped up at the suggestion, "your Uncle Jack would be so proud!"

It was a losing battle. I begrudgingly followed the clerk from hell out into the dressing room. He got me into a baby blue ski outfit that he thought was absolutely the top line and so *chic* on me. I swear he was snickering behind my back.

I walked out to Killa and Ray's raving reviews. To my dismay, Julie pushing the baby carriage and Marty trailing behind, came into the store. It didn't help that the damn clerk pushed the button and the ski suit sucked in. It was so tight, I had trouble breathing.

"I think he needs a bigger size," Killa said.

Ray was just laughing, even though Julie hit him in the arm. Even Marty's usually severe expression laughed.

Meanwhile, I'm dying of suffocation. It was Julie that went over and pressed the button when she realized I couldn't bend my arms to reach it. Instant relief.

"Oh let's get you a couple of sizes larger," the clerk quipped.

I was just about ready to punch the shit and tell him where he could take his suit but Julie interceded. "I'll come with you." She took my arm and led me back into the dressing room. "Why don't all of you go across to the ice cream place? We'll join you when we are done."

The Ice Cream Place! That was supposed to be me! Julie patiently supervised the refit. She thought I should change the color but Killa would be upset. I went with the baby blue ski outfit with a dark blue helmet and dark blue ski boots. Julie picked out dark blue gloves.

Then we went out and she picked out a nice brown coat, sheepskin boots and a brown canvas fur-lined hat that had flaps that could cover my ears. She even made me get a sweater and some thick shirts and ended with two pair of corduroy pants.

"Now you will look great!" Julie put her arm through mine as we headed toward the Ice Cream Parlor.

"Thank you," I pressed her arm. "Ray is a damn lucky guy."

"Well, I think so too!" she laughed. Her face lit up making her even more dramatically beautiful. She was from Sol, the capital of the Sol Sector. Her dark long silky black hair, dark brown eyes with skin an almost olive complexion only enhanced her exotic nature. She was smart, yet totally down to earth. She was everything my brother needed to keep him focused on his racing career. He was a lucky guy.

As we approached the Ice Cream parlor, Marty was rolling out the baby. Killa was behind her looking miserable and Ray was behind them carrying a chocolate ice cream cone which he handed to Julie.

"Hey, where's mine?" I asked.

"Killa wouldn't let me get you one. Guess she thinks you need to get into a smaller size ski outfit." He was trying not to smile but he didn't quite cover his smirk up. Julie punched him in the arm again.

I went to yell at my old nursemaid but she looked so miserable as Marty pushed the baby carriage that I didn't say a word. Julie took over the driving. Now we had two miserable old ladies.

"The skiing rentals are at the end of the mall," Julie told us. "I've booked us all for early morning lift tickets. Killa and Marty can watch Jim. I'll only ski the morning but I got Ray and Skip all day passes."

"I think I'll wait. I can't ski, so I'll look into lessons tomorrow," I told them. Of course I had no intention doing any such thing.

"Oh, don't worry, Ray told me to get you lessons. So you're all set to report to the "bunny slope" at 07:30."

"That's so thoughtful of you," Killa squeezed Julies arm affectionately. "He needs the exercise. Judy is always trying to get him to move his feet."

"Really?" Julie looked over at me.

"Lt. Hill is a pain in the ass!" I pointed at Killa, "The two of them are constantly conspiring to feed me crappy healthy food and even set the dogs on me!"

"I'm sure Judy is not going to like you not getting into that smaller suit..." Killa started to say.

"You are not to tell Judith Hill anything!" I pointed my finger at my nursemaid. "I mean it." I could tell Killa was going to ignore me and meant exactly what she said. Damn!

I had to patiently sit and try several types of skis on. Ray insisted on "old fashioned" style equipment. I wanted the type that were small and had "training wheels" to keep you balanced. Those skis used a new kind of "hover" technology but my brother shook his head. "That's not skiing," he told me, intimating I was not to be a coward. Oh well.

Afterwards we shopped a little more. Killa got to buy baby Jim a new ski hat that said *I love Grandma.* It pleased her when Julie put it on for the ride home. Of course, Marty just scowled. Otherwise it was a pleasant ride back to the chateau. I was looking forward to getting back to my book and finally to my brandy.

When we got back to the chateau, our entire set of mall packages had been delivered. On our front porch were our rented skis; ready to go in the morning. Whoopee. Julie and Ray went over to inspect. I walked into the house without a glance in that direction.

Marty was the first in the house. To Killa's dismay, the housekeeper had already gotten the baby undressed and was holding him. "It's time for his bottle," Marty said.

"Good, let's give Killa her first chance to feed him," Julie said taking Jim and putting him in the little Ligithian's arms. All smiles, Killa sat in a rocking chair and gave little Jim his bottle that Julie had prepared from her breast pump. Marty just scowled.

I couldn't help but smile as I settled into my soft comfortable chair. I put in a call to Hill and

Issam. Hill was all questions but I finally learned all was well with the dogs and the apartment. Issam had a regular day, no problems or I should say he handled all the problems. Content, I brought up my book.

"Hey, don't get too cozy," my brother informed me. "We have a manager's welcoming cocktail party to attend in about an hour. You need to shower and get dressed."

"I'm not going!" I looked at him square in the eye, using my best "Police Chief" voice.

"Oh," Julie sounded distressed, "I accepted for you. The resort's top manager himself called. He specifically asked for you. I'm sorry, Skip."

Of course I didn't like to disappoint Julie, though I was tempted. "That's okay. I'll go get ready."

She smiled and kissed me on the cheek, "besides, we wouldn't want to go without you, would we Ray?"

Ray just shrugged, "He always was a party pooper."

I just glared at him as I headed to my bedroom and the shower. I took one last forlorn look at my tabloid laying on my big cushy chair. Oh well.

Chapter Three

As we stepped outside, large snowflakes greeted us. Since we weren't that far from the main lodge we decided not to take a sleigh, but to walk. Julie strolled between the two of us. She wore a long double-breasted gray coat with a white fur earmuff and carried a matching white hand muff. The tall elegant woman looked almost like she had come from a fairy tale. Even in the fading light her waist length black hair shone. My sister-in-law was stunning, fitting right into the beautiful surroundings.

The snow was falling all over my new brown coat and the matching hat. I took off my mittens letting the flurries fall on my hands. It was hard to discern the different snowflake shapes before they quickly melted. The snowfall tickled, making me laugh. I definitely never laughed much on Fulton. The light airy sound of my laughter even sounded strange to my own ears.

What a winter wonderland! The sun was just setting, all the chateaus were sharp pointed silhouettes against the mountain ridge. We had somehow crossed over to a fantasy land. The Bassodian lizards had done a good job on this planet. I heard that when the Hildan Corporation had planned this planet, the CEO had waved a lot of money in front of the reptile engineers to get exactly what he wanted - a planet that tilts one way with only one season - winter. Of course that was centuries ago. It was a different ballgame now.

Individuals and even corporations couldn't afford their own planet. Now most of the planets were Federation built.

"Did you know no two snowflakes are alike?" I told them.

"Gee Skip, have you counted all of them to be sure?" Ray said getting a kick of snow from Julie.

"You're so funny," I said as I kicked snow at him too. My boots were nice and warm. I couldn't even imagine wearing them on Fulton where sandals were the norm.

"Ray behave yourself tonight," Julie brushed against him emphasizing her point. "He gets rambunctious when he's off racing season," she told me.

"I can understand that," I answered her. "When the pressure of winning isn't there, you become a completely different person. I know I was."

"Shit Skip, you're a different person minute to minute. Never know who we are dealing with, the grumpy brave Chief of Police or the skiing coward. Let's not forget, we also have the compassionate landlord who helps the disabled," Ray expounded as he stuck his tongue out at me.

"Well, I like them all." Julie squeezed my arm.

I didn't get to respond as we had arrived at the main lodge which was all lit up. Evening was descending rapidly; the light of Hilda's sun was going behind the mountains. Evening descends earlier on this planet as the mountains swallowed up the light rays. They had no moon so evenings were always dark. The mountains were crisscrossed with tiny dots of light outlining the ski runs. Their brochure bragged that avid skiing fanatics could hit the slopes all night. That thought sent shivers down my back despite the warm coat.

All the pine trees, which were neatly trimmed with small glowing bulbs, gave it a festive atmosphere. The sidewalk was well lit in radiant mellow yellow with the sides pulsating different pastel colors. The stained glass doorway opened automatically. Live music drifted out.

"Sounds like dancing music to me," Ray quipped as he grabbed onto Julie and spun her around as we entered the lobby. They made a great couple. Was I envious? You bet your ass. I'd love to find someone like Julie but my ex-wife, Charlene, kind of cured me of any serious relationships. Of course, marrying at seventeen I didn't know what I was doing. I doubted I still did.

We gave up our winter gear near the front desk and then followed the sound of the music into a huge side room. Servers were everywhere with drinks and hors d'oeuvres. I didn't realize how hungry I was, eating several fruit filled chocolate covered tarts. "Remember that ski outfit," Ray quipped after my third one. What, was Killa tutoring him on my diet!

As big as the lobby was, the side room was so large it contained two fireplaces, one at either end, with roaring fires in each. Real fires, with the smell of burning wood were a wonderful addition to the already rustic atmosphere. The room reminded me of Yuletide with balsam wreaths and electronic candles everywhere. The smell of pine permeated the room bringing back great memories of holidays with my parents and Uncle Jack.

There were quite a few people filling the room with the floor in the middle having been cleared for dancing. I watched Ray grab Julie and he swept her onto the floor. I never knew my brother liked to dance and he is good at it! My sister-in-law, with her elevated high boots, kept right up with him. With the high heels she was almost as tall as Ray. They make a nice looking couple.

Around each fireplace was a circle of big soft chairs. I found myself a nice comfy chair by one of the fireplaces and ordered a brandy. When the brandy came, it was of a high quality and went down real smooth. I wondered how Killa and Marty were making out. Julie had already checked on them when we came into the lobby. All was well; the baby was sleeping. Kids sleep a lot at this age. I had no way of knowing why but Julie seemed satisfied. It wasn't until Jim was born that I became aware of how little I knew about kids; not in my forte.

The fireplace was nice and warm, the chair relaxing. My mind went to Hill, would she like this hoopla? Probably. After all, she'd been brought up by her diplomatic father to fit into any situation. I had promised never to bring her family up but it still did linger in my mind. Well at least now I realized why she was so pushy - it was in the genes of her diplomatic family dynasty.

Now why are you thinking of Hill? I chastised myself. I was saved from further thoughts as Ray and Julie joined me. Ray had a martini with extra olives. Julie had a soda as she was nursing baby Jim.

"This is quite lovely," Julie commented sipping her iced drink by the immense hearth.

"Well, I'm glad you approve, Mrs. Brown," said a rather handsome man in an expensive suit with perfectly cut curly blonde hair. He was perhaps in his early forties. "I'm Lawren Streng, I manage the Sunrise Resort, including the casino." He took Julie's hand and kissed it. "And you are Ray Brown, this year's Racing Circuit Champion." He held out his hand to Ray, who took it.

"Glad to meet you, Mr. Streng," Ray nodded. Julie stood behind him carefully scrutinizing the manager with her big grey eyes. "I'd like you to meet my brother…"

"Oh yes, I know, Mr. Skip Brown," he interrupted my brother, coming over and vigorously shaking my hand, "I'm a big fan of both of you. I believe it is *Chief* Brown now?"

"Yes, I now go by that label, it's been a long time since I raced, giving it all over to my brother now, Mr. Streng," I told him as I extricated my hand from his firm handshake.

"Please call me Lawren," he told us and of course we told him to call us by Skip and Ray.

An extremely tall skinny bony woman appeared at Streng's side. "I'd like you to meet my wife, Hessina." He put his arm around her slim waist and drew her to his side. She towered over him by several inches. Now I don't mean to be mean but she was the ugliest woman I have ever seen. Her face was like a bird's, beady eyes, pointed sharp nose, large ears. I suppose she looked even uglier next to a handsome husband. Her long whitish striped hair was impeccably done in cascading curls but even this did nothing to help but only emphasized her almost completely white slanted eyes that had small black pupils.

"How do you do?" she shook my hand with her long boney fingers. I noticed a big diamond ring on her other hand. I was looking at her hands because I didn't want to stare at her face. Her rich designer clothes literally hung on her; the long red skirt let her bony kneed legs peek out and her large feet had matching slippers.

"These are the famous Brown brothers of racing, my dear," her husband's voice full of excitement, making me feel guilty for having such bad thoughts on his wife's looks.

"Oh yes," she had a high-pitched squeaking voice that fit her bird face. "I'm so glad to meet you. Are you the famous Brown mechanic?" She had turned to Julie.

"Well, I'd like to think I make a difference," Julie said, gracious as ever as she took Hessina's handshake. "Right now I'm happy to be just Ray's wife and baby Jim's mother."

"Oh, how old is he?" his wife bubbled over, but I could see the dark look that came over her husband's face.

Before Julie could answer he changed the subject, "So I hope you are going to enjoy our ski slopes."

"Yes, tomorrow morning, we will all be on the slopes," Ray quickly said as he saw the husband's dark look at the mention of the baby.

Julie also shut up but Hessina was not ready to let the subject go.

"How old did you say he was?" She had taken Julie's hand as if not to let her go until she answered.

"Oh, he's just two months old," Julie answered.

"We are hoping to start a family soon," Hessina's voice sounded excited.

"Let's not bore our quests with that," Lawren said a little too fast, bringing a frown from his wife.

We were saved by a slim but well-built woman coming up and grabbing Streng's arm, "Lawren, who are these quests?"

To put it mildly, where Steng's wife was not so pretty this woman was absolutely gorgeous. She had long auburn hair that hugged her oval face that was designed with a perky nose, big green eyes, and a sensuous mouth that had an easy smile. She was dressed in a velvety black dress outlined in tasteful sequins with tiny black matching slippers. Her petite delicate well-manicured hands were bedecked with several shiny rings.

"Oh, Lilac," Streng dislodged her grasp on his arm, "this is Skip Brown and his brother Ray. This lovely lady," he nodded at my sister-in-law, "is Ray's wife, Julie."

"Well, how do you do? You are the racers that Lawren has been so anxious to meet. Aren't you Chief Skip Brown? I see you on the telescreen news. You're more handsome in person."

"I'm not handsome anywhere," I told her as I had no intention of flirting with this woman despite her being drop dead gorgeous. She spelled trouble with a capital T. My police instincts went into high gear. I looked over at Hessina whose face showed pure hatred making her even uglier. Obviously, Lilac was not the manager's wife's favorite.

"How about dancing with me," Julie grabbed my arm. I took her onto the dance floor.

"Thank you for saving me," I quipped but I noticed her looking sideways. Ray was dancing with Lilac. The beautiful short sexy woman was clinging to my brother rather closely. I danced over and tapped his shoulder, "Let's switch." I tried to sound cheerful. Ray switched with me, I could see the relief in his eyes as he grabbed onto Julie.

"Well, Lilac, what brings you to Hilda?" I asked not being able to think of anything else to say.

"Oh I live here," she informed me as she moved closer putting her arms around my neck. I could smell her perfume which was the same as her name. Too sweet, came into my head, not good for my epileptic mind. The sweet smell bothered my senses, sending electric shocks to my sensitive brain. I could not, however, reach my pills. She obviously was oblivious to my discomfort as she snuggled closer. "I just love to follow crime stories on the telecom," she informed me. "I suppose you have to be big and strong against all those criminals?"

Her come on lines weren't even original. I cringed and my mouth completely deserted me as I could think of nothing to respond to her blatant flirt.

I was just thinking of how I could get into my shirt pocket and get my little blue pills when I felt a hand tap my shoulder. I looked over to see a young man, perhaps middle twenties trying to cut in.

"Oh, be my guest." I handed over Lilac who was frowning deeply.

"Really, Reich," her angry voice almost spit at him. "I'm working tonight. I told you to leave me alone when I'm here!"

Oh, so she'd been paid to keep us amused. *Good god!* I thought as I headed back toward my chair which was now occupied by a man who obviously hit the slopes. He was in a ski outfit and it looked good on him. I'd guess he was in his middle twenties.

"Oh, I took your place," he said jumping up.

"No, really stay where you are," I told him getting my drink from the table next to the chair. He stayed standing and held out his hand.

"Hi, I'm Marc Lulis," he told me shaking my hand. "I just got here. I'm going to do some night skiing. My friends are due here tomorrow but I thought I'd get some skiing in tonight. The ski runs are well lit."

I shook his hand. Lilac was walking over to us. Julie and Ray were also joining us. I introduced them and Lilac. Marc seemed taken with the beautiful woman. Still she tried to sidle up to me, asking me to order her a drink. It was Marc Lulis that got her the drink. She didn't even look at the skier when he handed her a tall fluted glass of champagne.

"So Chief Brown, are you here to arrest someone?" she quipped. "I have heard you're really dedicated to your work. Are you all work and no play?" She jokingly poked my arm batting her gorgeous green eyes.

I was tongue tied. I wasn't used to such openly come-on lines. Of course, my brother was of no help. "Cat got you tongue, Skip? He is the *big silent type*," he whispered to Lilac. She smiled at me, taking my arm. I was gonna kill him!

Julie touched her cell button on the collar of her sweater. I saw her walk away talking. When she came back, her face was one of concern. "I have to go, our baby Jim is acting up."

"I'll go with you," Ray pounced on the opportunity to leave.

"I'll go with you, too," I offered, pouncing just like my brother did, dislodging myself from Lilac's grip.

"Oh Skip, stay!" the small sexy woman grabbed onto my hand. "I'd love to get to know you better."

"Well, I'm really tired you know, long Jump." I took her hand and put it on Lulis' arm. "I'm sure Marc will take good care of you. I have to go call my fiancé," I lied. "You know how women worry?" I actually had no idea how women worry but it sounded good.

"Oh, I will take good care of Lilac," Marc bubbled over grabbing onto Lilac's hand. "Hope to see you on the slopes tomorrow. Goodbye, Julie, it was nice talking to you."

I saw Ray frown. Ah, he didn't like it when someone flirted with his wife!

As we got our coats and headed out, I looked back and saw Marc fawning over Lilac but her eyes were on me. I quickly looked away heading back to the outside and the safety of the snow. The cold fresh air renewed me to calmness. My blue pills stayed in my pocket. I tipped my head back and let the large snowflakes wash over my face.

"Your fiancé?" My brother was standing next to me. He seemed to be enjoying the cool evening as much as I was. "Have you been holding out on us Skip?"

"I had to get her off of me!" I told him. "It just came out."

"You should have just told her the truth," Julie came up between us, holding on to both of our arms to steady herself, although the walkway must have been heated because it was clear despite the snow fall. "Women appreciate candidness."

"Humpf," my brother remarked and got a punch in the shoulder from his wife. "Really, Julie, really? Candidness is the last thing a woman wants."

"You are wrong!" she told her husband.

We walked in silence, each appreciating the night, the stars, and the snowflakes until we got to our chateau.

The door, upon recognizing us, opened. The fireplace was going. Killa was reading in a chair and Marty was watching the news in the adjoining den. They both showed surprise upon seeing us. "You're early," both of them said at the same time.

"Didn't you call?" Ray asked. "Where's the baby?"

"Sleeping," they both answered again together.

I looked at Julie.

"Well, I thought I'd get us out of there," she half grinned. "I felt sorry for you Skip."

"So much for candidness!" Ray flopped into a chair by the fire. I just laughed. Julie went in to check on Jim, coming back with her big fluffy bathrobe and matching bunny slippers. She looked cute without a hint of being a racing car mechanic.

"The baby is a happy camper. I just fed him so he'll sleep until morning now. We've been lucky, he sleeps through; makes life a lot easier."

Marty handed Julie a hot cocoa, while Killa handed Ray and I hot steaming cups of java. I also got a bowl of fresh fruit while Ray and Julie got chocolate muffins. "Hey!" I yelled at Killa, "I want one too!"

"No," my old nursemaid told me, "the fruit is good for you. You need to lose some weight."

I just slumped down, sipping my java. I knew when it was hopeless to argue, at least Hill wasn't here to lecture me also.

"This is a stunning place," Julie remarked putting her bunny slippers up on her chair's matching ottoman. "I can't wait to hit the slopes. How many resorts does Hilda have?"

"Four," I answered her. It was my job to know the basics of the planets. "This resort, however, is the biggest and most luxurious. It was the original Hildan hotel with the best slopes. I believe Hilda is now completely developed, the planetary council has put strict conditions on immigration and business expansion."

"I hope we can get out and see the other mountains. I hear they even have hot springs!"

"Hildan had the engineers put in a few underground fissures. My superintendent of the police here, Chet Kodis, complains a lot about them. I guess people drink and go into the springs, which are over 100 degrees and end up in the hospital from the mixture of heat and alcohol."

"Oh," Julie said, "I'll remember that!"

"Like you're such a big drinker," Ray teased. "Maybe Skip can bring his fiancé?"

"Oh, you're so funny!" I chided him. "It is the only real problem Chet has. The crime rate here is low. It is one of my *easy* planets."

"Speaking of easy," Ray looked over at me, "it's too bad you didn't like Lilac. She sure liked you! Do you always have women throwing themselves at you?"

"Please," I took a big sip of my java before answering him, "I haven't had a woman throw herself at me ever! I certainly don't encourage it in my line of work. That woman is trouble!"

"Did you see the look Hessina gave her? I don't think she likes Lilac at all," Julie said. "Perhaps she's afraid that woman will come on to her husband."

"Well," Ray reached over to take his wife's hand, "Lilac grabbed onto Hessina's husband pretty familiarly. I don't mean to sound awful but Hessina isn't the most…." Ray hesitated then said, "pretty woman, as a matter of fact I haven't seen one uglier."

"Ray!" Julie took back her hand, and then pointed accusingly at him, "That's an awful thing to say!"

"So much for candidness," Ray looked over at me for help.

"I'm not getting you out of this one," I told him laughing. "Hessina seemed nice and her husband did seem devoted to her. To tell you the truth, I'd rather have a hundred Hessinas to one Lilac."

"You are right!" Julie emphatically announced. "Remember that Ray!"

"You don't have to worry," he told his wife. "Where would I ever get such a more competent mechanic, never mind such a beautiful one?"

Julie blushed and squeezed his hand affectionately.

The baby cried. Julie jumped up; Marty jumped up and of course, Killa jumped up. It was Julie that went into their bedroom with the other two women watching her intently. When Julie emerged with little Jim in her arms, she walked over to his father and handed the baby over. "He needed changing, he is happy now. Just hold him for a while and he'll go back to sleep."

Killa and Marty both left. Marty went to the den to watch the news and Killa went to the kitchen to putter - neither of them happy at not getting the baby.

To my surprise Ray handled the baby just fine, slightly rocking him. I could see Marty and Killa were both disappointed but neither said a word. "It's good he gets to know his father too. Once racing starts up again next week, he'll be busy. So I want to get as much fatherly time in as I can," Julie explained.

"How are you going to manage?" I asked her. Being Ray's crew chief and main mechanic took up a lot of time.

"I have Marty," she said softly, looking around to make sure Killa wasn't nearby. "She really is a big help. I just wish her and Killa got along. Jim can love everyone. No child can ever get enough love. Plus I'll have to get more crew help."

"Give them time," Ray interjected, "I know Killa will adjust to Marty. Just give them time."

That was my brother, pragmatic to a fault. Marty came in and sat by the fire, "We will need some more nursing bottles for tomorrow morning."

Julie just shook her head. "Yes, I'll take care of it tonight. Please Marty, let Killa feed the baby tomorrow. You'll have Jim all to yourself after we leave for home."

Marty's mouth went into a pout and nodded. "It's just that he can get a really upset stomach if not fed right."

"Well, let's give Killa a hand." Ray actually turned to Marty, almost confrontationally, very unlike him. "She helped raise Skip and I under very stressful circumstances. She deserves to have time with her grandson. Do you understand Marty, it's important to me?" Ray looked down at his son, sleeping soundly against him. "It's important to my son that he knows his grandmother."

To my surprise Marty just shook her head, "I will try." I could tell the stern woman was conflicted but she sounded sincere.

"Where is Killa?" I asked, looking around for my old absent nursemaid.

"She's in her room," Marty answered, obviously keeping track of her perceived rival.

Julie stood up and took the baby and headed toward Killa's room. When she came out the baby wasn't with her.

"Speaking of tomorrow," Ray relaxed, putting his stocking feet on the ottoman, "did I hear you offer that skier, Marc Lulis, to meet us for breakfast?" The lightness in my brother's voice did not match the frown on his face.

"He really is nice," Julie countered. "Right now he's all alone. His friends are coming in tomorrow afternoon. He is so pleased to get our original chateau. He just had rooms in the lodge and they gave him a discount if he and his friends took next door. I didn't tell him it was because we switched to this one."

"He's pushy," Ray looked at his wife. "I get enough pushy fans all year, I'm looking forward to it being just you. And you too Skip," he added me as an afterthought but I didn't mind. I remembered the crush of the fans during the regular racing season. Privacy was at a minimum.

"You don't have to worry about me, I'm not skiing much," I told him but thought *none at all if I can help it.*

"Oh Skip, I'm looking forward to us all skiing. I'll help you." Julie smiled that smile at me, my resolve to not skiing melting away.

"I'll try," I grumbled.

"Thank you," she reached over patting my leg. "We see so little of you and Killa, it's nice to be a family."

Oh boy, she was playing the *family* card. I had no defense at all. Skiing, here I come!

I snuck into the kitchen grabbing a muffin but as I turned around and Killa was right there with the baby in her arms. Her frown made me put it back. It was time for bed.

As if on cue my cellbutton buzzed. I touched the button, hearing *10:56 federation time, call from Ms. Hill.* My heart skipped a beat as it was late for her to be calling.

"Yeah, Hill," I said rather loudly. Panic must have been in my voice as Hill answered me quickly.

"Hi Chief," her voice had an edge to it so I knew something was wrong. "We had a little accident here."

"Accident?" I said too loudly as Julie and Ray looked over at me with alarm in their faces. Killa came out of the kitchen still carrying the sleeping Jim.

"Well," Hill stammered.

"Tell me!" Pictures of a burnt out apartment was circulating around my head, my hand went to my pocket for my blue pills.

"There was a fight and Bear has four stitches on his nose but he's okay and all..." she stopped talking I suppose waiting for my reaction. I saw Killa hand the baby to Julie and was sitting next to me on the arm of my chair. I didn't want to alarm her.

"And..." I encouraged Hill to continue.

"Well, Hoover has four stitches and he's fine too. Stanley is really sorry. She's been licking their ears all night."

"Licking their ears?" The statement astounded me. My two 190 pound Hiberian Hounds were letting a 26 pound Amise cat lick their ears?

"They are all sleeping on your bed together. Artchie helped me bring the dogs to the vet who says they'll recover perfectly fine. Even old Mrs. March, who covered the front desk by the way, says they look fine."

Killa took my cellbutton and put it on her collar, "Judy, is everything alright?" The small Ligithian's eyes were dark purple and her hair was standing on end, her ears twitching; a sign that she was concerned. She must have gotten the same story as I did. Her eyes returned to light purple, her hair settled down as did her small pointed ears. "Oh, they'll be fine now. Make sure you take out the blanket in Skipper's closet and give them something to cuddle up on. Oh yes, the baby is beautiful. We are having a great time. Skip is learning to ski tomorrow morning. Okay, here he is."

She handed me back my cellbutton. After attaching it to my collar, I asked Hill, "Why are they sleeping on my bed?"

"They like to sleep with me, makes me feel safe," she answered.

"I would think your gun next to the bed would be sufficient," I told her.

She laughed, it was rather a nice sound, I must admit. "You're so funny Chief. The dogs miss you. Artchie said to tell you all is well. He's so nice. He's handling the front desk very well. He says the experience will help him after he graduates." She laughed again. I could picture her with the two dogs and cat lying on my bed. It must be quite a sight. I almost wished I could be there but not quite.

"Glad to hear all is back to normal. Don't spoil them Hill." I admonished her knowing damn well I was blowing smoke up my ass.

"Oh, don't worry," she said as I heard two "woofs" from the dogs and one loud meow from the cat. How did my life get so complicated? Hill, of course!

"All is well at the office," she was half laughing. Why was she bringing up the office, I thought? Then she continued, "I told Issam we should all go and join you. Lara agreed but I'm afraid crime is not waiting for you to return. We had three murders on Mody yesterday but," she seemed to catch herself, "don't you worry, Helen and Sam headed out there."

I already knew since I had talked to Carl Issam earlier before the cocktail party. "Well, goodnight Hill. I'm fine, Killa is fine, and the baby is fine. I will be skiing tomorrow."

"Don't sound so unhappy about it," she must have heard the lack of enthusiasm in my voice. "You need the exercise!"

There she went ruining a perfectly good conversation. "Good bye, Hill."

I took a quick shower, set my cellbutton for 06:00 and grabbed my book. I put my gun in the voice activated side draw, usually it went under my pillow but not here. I think I got all of three paragraphs read when sleep overtook me. So much for catching up on my reading.

I was dreaming when the loud knocking interrupted my last lap with my Blue Horizon race car. At first I thought it was a flat tire on my speeding car. Then I realized it was real as the banging continued....

Chapter Four

I sat up as the pounding continued. I went to grab my gun under the pillow and realized where I was. Throwing the covers off, I stood up and grabbed my bathrobe on the bedpost. I put my hand on the drawer, told it to open. It took a few seconds for the voice and fingerprints check, and then the gun was in my hand.

I crossed to the bedroom door, flinging it open. I saw that both Killa and Julie were coming out of their rooms. "Stay where you are!" I shouted at them. They both froze. My thunderously loud commands are rarely disobeyed. It comes from years of being the Chief of Police and handling the public.

The pounding was coming from the front door. I crossed the living room and kitchen and looked out the peep hole. It was Marc Lulis. Even in the small peek hole I could see he was covered in blood. I swung the door open and he literally fell in, flat on his face. Management was not going to like the stains on the foyer carpeting.

"Help me!" he mumbled as he tried to get up. I grabbed his arm, careful of my bathrobe and pulled him up.

"What the hell!" I heard Ray from behind me. Then I heard him gag. Civilians never handle blood well.

"Ray, get back," I ordered him. "Lulis, what's going on?"

"She's dead, she's dead." He grabbed on to me, there went my newly bought bathrobe.

"Who?" I shook him, and then said loudly, "Who are you talking about?"

"Her, her…" was all I got out of him.

"Get yourself together!" I ordered him. "What the hell happened here?"

"My police voice snapped him somewhat out of it. Lulis started again, "I was skiing, honest." Now I knew he was coming out of it because he was already trying to protect himself from any blame.

"Just goddam tell me what's going on!" I told him. He was shorter than I was, he looked up, terror filled his face.

"I got home. She's in the living room." For the first time he must have realized his tight fitting spandex ski outfit was covered in blood. He looked at it in disbelief, "I tried to help her."

He got no further as I grabbed him and headed out the door. I only had my pajama bottoms and bathrobe on. The snow bit into my bare feet. The wind ripped at my bathrobe and chilled my chest. It must have been really snowing as even the heated walkways were covered with wet sloshy snow. My bathrobe flew wide open as I dragged him as fast as I could to the chateau next door. My brain was working overtime. I had to get to the girl, perhaps she wasn't dead.

I dragged him up the stairs onto the porch. My brain registered his skis and poles were outside, leaning against the clapboards. The door was half opened. Just inside was blood, probably from him. The bloody footprints lead me right into the living room.

There she was, her back to me but a pool of blood lay under her body. The footprints went right up to her. I let him go, hearing him whimper as he fell to the carpeting. I turned her over. It was Lilac and she was definitely dead. Her neck had been cut. Shit. I recoiled from the brutality of it. My mind registered the whole scene. The first thing I thought was *this is a mob killing*. No that's not possible, I realized. Not here.

I remembered that my cell button was back in my bedroom. I looked up to see Ray and Julie in the kitchen. "Ray get my cellbutton," I told him. "Julie go home!"

My sister-in-law was as white as a sheet. "Is that, is that…" she managed to get out.

"Yes, now get back to the house, now!" I saw her eyes widen, then she turned and left.

Ray returned with my cellbutton and he was carrying my slippers. I sent him home to his wife. I made Marc sit on a chair before he passed out. He took a seat on the other side so he could avoid looking at Lilac.

I pressed the Giles police station, getting the dispatcher. Although I had my Hilda superintendent, Chet Kodis' number, I had always stressed using the proper channels. Dispatchers had a hard job, especially with people going over their heads, so it was to her that I made the first call. "This is Chief Brown over at the Sunrise Snow Retreat, Chateau 14. There has been a murder of a young woman. I need you to send some officers and the crime unit over."

"You say a murder, are you sure the woman is dead? Do you need a medical unit?"

"Yes, the woman is dead," I firmly told her. "Can you get me superintendent Chet Kodis please."

"Certainly Chief Brown, the officers you requested are on their way." She sounded very efficient. I would have to compliment Chet on his great personnel.

Chet came on the cell almost immediately, which led me to believe the dispatcher had gotten a hold of him as I was talking to her. "Chief, I'm on my way. Should be there in about ten minutes. I live only a few miles from the resort. The duty officers will be there in a few minutes. I've also gotten hold of Lawren Streng. I got him out of bed so I presume he'll be there pretty soon. Streng sounded very upset, almost hysterical, so be prepared."

"Thanks Chet. Not a pretty scene, someone really is trying to make a point."

"Great. See you soon," he signed off.

I looked up to see Lawren Streng coming in the door with two police officers right behind him. The resort manager got as far as the kitchen, looked at the body and went to the sink and threw up. Great, now I had to worry about contamination of the crime scene.

"Please take Mr. Streng outside," I told the officers. Have him sit on one of the porch chairs. I'll be with him shortly."

"Yes, sir." One of them gently took Lawren by the arm and led him outside. I saw Marc Lulis start to get up. "Stay put," I order him. He started to say something and then shut up and sat back down.

Wearing my slippers, I carefully examined the scene. The girl was cold but not stiff. Whoever killed her did it in the last couple of hours. I hit my cellbutton hearing in my ear, 04:02 standard federation time. I clicked it off. So I figured the murder had happened around two but it would be up to the coroner to establish the time of death.

"When did you last see her?" I asked Marc.

"I don't know," he mumbled.

"Think!" I had enough of pretending trauma.

"It must have been around 01:00, just as I was leaving the reception. I wanted to make the next lift to Astin Mountain top. They just groomed Snake Run."

"When did you get back here?" I asked as I noticed a very expensive diamond wrist bracelet on Lilac. I took a pencil from my bathrobe pocket and slightly lifted it. I noticed also she had matching diamond earrings. Whoever killed her wasn't robbing her, that's for sure. I would bet the diamonds alone were worth half my salary.

"I don't know, about, about 03:45. I only made one run down and was tired."

Just then Chet came in with his whole forensic team, which wasn't a lot - a doctor and a photographer.

"Crap Chief, you can't get a break! For god's sake it's your vacation." Chet shook my hand. "You know your bathrobe is ruined."

"Yeah." I motioned to Marc Lulis, "he found her and ran next door to our chateau."

"Is this your chateau, Mr. Lulis?" my superintendent asked in a strong clear voice, almost accusingly.

"Yes, yes...," the man stammered, obviously very intimidated by all the cops now entering the lodging. "I was skiing...I was skiing," he was almost whining.

"We will check that out." Chet nodded to one of his officers, "please take Mr. Lulis down to the station and take his statement."

"Can't I change my outfit?" he was looking at the blood covered skiing outfit. "I can't be seen like this!"

"We will let you have something downtown." The officer took his arm. "We'll need to properly bag what you are wearing."

As Marc Lulis was being escorted out, I heard, "I want a lawyer!"

"Of course," the officer assured him.

After he'd left, Chet turned to me, "What's the chance he did it?"

"To tell you the truth, practically none," I gave my opinion, "he doesn't seem the type to cut a young woman's throat and he seemed genuinely in a panic at my door. He'll be easy to check if he was on the slopes."

Chet nodded as he bent near Lilac's body. "Nice looking girl." He also noticed the bracelet and matching earrings.

"I met her at a welcoming reception earlier this evening. Why don't you take my statement now, then you can take Julie's and Ray's statements. They were there too."

"Good idea." He looked over at the photographer. "He'll be awhile, let's go back to your place."

We spent the next few hours going over everything that happened at the reception earlier the night before. An officer recorded everything

The best way to do a statement is to start from the very beginning. I told him about going with Julie and Ray to the Lodge. Still, I let the interrogating officer set the dimensions. Chet wanted me to start when we had first entered the reception. He was interested in impressions. He questioned me about Streng and his wife Hessina then went on to when Lilac first appeared. He was very interested when I told him that when a young man named Reich had taken over the dance I had with her, that Lilac had said she was *working*.

"Working?" Chet looked surprised, "Working what?"

"I think Lilac meant she was working the reception, keeping us male guests happy."

"Well, I've got some pointed questions to ask Streng, but I already sent him home," my superintendent informed me.

I shook my head, "Don't know what Lilac meant by that."

Ray and Julie gave their renditions of the reception. I heard Ray in the kitchen speculate on Hessina's dislike of Lilac. Then I heard Julie later confirm it. I felt bad for Streng's wife. She would be under a lot of scrutiny and I liked her somehow. But personal feelings mean little in a murder investigation.

When Chet was done I came and sat next to him in the kitchen. Killa had gotten him a cup of java, which he seemed to clench in frustration.

"This is not going to go over very well on Hilda. Anything that ruffles the feathers of our tourist industry is catastrophic to the resort owners. I've gotten hold of Isaam and he is sending two homicide detectives. They'll be here this afternoon, it all depends on what Jumps are available."

I nodded. I wasn't going to force my way into this investigation. It was Chet's and I'm big on personal duties. This wasn't mine. He would work with Carl Issam. I have to admit I was tempted but nothing is more demoralizing than to have the "Chief" take over.

"Well, I'll let you get on with your vacation. If I have any more questions I'll get hold of you. I hope you won't mind that if I run into trouble, I can ask you for some advice? It is not like we get many murders out here."

"If you need me, I'm here," I sincerely told him. After he left I sat nursing my cup of java. The murder bothered my sensibilities. It wasn't that I even liked Lilac but she was so young. The *Why?* came flooding back to me.

It was close to 06:00 when Julie came into the kitchen with Jimmy in her arms. She was followed by Killa and Marty both looking anxious to help with the baby. To my sister-in-law's credit, she put each woman to work. Killa was getting the baby bottles ready, while Marty was setting out his outfits and diapers for the day. I'm sure Julie could have done everything herself but both women were content.

"Anything on that poor girl?" Julie asked me.

"No, we won't hear anything more. Hopefully the press won't get our names and we will be left alone."

"Oh, good grief, Ray will have a fit. He's been looking forward to having some *no fan, no press* time."" Julie gave Killa the baby to change and get him dressed. Marty hovered close by watching with anxious eyes. My nephew cooed and babbled over the attention.

"We will see." I looked out at the snow-covered wonderland. It was time to get dressed for my skiing lesson. I felt conspicuous and out of my comfort zone as the outfit closed tightly, despite Julie's assurance that I looked fine. Of course, her and Ray looked great in their ski outfits.

I followed them over to the ski area. It was bustling. They headed for the slopes, I followed the sign pointing to lessons. The sun was full out and the smell of fresh cool air was wonderful considering Fulton was the exact opposite. I took off my hat and mittens just to get the feel of total freshness. I stood there taking in the mountains, the blue sky with white puffy clouds. Yet, the murder intruded into my brain. I couldn't let it go, damn!

"Mr. Brown?" A woman with a tabloid opened in front of her broke into my thoughts. "Are you here for a beginner's lesson?" She stood there looking like some Alpine Amazonian. I was waiting for her to break out yodeling.

I almost quipped that I was here for a suntan, but I held my tongue and just nodded. The ski teacher looked like one of those strict army sergeants with her tight blonde braids. You know the kind that would beat the shit out of anyone who was disobedient. Standing there in my skis, having trouble keeping my balance, I was no match for her. I took a blue pill; this was going to be a strenuous, long, arduous morning.

"Please get in line. We are going over some basics first," she said pointing to about twenty skiers. I cringed - half of them were children. Wonderful! Snow castles were looking better and better. I took my place next to a little squirt who kept hitting me with his ski pole. On the other side was an older lady who kept grabbing my arm to keep from falling.

And so the morning began with basics and then we put our helmets on and carefully followed the instructor to the "bunny slope" lift. Half of the class kept falling, while the other half almost fell. The poor older lady actually held onto me the whole way. When we finally got there she totally lost her balance and brought me down with her.

"Oh, I'm so sorry," the gray haired older woman half cried.

I got myself up and then helped her. We sat together on the lift, as we swayed toward the top of the small hill. She explained she was only there to watch her grandson. Now that's a dedicated grandmother!

At the top, we each took our turn slowly gliding down with our snowplow V-type movement. The ski instructor's voice came into our helmets, encouraging us to keep to our form. Yeah, right. I just wanted to keep upright.

I hated the kids, who seemed to do much better than us grownups. "Come on, Mister, get out of the way," one kid yelled at me. By noon I was exhausted. I sat on a bench at the bottom of the beginner's slope watching the kids that already were skiing circles around everyone. I had at least learned to stop after plowing through a few fences that had been put up for the protection of non-skiing spectators. Some people just loved watching us beginners tumble down. I ached everywhere; literally everywhere.

"Mr. Brown, time for lunch," the blonde bodybuilder informed me, sounding even more like a drill sergeant. "Need that energy, think of all those calories you've burned up!"

I'd rather not. I'd rather just sit here and suffer. "I think I'll pass. I think I'll call it a day," my voice sounded like a pleading toddler.

"Oh, come now. You paid for the entire day, you are made of stronger stuff!" Her demanding voice assured me that she'd drag me back if I tried to escape.

Yep, a drill sergeant. I'd bet money that she had done a stint in the Federation Marines. Leaving our skis behind and pushing the button to loosen my ski suit, we followed her to nearby picnic tables. I must admit hot chicken gumbo soup followed by a potato steak casserole with hot buttered rolls was heavenly. It was only ruined by knowing I would be heading back to the slopes when I was done. Of course, after eating so much, I wondered if the suit would fit but it snuggly shrunk again, making me feel like an Atlise walrus or even better a Mody blue whale.

I didn't see the older lady; she probably had made her escape. I had to admit I was getting better. I could actually make it down without falling but I still stopped just short of the fences. It was midafternoon when I had my day totally ruined.

As I was careening down out of control with my arms flailing, trying to snowplow to a stop, I noticed Lieutenant Judy Hill at the fast approaching fence. I totally lost it. I hit the thankfully soft fence and bounced back to fall flat on my ass.

"Chief?" she yelled as my detective jumped over the fence. "Are you alright?"

I was covered in snow, my ski glasses were askew, leaving my eyes caked with the white stuff. I'd lost one of my gloves and my skis were sticking straight up. Hill helped me stand up, brushing me off.

Taking off my helmet, I finally found my voice or part of it. "What are you doing here!" I gruffly croaked it out. "How did you find me?"

"Nice to see you too, Chief!" Hill sounded hurt, making me back off a little, although I'm not known for my diplomatic skills.

"I repeat Hill, what are you doing here?" I had dragged my skis over to the bench, dodging the now proficient kids that were doing circles around me.

"Issam sent me here," bluntly said, "Fred came too."

"Fred!" I sat down in a huff. "Fred?" I repeated. "Is Issam losing his mind?"

"Now what do you mean by that?" Hill sounded angry. "Is he crazy for sending me or Fred?"

"Both, why didn't he call me? Who's watching the dogs?" I grabbed my skis and headed toward the outdoor restaurant with the picnic benches. Hill followed me, gabbing all the way.

"Artchie is more than capable of watching ALL the animals. I noticed you didn't ask about Stanley. Mrs. March is pitching in. So is Mrs. Hippnow."

"Hippnow! Good god Hill, the grumpy old bitch will call the animal league!" I stared at her, what had she done now?

"She is a very nice lady. I got her into the OPD and she's very grateful."

I shook my head, I doubted the Old Person's Depression League would help the old bag. My head hurt and she'd only been here a few minutes. "I'm gonna kill Issam!" I exploded getting some worried side-glances from the other patrons. I popped another blue pill and tried to relax. Not easy with Hill around.

"As for Issam, I do believe he's been trying to call you, he even sent a message to the front desk but you didn't answer." She made me sound like a blooming irresponsible idiot, which I quickly realized I was. Damn, my cellbutton hadn't rung once. I'd been so busy trying to keep upright that I hadn't noticed. *Good going Chief of police,* I chastised myself. I stopped, sitting down at a picnic table. I fooled with my cell, it was turned off. Damn Killa, I would bet my old nursemaid had something to do with this. Wait 'til I got back to the chateau, heads would roll!

I realized I hadn't had a cup of java all day. No wonder my hands were shaking. I ordered one and Hill had a cup of black tea. "Okay, tell me how you found me. No, let me guess, you've seen Killa." I pressed the ski outfit's button, feeling the relief as if expanded. I noticed Hill's eyes widen with amusement as she saw it expand.

"Wow, that's amazing. The baby's cute by the way. Though I hate to mention it, I did sense a kind tension between Killa and Julie's cousin. Killa just told me you were on the beginner's slope, getting lessons and to look for someone with a baby blue ski outfit."

I think I blushed about three shades of red. "I did it for Killa, she wanted me to wear the colors of my *Blue Horizon* car," I sputtered out, knowing damn well it was a waste of an excuse.

I got one of those incredulous looks Hill is so famous for. "Well you certainly are easy to pick out. Killa told me of your time at Belcher's. She told me the suit almost choked you to death. Thank goodness for Julie. You should have known better and started with a bigger size."

"I'm very capable...," I started to yell at Hill but noticed people were looking so I quieted, "When did you become an expert on my clothes? I can do my own shopping thank you. I got my own hat and coat... and boots!" I quietly snarled. "The suit isn't that big, the clerk was a jerk!"

"Good for you. Now about the murder." Hill could certainly change topics quickly when it suited her! "I talked to Chet. I guess that Marc Lulis' alibi has been substantiated, although still something funny there. Fred is out looking for that Reich Hisner. He is one of Lilac's local boyfriends. She had several by the way."

"Look Hill, I can't get totally involved in this. Chet Kodis is a very capable superintendent of the Hilda police. I'm not going to step on his toes." As if he'd heard his name, Chet came walking over, a cup of java in his hands. He was dressed in all browns that made him blend in with the surrounding atmosphere. He looked the "outdoor" guy; hearty and very masculine with heavy boots and deerskin jacket. He took off his sheepskin gloves and matching hat and sat down.

"I see you found him," he nodded at Hill. "How are the lessons going Chief?"

"Don't ask," I told him. "Look, I was just explaining to Hill, you are more than capable of handling this. I don't want to step on your toes."

"I could use some stepping," he interrupted me. "Have you filled him in?" he asked Hill. "I got a feeling Chief that this isn't going to be pretty. The newspaper has an article about it in today's tab. So far, you and your brother haven't been mentioned."

"I was just starting to fill him in," Hill explained sipping on her tea.

"I could use all the help I can get. I don't want to ruin your skiing vacation but I just don't want to miss anything crucial. If you could help a little it would be appreciated. I've already heard from both of Hilda's senators and both mentioned your name."

Wonderful, that's all we needed, the Dome government getting involved. My aching body was not regretting the interruption of my bunny hill experience. "Okay, what do you have so far, Hill? I'm still calling Issam and wondering if he's on drugs."

"Oh funny, Chief," Hill exclaimed. "It seems the last people to see Lilac Floe were Marc Lulis and that Reich Hisner guy. I guess Reich caused a scene over Marc's attention to Ms. Floe after you had left."

"Have you asked Lewren Streng about her *working* the reception?" I asked Chet.

"I grilled him for several hours. His lawyer was there as was his wife. He wouldn't say much about the girl, claims he didn't hire her. He knew Ms. Floe as I guess she was quite the skier, on ski patrol and has won several local ski competitions."

"What did his wife say?" I asked.

"Not much, but she didn't look happy. I asked her what she thought of Lilac and got nowhere, claims she hardly knew the girl." Chet slouched in his chair as if he was completely disgusted. "The Strengs have a sharp off-planet lawyer, who also represents the Hildan Corporation. Think he's from Fulton Station."

"Who is he?" both Hill and I asked together.

"Nove Deck," my superintendent answered.

"Shit," slipped out of my mouth. Deck was not only one of the top lawyers for the Dome representatives; he was the top lawyer for everyone important! "How did he get here so fast?"

Chet shrugged. It was Hill that knew, "He was on our Jump. I noticed him, so did Fred."

"Yeh, I noticed the bastard." Fred was walking up to our table. He looked like a huge lumberjack.

"Where's your axe?" I couldn't help but ask him, getting an uncomprehending look from my detective. "I know you don't like Deck."

"He's gotten some of the big drug mob guys off. He's not too fond of you Chief, especially since you got the Blithies put in jail."

I shrugged, Deck was the least of my worries. He was just a slick slime guy but also a very competent lawyer. We need to find the killer of Lilac and if Deck got in my way I'd plow him over.

Fred sat at the picnic table and the seat groaned. Fred was one big guy, not fat but just big, standing about 6ft. 6in. He was my best drug enforcer which is why I couldn't understand Carl Issam sending him here. Maybe I was missing something. "Did Carl send you because there is a drug connection?" I asked the big guy who had ordered two hamburgers and double fries.

"Not that I can tell. That Reich Hisner guy is a pansy!" His first bite took half the hamburger.

"Really Fred!" Hill exploded. "You can be such a pig sometimes."

"Well, he is a pansy!" Fred finished the hamburger on the second bite.

"It's the way you eat, dummy, and yes the pansy remark is very unprofessional also," my lieutenant curtly informed him.

"Well he wouldn't stop crying," Fred frowned, "it's hard to interview someone when all they want to do is sob uncontrollably."

"I gather he took Lilac's death hard," I conjectured. "Did you get anything out of him, any suspicion he did it?"

"Don't think he has the balls to do it." Fred Stoshingburg dug into his french fries. "He's a stripper at a local nightclub. He has *talent*, he told me." My detective smirked, waving his hand in disgust.

"He's a stripper?" Hill almost fell off her bench. "Aren't they mostly gay?"

"Now who's unprofessional?" I told her. "Please ignore my uncouth detectives, they usually show better judgment, Chet." I pointed my finger at both of them but they ignored me.

Chet, however, was laughing, "He must work at the Chippy Chip Bar and Grill."

"Yep, that's the one," Fred nodded as he finished his second hamburger. "Told me that him and Lilac were going to get married as soon as he hit it big time."

"Oh I can't wait until our news guys get a hold of this," Chet held his head in his hands. "They are going to have a field day with this!"

"Well, between sobs, Reich told me he left Lilac at about 01:00 in the morning when they argued about some guy she was flirting with. I pressed him hard, kinda scared him I think when I grabbed him by the shirt and accused him of killing her." Fred wiped the ketchup off his face, "but he cried he didn't do it!"

Only Stoshingberg! I cringed but I had to admit Fred got results so I chose to ignore his tactics. I also knew that my big detective knew how and when to stretch the rules. If Nove Deck was Reich's lawyer, Fred would have stayed clear. Was it right or wrong? As usual the gray areas dominated the law and criminals knew it!

"I should have the forensic report tonight," Chet informed us. "The coroner was curious to see if she died before her throat was cut."

"I don't think so," I conjectured, "too much blood. I'm more interested in if she was unconscious or did she fight her attacker? That will tell us a lot."

"What's next?" Chet asked.

"If you agree, I think Hill needs to get into Lilac's life, every aspect. Fred, I need you to find out about Streng and his wife. Is he liked, is he cheating on his wife? How well did Lawren know Lilac Floe?"

Both Fred and Hill nodded and started to get up when Chet touched his cellbutton and held up his hand to us. When he got off he looked like someone had struck him.

"They just found Lawren Streng dead, apparent suicide with a note that is a confession of killing Lilac!"

We all stood there stunned....

Chapter Five

All of us took off at the same time. Of course, I had my skis and was still in my ski boots and outfit. I did not make good time, even with Fred helping me. He came back and took my skis and poles. The damn boots were hard to walk in but I couldn't change them unless I went back to the chateau. I decided to go straight to the lodge with the rest of the crew.

There were several police hovers and an ambulance in front of the main lodge. Two officers greeted us at the tall stain glass doors that stood wide open. Once inside, Chet must have known where Streng's office was because he headed right up the front staircase, taking two at a time. Hill was right behind him.

Fred put my skis and poles against a wall and followed Hill up the stairs. I sat on a chair and took the damn boots off, throwing them with the skis. I then trudged up in my stocking feet. I did not take the stairs two at a time but huffed and puffed to the top. On the second floor was a long hallway but it was at the first door that I saw two officers standing.

"Sorry, Sir. You can't go in there," an older patrol guy put his arm across the door barring my entrance.

"I'm the Police Chief," I said and ran into his arm as he did not remove it.

"Sure you are, and I'm the Governor General." He took in my baby blue ski outfit, socked feet and gave his partner a smirk.

Now I'm reasonable most of the time. I'm lying; I'm on a short lease. "Listen, let me in or you'll be walking the cold streets of Giles doing foot patrol for a month in your stocking feet!"

When I'm in my "Chief" mode, few question me and his eyes went wide and saw beyond the blue ski suit, taking his arm down and letting me enter.

Inside was a large office with a panoramic view of the ski area. The mountains loomed large with blue skies framing them. Most of the office was taken up by an immense oak desk that had two carved high-backed cushioned chairs in front. To the side was a couple of couches and chairs with a wide telescreen. On the other side was a conference setup with a round table with computers at each of the plush office chairs. It was all beautifully decorated in shades of grays and tans and complimented the outside view instead of taking away from the mountains' background scenery.

It was, however, the body of Lawren Streng that took precedence. His head was down on the desk top, his arms spread out in an awkward position. The police photographer was already taking pictures and I saw when they rolled him over that a bullet hole was in his front forehead. The projectile gun must have been up against his forehead because the wound was large and gaping. It looked like a burn discharge was also quite prevalent.

I noticed the gun near his right hand. Chet was looking at it before they bagged it for evidence. "He shot himself." My superintendent looked at me with questions on his face. It is rare we deal with projectile guns. Most weapons are electrical charged stun guns. It's an ironic term since stun guns usually kill.

"They say he was all alone up here," Lt. Hill remarked, "but they can't be one hundred percent sure since there is a back stairway."

"What about this note they claim to have found?" I asked.

"It is on his tab," Hill remarked but I could tell from her voice she was skeptical of its authenticity.

I walked over to the desk touching the computer tab that was just beyond his left hand. *I cannot go on! I killed Lilac. I loved her but she was threatening to tell my wife and ruin my career,* came popping up. The holographic screen's letter appeared double-sided. Now wasn't that thoughtful of him.

I could see why Hill was skeptical. It sounded hastily written, perhaps the killer didn't have much time to think it through. I realized at that moment I was considering it murder. I didn't, however, say a thing. Let the person who did this think the cops were fooled.

Fred was over by the telescreen. The big man was wearing investigation gloves that half fit his big hands. He had a big frown on his face. "What's going on?" I asked him.

"I've been playing with his remote telescreen buttons on this chair. You can see by the worn indent in the seat that it was where Streng sat when over here." He saw me take note of it and continued, "He was watching the local ice hockey game." Fred pressed a button and up came the Planetarians vs. Celestrians game with the time it had been on - just a couple of hours ago! "The game actually ended just a couple of minutes ago. The local team, the Planetarians won. It wasn't shut off by the way, but timed out."

"I think we'd better check this out, why would he kill himself in the middle of a hockey game he was watching?" My eyes went to the wall opposite, a picture of Lawren Streng and what appeared to be a famous well-known hockey player was prominently displayed. They were in a buddy stance, smiling for the camera. Lawren was holding a disc puck. Planetarian banners and other photos surrounded the picture.

"It gets worse," Fred nodded toward the chair. "Streng was drinking a ColaCool. His glass is next to the chair, there is still some ice in the glass. Also he was smoking a cigar, it's in the ashtray. The butt is half finished. I'd say whoever shot Streng, interrupted him watching the game and got him to go over to his desk." So Fred had come to the same conclusion as I had.

"Why use a projectile gun?" I was trying to make sense of this, "Wouldn't they hear it downstairs?"

"Maybe not if the door was closed. They may have heard it and not understood what it was," Hill said as she came over. "Fred, doesn't the drug cartel use projectiles - like a signature kill?"

"Yup," Fred simply said. "The Blithie and the Nixitie families come to mind but then it could be a copycat or someone trying to screw with our heads."

It was the second time I had thought of the mob and my hair stood up on my neck. I needed to talk to Issam and see what he thought but I'd wait until later when I was alone.

"There is something wrong with this," Chet Kodis had come up behind me. "This doesn't smell right."

"We agree but let's not concede that it is anything but a suicide," I told the Hilda cop and he nodded his agreement. We didn't get to talk any further as Hessina had come rushing in. She stood in the middle of the room and screamed. It was a high pitched scream that hurt the ears. An officer who had been following Hessina in caught her as she slumped to the floor.

"Someone get the doctor!" Chet yelled then demanded, "Who the hell let her in?"

"Sorry sir, she ran right past me. I tried to grab her but I missed." The officer sounded contrite as he bent down to the woman sprawled on the floor.

To my surprise, Hill ran over, stooping on one knee, she cradled Streng's wife's head in her hands. "Hessie, Hessie it's me, Jude," she softly murmured.

The doctor had come over and was feeling for the woman's pulse. "She's fainted." He rubbed Streng's wife's face. Hessina's eyes flickered open.

She looked at Hill, "Jude, is that you?" She grabbed onto my lieutenant's arm and sat up, a wild look on her face. "Where am I..." but then it must have dawned on her where she was. "Oh my god, what has happened?" She tried to get up, her bony legs seemed unable to support her. Hill helped her and tried to turn her away from the sight of the body which still was slumped over the desk.

Hessina, however, was determined to look at her husband's body. "Oh Lawren, what has happened?" Tears flowed down her prominent cheeks; her long fingers were clasped tightly in front of her. She turned to Hill, "They told me downstairs he'd been shot. He's dead isn't he?"

It was Hill that took charge, "Yes, there is nothing you can do. Come with me, Hessie. There is nothing you can do here." She firmly grabbed on to the tall thin woman and led her out the door.

"I gather your detective knows Streng's wife," Chet Kodis turned to me.

"Hill knows a lot of people, let's leave it at that," I dryly informed him. I wasn't going to get into Hill's pedigree.

"Frig," Fred had come over, "wife's a little upset. Wait 'til she hears about the note."

We quickly went through Streng's desk but found nothing unusual. I didn't dare go any further until we got a search warrant. They were taking the body away and the crime scene was being taped off and sealed when Nove Deck showed up.

"I demand to know what has happened to my client!" he said in his most authoritative lawyer voice, which of course got my hackles up. He was dressed in his lawyer uniform of a three piece tailored gray suit. I noticed an old fashioned watch was hung on a chain dressing his vest pocket. I was not impressed because it was there just to impress.

"Demand away," I quipped. "I'm sure you'll get a full report when it is ready later today. Until then stay out of the investigators' way." Gripe, I couldn't stand the guy on hot Futon Station, in this beautiful cool surroundings it seemed to emphasize his sleaziness - I hated him more. "Please remove yourself from the crime scene."

"Crime scene? I heard it was a suicide?" he almost shouted it at me as if I was hard of hearing.

"My, aren't your ears on fire?" I snapped at him. Fred snickered behind me, "Whether it is a suicide or a murder, it is a crime scene. So out!" I pointed at the door.

"You'll pay for this Brown. Baby blue suits you well, pansy clown, you asshole." Deck yelled back at me as he left the room.

No doubt I'd probably made his day, I thought as I turned to Fred. "Find out where he's staying, let's keep tabs on the bastard. I got a feeling he's more than just Streng's lawyer."

Fred nodded and left. Chet left assuring me he'd call when the autopsy on Lilac came in. I told him I'd be downtown as soon as I could.

Unfortunately, Fred had come running back. "Hey Chief, the press is here." Wonderful! "They have Chet Kodis cornered. He's trying to assure them but I think Nove Deck set them on him. How else would the reporters know you are here? The vultures are asking for you."

Shit. Hill came strolling in. "The doctor has her sedated. Until she's rested I'm not going to get much out of her."

"How do you know her?" I asked trying not to break my promise of bringing up her father, though I had a feeling it was through family ties.

"We grew up on Lobo together. Her father is a big time attonium fuel baron. He heads the XIL Company in our sector."

"Well that explains her marriage," Fred spurted out, "the woman is ugly as hell."

"You clod," Hill exploded at him, "she's a wonderful person, one of the nicest people I know. I heard through the gossip vine that it was a marriage of love, she could have done much better!"

"Hey, don't go all emotional on me!" Fred backed away, "Just calling it as I see it."

"Well you are wrong!" Hill pointed her finger at him then me, "Don't go judging people by their flimsy covers."

"Fine. We have a bigger problem, the news media is downstairs. I really don't want to see them yet. I need to change out of this friggin buffoon suit."

"Isn't there a back way? We could slip out." Fred pointed down the hallway. I checked it out, looks like only employees use it."

"Fine, let's go." I headed out the door. Down below in the lobby I could hear the news people badgering Chet.

"Come on, give us the real deal," one reporter was shouting at my superintendent, "where is Chief Brown, what's he doing here? We heard the woman's murder is connected to this suicide? Was he the girl's lover?"

"Please, we will have more for you this afternoon. We have a press conference scheduled for later today. Until then I don't have anything!"

We headed down the long hallway passing several conference rooms and even a small kitchen. The steep stairs were at the very end with a small windowed white door at the bottom. We headed down, Hill leading the way. She opened the door. I could feel the cold draft. My mind drank in the freshness of the air, something we never see on Fulton.

The snow was dazzling, blinding our eyesight. I hadn't gotten two steps out when I realized my stocking feet were going to freeze me. Oh well.

We hadn't got two steps away when I heard, "Aw, Chief Brown?" There stood a woman reporter with several camera crew members all pointing their equipment at me! Shit!

....

Julie handed me a brandy, "I think you need this Skip." She patted my arm as I sat in the big easy chair with my still frozen toes pointed at the roaring fireplace.

"He needs more than that," Ray quipped in, as he sat watching his tabloid, "he looks just great in his baby blues on the news feed."

I moaned, Julie patted my arm again. "Don't worry, no one will pay any attention to what you're wearing," she tried to console me.

I moaned again. After finally escaping the news people, I'd come the back way to the chateau. No one was there; Ray was still skiing, Julie had taken the baby and the two ladies shopping. I was glad they weren't there to see me fume with humiliation; another great outing with the press. I'm sure they'd all get a big kick back on Fulton of me in my big blue outfit with no shoes.

When I got back to the chateau, the first thing I thought of was to get rid of the outfit.

Unfortunately, I couldn't manage to squeeze out of it. I kept pressing the button but it didn't seem to work. The more I tried the more frustrated I became. The arms seemed too tight to get out of their sleeves. I couldn't believe it.

I called Hill. "Where is Fred, he's not answering his cell?" I demanded.

"He's on his way to check out where Nove Deck is," she answered.

"Where are you?" I asked.

"I'm in the main lobby asking the staff questions," she answered.

"Well, get over here, I'm in the chateau, hurry!" The thought of spending any more time strapped into this outfit was driving me crazy. I managed to take another blue pill, calming me. That's all I'd need, to have an episode.

Ten minutes later Hill got to the chateau. "You called me because of your ski suit?" she couldn't help but smile although she tried to hide it behind her hand. "I ran all the way here, thinking you are dying and you just can't get out of the stupid tight suit?" She was shaking her head in disbelief. Damn woman!

"I'm struck! Help me out of this outfit from hell!" I shouted at her. "Pull on the arms!"

"Gesh, you could at least say *please*." She walked over taking one of the sleeves and pulled. It slowly came loose and then she pulled on the other. What relief!

I quickly peeled the rest of the stupid ski outfit off, throwing it as far as I could in frustration. I sighed deeply, feeling the refreshing air - then I realized I only had my underwear on.

At least Hill had the sense to avert her laughing eyes. I walked with as much dignity as I could to my bedroom, slamming the door behind me. After I'd dressed in my new corduroys and sweater, I walked out to find Hill patiently waiting. She'd made herself a cup of tea and handed me a cup of java as a peace offering. I gladly took it.

"Explain Hessie to me," I pointed my mug at her, "sounds like the two of you were close."

"We went to the same private elementary school." Hill started to explain but got up and went to the window, looking out as if the past was out there. "Hessina was always an awkward kid - awkward looking and awkward socially. Of course, because her father was so rich and so powerful, none of the kids teased her. In reality, they all tried to be friends because of the influence her family had on Orbo. I never tried to connect with her family, so she liked me because I was a *real* friend."

"What's wrong with her?" I asked. "She is almost bird-like."

"She has Chroame's Disease or commonly known as Bird Disease. It causes a tall bony structure. She is over six feet five inches tall. Her bones are almost hollow. The body takes on a birdlike quality. High voice, pointed nose, small eyes that turn red easily." Hill turned back from the window, looking at me with a frown, "It hasn't been easy for her but she's a nice person. When she lived on Orbo she did a lot of charity work. She knows people make fun of her behind her back, despite that she isn't a bitter person."

"How did she meet Streng?" I asked. "How did that happen?"

"I'm not sure. I heard from my brother Matt, who's friends with her brother that she'd married someone who really loved her and that she adored him. He never told me the particulars."

"Well, what little I saw, he was affectionate towards her," I tried to sound sincere but Hill shook her head.

"No, you are like Fred. She's ugly so how can a good looking man like Streng adore her?"

"I think you are judging me a little harshly, Judith!" I grumped at her, although I felt guilty even as I said it.

"I should call Matt and tell him to call her brother and get some family down here."

"Use the police Jump data line, it is for official business," I told her.

My lieutenant touched her cell, putting an off planet call to her brother's cell via the quick police Jump line. It took just a few minutes before her brother answered. She told him what had happened. Matt assured her he'd call Hessina's family. "Matt will tell them with the right compassion. He'll make a good Consulate General someday."

"So he's your father's heir?" I saw her nod. I saw a strange look come over her.

"My father's calling, damn," her face took on a grimace look but she pressed her cellbutton. "Yes, father?" I heard the uncertainty in her voice. "No, I'm fine. Yes I'm the investigating detective. I'll be fine! No, don't you dare come here! No, don't send Matt! I mean it. Yes Mr. Brown knows I'm here, he's also here. Fine good bye."

"Remember, he's your father, he can't help but worry." I'd met her father, also known as

Consulate Assembly General Thern Pinote. He was probably one of the most powerful politicians in the humanoid universe. He had promised to leave Hill alone but I wondered for how long.

"Well, you obviously got his respect, your name stopped the badgering. If only he could have seen you in your baby blues," Hill said rather sarcastically.

"That's a low blow, Judy. Don't take it out on me because your dad has angered you."

She didn't say anything but I could tell I'd made my point.

Just then, Julie returned with Killa and Marty bringing up the rear. Supersensitive Killa picked up immediately on my mood. "Skipper, what has happened?"

"He is having a bad day," Hill chimed in as she gave Killa a quick hug.

"Thank you for answering for me," I frowned at my lieutenant but of course it had no effect, she just continued unabatedly. The woman had no sense of propriety.

"He had a run in with the local press and he was still in his blue whale suit and didn't have any shoes on to boot." Hill was laughing. I'm glad I had brightened her day.

Julie started laughing. Even Killa and the dower Marty had smiles. I'm so glad my life amuses everyone but me.

My sister-in-law suddenly became very serious. "We heard that Lawren Streng was found dead. Is it true? It's all over the news. He committed suicide?" It was then that she got me a much needed brandy.

I nodded as the brandy slid smoothly down my throat.

"Oh that is terrible," Killa said what they were all thinking. "His poor family."

My cellbutton rang, it was Chet wanting a meeting after supper in his office to go over all the autopsy reports. I'd be there. Hill left to continue her questioning of the staff. I would see her and Fred at the chateau here for supper then we would all head to the Hilda police station together.

And so here I was drinking a brandy, trying to get my dignity smoothed out, taking another blue pill to calm my shattered nerves. My brother Ray, who had returned from a day of skiing, was not helping my mood.

"I think your outfit looks rather stunning on the video. The lack of shoes, that really finishes the whole outfit, especially appealing as you are running away from the cameras." The amusement in his voice didn't help my headache.

"Shut up, Ray," I managed to get out between sips, "it's you guys that made me get that outfit."

Marty had come in carrying the baby. She handed little Jimmy to his father. "Julie says it's *Dad Time*." Killa, of course was right behind her and sat on Ray's chair arm.

"You are supposed to be on vacation," my old nursemaid looked disapprovingly at me. "He and Judy work all the time; work, work, work." Her white hair whirled around her little head showing her Ligithian disapproval; her eyes were dark purple, her small ears twitching away.

Now how did Hill get into the conversation? "It's our job. I'm Chief of Police, it is not a nine to five job!" I sent my remarks in Killa's direction, getting a big Ligithian frown in return.

"You should have some life, Skip," Julie had come over sitting on the other arm of Ray's chair.

"I do. It's just like Ray when he comes across fans or sponsors, he still is the *race driver*." I put my brandy glass down; somehow it had lost its taste. I was tired, frustrated and my life, according to everyone else just wasn't up to par.

"No, no," Killa interjected, "Skip does a lot of good but there is a *time* for vacation." I watched fascinated as my old nursemaid's ears twitched even faster.

"Well, most vacations don't have a murder happen," Ray pointed out. "It seemed so perfect when the resort offered me such a deal."

"They called *you*?" I asked.

"Yeah, they wanted to congratulate me on winning the cup. They offered me this chateau almost free. They didn't even ask for any endorsements - nothing."

I didn't get to ask any more questions as Hill and Stoshingburg showed up. I introduced Fred as Ray and Julie had never met him before. The big guy shook hands with Ray and the baby started crying, bawling really.

"Gee, sorry," Fred looked horrified at the screaming baby.

"You're such a clod," Hill expounded.

"And you're a pain in the ass, oops sorry," he looked at the baby as if the kid could tell he swore.

"It's alright, Fred," Julie said. "He needs to cry every once in a while. I'm sure you had nothing to do with it."

Marty had run over taking the baby, she was rocking him back and forth.

"No, no," Killa said, "here give him to me." She reached up to take Jim from Marty. I thought for a second it would be a battle. Julie tensed. Marty, however, finally let go.

"Here, here Jimmy." Killa snuggled the baby close to her face. I noticed her eyes, hair and ears were back to normal. The baby stopped crying and actually looked up and laughed. To my surprise, Killa gave the baby back to Marty.

We all stood silent for a minute but Jimmy didn't cry anymore.

We had a quiet dinner that Marty had put together. Of course, Fred ate three times what we did. The big detective could really pack it away.

It was time to go visit Chet. I quickly put on my regular boots and we headed out before the baby could notice Fred again. Chet had sent a police hover and we drove right into the city of Giles.

On the way I called Issam. I got him at home interrupting his vegetarian dinner - it's all Carl eats. I'm sure my Castorian Captain has never heard of dessert. "I have been trying to get hold of you today." Issam sounded annoyed with me, a rarity.

"Sorry, Killa must have shut off my cellbutton, she's big on this family vacation thing, sorry." I tried to sound contrite and it worked, his angry tone let up. Carl had a soft spot for my little Ligithian, maybe because he was small too.

"Well, it's the usual at work but I wondered if Hill and Stoshingburg are working out?" my Captain asked. I heard Lilly and the kids in the background.

"By the way," now it was my turn to be perturbed, "why did you send those two? I would have thought Marcus or Lionel more suited for a brutal murder. They have more experience, although Fred does deal with the mob violence. But Hill?"

"Sorry, I was going to warn you they were coming but your cell didn't answer and the front desk had no clue where you were. Borger told me to send them, something about a request from the Hilda Dome reps? He was adamant by the way, very unlike him."

"What the hell!" I sputtered out. "Well, I will call him tomorrow and find out what gives with that!" I then filled in Issam about the two murders. He offered to either send two more detectives or have them at least investigating from Fulton Station. "Hold off until I talk with Chet Kodis. I'm just assisting him. I'll let you know but could you have someone checkout Hessina and Lawren Streng? Where were they before Hilda?"

"I heard Nove Deck is out there?" Carl made it a half question.

"Yup" I told him of my run in with the slimy lawyer.

"Be careful, he has connections," Issam warned me. "Wait a minute, Lily wants to talk to you." Lily Issam was Carl's wife and my therapist, a damn good one.

"Skip," she came over, her voice calm and sweet, "how are you feeling?"

"A little stressed," I told her honestly, "but I have it under control. They are trying to get me to ski!"

Her laughter came over clearly on the cell. "Well I think it would be good for you!"

"Not you too?" I moaned.

"Just remember to breath deeply and keep the pills nearby." Her voice became serious, "Do not take chances, keep the pills handy."

"I will, I promise." We closed off.

"What was that?" Hill yelled at me, "*Why Hill*? You said, *why Hill*?"

Oh no, here it came. I tried to placate her, "It was a rhetorical question." I shrugged my shoulders, which is hard to do with the three of us in the backseat of a squad hover, especially with Fred squeezing me.

She managed to point her finger at me, "I'll have you know I'm very competent. Maybe I won't tell you what I found out this afternoon questioning the lobby employees! After all, Marcus would have done a better job!"

"Stop being such a bitch!" Fred quipped. "He wasn't really kind to me either, don't see me throwing a fit! Although Chief you did kinda trash me."

I decided to ignore Stoshingburg. "Hill, just tell me what you found out or you've proven my point to Issam!"

I saw her grind her teeth. No foolin', she could grind her teeth! "Fine! No one heard the firing of the gun but it's not surprising as I took a couple of kitchen pans and banged them together in Streng's office. No one downstairs heard that either - with the door closed, it is almost sound proof."

"Real scientific, Hill," Fred slyly remarked leaning across me, causing me to lose my breath. I shoved him back, taking a deep breath.

He got one of Hill's deep hated looks, he shut up. She continued, "They all knew Streng was watching the hockey game. He never missed it. Usually Hessie watched with him but she had a doctor's appointment. So Fred, looks like you were right."

"I'm always right," he quipped and this time got a glowering look from me.

"Anyway," Hill continued, "the staff all liked Lawren but didn't see much of him. He left the running of the lodge to Paul Bell. They did tell me that Streng, lately, went on a lot of off planet trips, at least three times a month. I'm going to try and track those down or maybe get the info from Hessie."

"How's she doing?" I asked.

"Not well, she's confined to bed by doctor's orders. I only got to see her for a few minutes and she's really sedated. The doctors say she should be well enough to get up tomorrow. I have a notebook that's full with reports on each front-desk employee. It contains where each clerk was and I noted anything suspicious."

I turned to Fred, "Anything on Deck?"

"He's staying at one of the chateaus on the other side of the lodge. Unlike this side, they are privately owned. I guess it's his. He bought it two federation years ago. I think he comes here often enough to use it. I checked with the cleaning personnel. They say he's erratic in his use but get this, he doesn't ski!"

"A man after my own heart," I quipped. "He's got more brains than I gave him credit for."

"Really Chief, think about it. He owns a chateau condo on a ski resort and he doesn't ski! That's weird!" Fred shook his head to emphasize his bewilderment.

"Maybe it is for an investment," Hill interjected.

"Maybe the Chief's right, you should have stayed home," Fred shot across. I leaned back as Hill hit him, square to the chest. He shut up. Hill has a wicked uppercut. Of course, Fred would never admit to even feeling it but I saw the grimace on his face.

We were saved by arriving at the Hilda Police Station. It was a two-story building that looked like it had come out of a fairy tale. It had a peaked roof with light shingles. Even in the fading sunset it looked charming like all of the city of Giles did.

Inside it was warm and cozy but very efficiently laid out - on the first floor was the regular police foot soldiers with a reception desk gracing the front. All had nice cubicles, twice the size of ours on Fulton and the lunch room had a fireplace. Of course it was a fake radiant hearth but it still looked good. They had lunch machines everywhere; anything from a hearty breakfast to a myriad of deli sandwiches and several kinds of java. I grabbed a large insulated cup and helped myself to the extra strong java blend before going upstairs to the actual offices.

"On Fulton, we have two selections in our lunch room machines - ham and cheese or ham without cheese. Our java really sucks," Fred commented on our way up to see Chet.

"Yeah and you empty them every morning," Hill snidely remarked.

I shook my head, I'd long ago given up trying to stop the two from arguing. Chet met us. "I think you'd better come into my office and sit down. You aren't going to be happy when you see what I have."

Great, an appropriate finish to a lousy day.

Chapter Six

Chet's office wasn't much bigger than mine but it was a hell of a lot more comfortable. While I worried about sweating myself to death on Fulton Station, Chet was concerned whether we were warm enough on chilly Hilda.

He reached into his desk and brought out one of the new Vorus tabloids that were just out. They came from the planet Mody, our high tech manufacturing part of the sector. I couldn't afford the new high designed computer tab but Chet had arranged for the city of Giles to fund his entire police force of one hundred with the new tabloids. I had to okay the deal too; jealousy almost overcame me!

One touch of the tab sent up a report screen, another touch it became two sided. The writing was clear and crisp, not like the opaque screens we had with our tabloids. I saw Hill lean forward fascinated at the clarity.

"As you can see," he pointed and the first section enlarged and highlighted, "Lilac Floe received a strong hit to the back of her head. Whatever hit her crushed part of the back of her skull, rendering her unconscious - this is a strong subjective conclusion from the coroner. Which means, by the way, it could be challenged in court. He feels by connecting her blood flow from the back of the skull to how far the blood leakage went to her lower body parts that she was struck at another location and carried to where her killer slit her throat. She was obviously alive when the throat cut was done as the amount of blood flow from the heart shows it was still pumping after the knife slice."

I nodded my understanding as the autopsy pictures showed on a second screen. Another tech features our tabs did not have. All three of us leaned forward, noting the brutality of the throat cut. It had almost decapitated her.

"Whoever did this had to be strong enough to carry her and strong enough to slice her so deeply," Chet explained.

"Yeah, someone did it angrily," Stoshingburg pointed out. "I'm used to dealing with this kind of murder with the drug retaliation squads. They want to make a point and send a message. I'm puzzled as to what message could it send here? It could have been done by someone who used to work for the mob or who knows their modus operandi. Maybe it is someone who is copycatting them."

"It gets better," Chet warned us. "The autopsy showed Lilac was pregnant."

We all leaned back in our chairs, astonishment must have shown on our faces. "How far along was she?" Hill asked, her voice quivering. I knew what she was thinking, could it be Streng's?

"She was in to her third month. And," he paused as if he didn't want to tell us, "Lawren was the father. Almost one hundred percent match to him."

I heard Hill gasp. "This will kill her. Really, kill her." My lieutenant stood up, grabbing onto her chair. Tears, so unlike Hill, filled her eyes. "She doesn't deserve this. I remember my brother telling me how happy the family was that she had found someone who really loved her."

It was Fred that jumped up, taking Judy by the shoulders. "Sit down. You need to let this soak in. I'm going to get you a cup of tea." He left, heading down to the cafeteria.

"He's right," I told my lieutenant and was glad to see her take her chair, all life seemed to have drained out of her.

"I'm sorry, I know she is your friend." Chet continued, "I have several of my cops checking with local criminal contacts to find if Hessina could have had someone kill Lilac, perhaps Mrs. Streng suspected her husband's infidelity."

"I know Mrs. Streng didn't like Lilac, it was quite evident at the Manager's Welcoming Reception." I pointed to the autopsy pictures, "Could she be sending a message to her husband?"

"No, Hessie wouldn't do such a thing." Hill leaned forward, "It just doesn't make sense, why kill her husband too if she was trying to make a point to him? How would she know anyway? If I understood you, Hessina seemed happy with her husband."

"Well both women share the same doctor who is a top notch gynecologist specializing in fertilization. I'm guessing that is why Hessina was there."

"I know she was all gun-ho on getting pregnant." I tried to recall the conversation at the manager's reception, "Mrs. Streng was excited about Julie having a baby. She told us how her and Lawren were trying to start a family, to which

Streng quickly changed the subject by the way. He didn't want his wife discussing it."

"I'll go over and talk to the doctor," Hill suggested, "also let me tell Hessina about her husband's infidelity, please. It has to be done carefully."

"Fine, but make sure a medical backup is there and Chief you'd better be in the background just in case as a witness." Chet closed down his tab.

Fred had returned and gave Hill her cup of tea. To my surprise, she smiled up at him and gratefully took it.

"I made it extra sweet, supposed to help that way," he commented while taking his seat or I should say squeezed down into it. "Lara taught me how to make the tea, she said it would help me handle hysterical witnesses."

The big guy never ceased to amaze me. He really was a big teddy bear as my senior sharp shooter detective, Lara Null, called him. She also had a few expletives that were usually included. It still amazed me that my exotically beautiful gun expert and Fred were a number.

We filled in my Hilda superintendent on what we'd heard and he took note of everything. "This is a nightmare. I gave a press conference this afternoon and the press was hell. Now I hear we are getting an influx of reporters from the entire Crab sector."

I had seen the conference on the telescreen and had remarked how brutal the reporters were being to the head cop on Hilda. Murders were rare on Hilda and with Streng's death it was now getting sector coverage. "Anything else?"

Chet shoved his chair back, "This won't make your day. Nove Deck is making our lives miserable. He's closed all the resort's and casino's records. If we want to get into them we will have to get a judge to open them. That's going to take time, that damn lawyer is especially good at this. I did find out before Deck closed the door, that Streng was part owner of the Planetarians hockey team, I guess he owns 49 percent of the team. Hilary Doss owns the other 51 percent. She's a big time socialite here on Hilda. Ms. Doss owns a big stonework mansion on Iginot Mountain and is on the Board of Directors of every resort here. When she talks, Hilda listens."

Hill piped up, "I've heard of her father. He was a big shot XIL executive. He ran the Crab Nebula Sector wing of the company for the big fuel conglomerate. He left her a very rich woman."

Chet sat back down again bringing up a picture of a well-kept middle-aged woman. "Hilary inherited her money from her parents," the file confirmed what Hill had reported. "Ms. Doss has never married but has a teenage daughter that is sheer hell. Zoe has been in and out of trouble most of her life. At three years old the girl wandered off and had the entire planet looking for her. They found her playing hide and seek in the cellar of the mansion. Been downhill ever since. I think Hilary has given up on her, although the girl is smart, just out of control."

"I'll take that assignment," Fred announced, "I'm great with socialites."

A loud "guffaw" came from Hill but she didn't say anything else, perhaps the tea was having an effect.

"Well, at least I know hockey," Stoshingburg followed up. "I'm a big fan of Fulton's Nebulars. We go to the games all the time, don't we Chief?"

Hill looked surprised, "I never knew that!"

As if she knew my whole life, "Really, Hill, really? I do have a life outside of yours! Killa doesn't like hockey. It's too violent for her. Must be it just skipped your nosey grilling!" I guess everyone thought my life sucked! Damn woman!

I noticed Chet cover his smile with his hand, glad he found it amusing. "I'll have Streng's autopsy hopefully tomorrow. I'll cell you when I have them. Anything else?"

We left the Giles police station, going back to the chateau. Hill, Fred and I sat at the kitchen table going over everything we knew. Killa kept feeding us coffee and tea. She also put out a bowl full of fruit. I would have preferred muffins but fruit it was! At least Hill enjoyed it and Fred, well Fred likes everything.

During our discussions, Killa went over and hugged Judy, "I'm so glad you are here, aren't we Skip?" My old nursemaid looked expectantly over at me. Don't know what she expected, the best she got was a shrug. "Of course, I wish it was under better circumstances." I rolled my eyes and Fred had a good laugh.

"I'm glad she's here because she's going to question everyone at the doctor's fertility clinic and she's going to keep an eye on Hessina," I quipped. "Let's see what else I can think for you to do to keep you out of my hair!"

Killa hit me in the shoulder but Fred nodded.

Hill ignored us, "Yes, I've already checked, the clinic opens at 09:00. I'll be there. The police medical doctor seeing Hessina says perhaps tomorrow afternoon I'll be able to talk to her. There is a nurse staying at the penthouse. The doctor says his patient is starting to come around but Hessie is still heavily sedated. I'm also going with one of Chet's police woman to talk to Lilac's parents. The Floes have generations of Hildanite ancestors, almost from the inception of the planet. Their daughter was born and raised in Giles."

"Good, we need to talk to them. Also if you get a call from Hessina's nurse, let me know, I'll be there," I told her. "Fred, you are coming with me to Hilary Doss' mansion. I called Karine Button..."

Hill rudely interrupted, "You called Judge Button? How close are you to her! How many favors does she owe you?" She had her fiery mad eyes glowering at my head.

I exploded, I admit it, "What is it to you! Nosey aren't you! Keep your remarks to yourself, *please*!" I pointed my finger right in her nose. "Although it is none of your business, Karine is just a good friend!"

I heard Fred snicker. He probably knew I had dated the judge for almost a year. She is ten years older than me but she fascinates me. We both drifted our own ways but remained good friends. I'd helped her on a few important cases and she had helped me in return.

"Anyway," I continued ignoring Hill's scowl and Killa's frown, "she's gotten me an introduction to socialite Doss. Hilary has agreed to see us at 10:00 tomorrow morning." I saw Killa mouth to

Hill, *I'll tell you later*. I glared at Killa but she ignored me. I swear my life is a friggin open book - not really interesting enough to read, but Hill has her nose in it!

Ray and Julie were out at the fancy restaurant in the main lodge. Marty had the baby until ten o'clock and then Killa took over. At ten o'clock, Killa darted out of the kitchen to take the baby. She sat with little Jimmy in the rocking chair by the fireplace, softly singing to him. Marty went pouting to the den turning on the news and ignoring all of us.

I just shook my head. Fred and Hill left for the main lodge. They had two rooms there. "Hey, let's stop in and get something to eat at the Sun Café," Fred piped up.

"No thank you!" Hill answered him. "I've had enough. We have busy days tomorrow!"

"Hold up Fred, I'll go with you!" I grabbed my coat and hat. "I could use something." I said quietly enough that Killa, who was busy with the baby, didn't hear.

The lodge was bustling, skiers returning from the slopes, guests hitting the bars and restaurants. I entered the lobby and suddenly it hit me. "Where did my skis, poles and ski boots go? I'd left them by that wall when I had run upstairs to Streng's office," I told Fred.

I asked at the front desk. No dice, they hadn't seen them. I asked at the coat check. Again I got nowhere. Crap. I went to Lost and Found. My skis were gone! Someone stole my skis and boots. I hated to think how much the rental equipment would set me back. Not even the poles! The brazen thieves had stolen them from the Sector Police Chief. Good god I hope Issam never found out, I'd be teased forever. How many schools have I preached the gospel of how to be careful not to be robbed?

I walked downhearted into the café/bar. Both Fred and Judy were there. Fred had a mound of nachos covered in beef and cheese. Hill had a cup of tea, black tea; it looked thick like sludge. "Thought you were going to bed?" I pointedly asked my lieutenant.

"I changed my mind." She sipped her mud then reached over taking a nacho from Fred. Somehow, I'd lost my appetite. I ordered a mug of java with a double shot of cognac in it and topped with thick whipped cream.

"Find your ski rental equipment?" Fred asked.

"Nope, I can't believe someone stole my skis!" I moaned.

Of course I got no sympathy from Hill, "That was very careless of you Chief."

"There was a murder when I left them by the side wall. I've been kinda busy!" I sipped my java, letting the liquor enhance the flavor, the sweet cream covering my upper lip. "Don't tell anyone, do you understand Lieutenant Hill? I know you don't want to do a month of department expense reviews."

She just shook her head. "Didn't realize this was your first murder," Hill quipped.

"I could also add a few days a week of foot patrol down by the docks for a year with an old hot patrol suit!" Just picturing it made me smile.

It shut her up as she reached for another of Fred's nachos. "Get your own!" he grumped.

I went to the bar and ordered another bowl of cheese-covered nachos, adding some hot jalapeno peppers. I noticed over to the side of the bar a man's face that looked familiar, but I couldn't think of where I'd seen him before. The man was nursing a beer. He was sitting by himself. He was stocky and rugged. His face had the beginnings of rough beard. It was his hands that I noticed. He had boxer's hands, callused and stubby. Good fighting hands. He looked up and for a brief second our eyes met - pure hatred. It was so intense, I lost my concentration but before I could get to him, he quickly left, leaving his almost full beer.

"Do you know who that man sitting over there was?" I asked the bartender.

"Nope," was all I got.

I explained to both Hill and Stoshingburg what had just happened. They looked around but the man was not in sight. I helped finish the new nachos and left still pouting about my stolen skis. Everyone was home when I walked into the chateau. They were all around the roaring fireplace. Killa held the sleeping Jimmy but at least Marty had joined them.

"I don't suppose you are skiing tomorrow morning?" Ray piped up.

"I can't, it's gotten complicated. Chet has his hands just full with the reporters." They looked at me like I was just making excuses. Killa just shook her head, her purple eyes getting darker and her ears twitching in anger.

I went to bed. *To hell with them.* I didn't mention the stolen skis; I'd had enough criticism for one night. I tried to wash away my *feel sorry for myself* mood with a hot shower but I still hit the bed pissed off and dreamed of racing my Blue Horizon racing car. I remembered dreaming that I was gonna change the color to bright red! I took a blue pill when I got up, my head was cloudy and until I had my cup of java, I couldn't think straight.

....

I met Fred at the main lodge. Chet sent over a patrol hover. Our driver knew where the Doss mansion was located, it was out past Giles on the other side of the city toward the other ski resorts. Once we passed the city, we traveled up a ragged mountain road. Although the other resorts lined the roadways, none could match the Sunrise in either luxury or size. The mountains were still beautiful. Each had plenty of trails and plenty of snow. We turned on Iginot Road, which sharply headed up Iginot Mountain. No resorts were found here, just a well-paved driveway leading up to a large plateau that housed the Doss estate.

Although there was a large wrought iron gate, it was wide open with the guard station empty. The drive got quite steep. I couldn't imagine this road if it were bad weather. It leveled out at the plateau where a good-sized gray stone building loomed against the skyline. This was literally the top of Iginot Mountain.

The circular driveway led right past a thick double wooden doorway. He dropped us at the entrance. "I'll be right here when you're done with the lady, sir," our driver announced.

A gong-type knocker was in my hand when the door opened. A maid in a pretty pink outfit smiled at us, "I presume you are Mr. Brown and Mr. Stoshingburg?" Her accent was definitely not of the Crab – definitely off sector. She had a tinge of green to her complexion and her oval dark green eyes showed lots of intelligence. I was betting her bleached blonde hair was really auburn. I was guessing she was from the far side of Pinwheel, maybe from the planet Hilliot.

I was still trying to place her origins when Fred said, "Titan, Pinwheel?" She nodded. Well I was close.

"Very good, very observant," her cute little nose turned to Fred causing him to blush. "Please follow me, Ms. Doss is waiting for you."

The house was a rambling two story open floor layout. The foyer was divided by a huge marble stairway that split in two at the top, fanning into the upper floor. Downstairs, the left side led into what looked like a large ballroom style dining room. The other way, which the maid led us into, was an equally large living room. As is typical on Hilda, a large massive stone fireplace took up most of the far wall. The room was separated into several smaller sections by nicely arranged comfortable plush furniture. The furnishings looked expensive and I'd bet from far off exotic sectors. Right in front of the fireplace there were arranged two long white leather couches. From one of them, Hilary Doss stood. The tall sleek woman was dressed in gray slacks with a matching cashmere sweater. She wore a string of pearls with matching earrings. She now stood near the fireplace with a drink in her hand.

Doss stepped forward giving us her long fingered palm as she greeted each of us. "Can I have Angeliae get you anything to drink? Perhaps a glass of champagne or even a cup of java?"

Fred declined, but I took her up on the java. It came in a large decorated sculptured mug and was probably one of the best javas I've ever had. She explained that it was made in an Amise press. The woman evidently had class.

After giving her glass to the maid, Ms. Doss sat down on one of the couches, crossing her legs, her hands folded neatly in her lap; the ideal picture of a well decked out socialite that is conscious of her status. She regally nodded for us to sit on the couch opposite her. We dutifully did.

"Now what can I do for you Mr. Brown and Mr. Stoshingburg?" She sat back waiting for us to answer.

"Well," I took out my Chief of Police identification. Her eyes went wide. "I am here investigating with a few of my detectives," I motioned at Fred, "into the murder of Lilac Floe and into the alleged suicide of Lawren Streng."

"So, how do you know Karina Button?" You could tell that it bothered her social sensibilities that a good upper class friend had recommended that a policeman see her.

I almost decided to tell her I'd had an affair with Karina but that would put her over the edge and I did not need to slap her sensibilities but to get information out of her. So I just quickly answered, "We've worked together, she is a Parley Judge after all."

"Oh, yes. Why Karina decided to *work* and leave behind her upbringing is beyond me." The socialite shook her head as if to emphasize her confusion. "Her father was the grain baron on Casey. She was engaged to marry Harald Harkin, the *Farmer's Equipment* CEO and would have been a great help in promoting good charity works and she knows the art world. But then we all make our choices." Her sad voice obviously thought Judge Button had made a wrong choice.

"Yes, we do," I tried to keep sarcasm from dripping into my voice. Karina was one of the most accomplished women I knew. Hilary was a pale excuse of a woman compared to the Judge's life but again I needed info so I kept my mouth shut. I could tell Fred was shifting around in his seat. I suppose he was thinking of Lara, another woman that made this woman look frivolous. I gave him a *don't say anything* look.

"Did you know Lilac Floe?" I asked.

"Not really," her nose couldn't get any higher. "My daughter knew her slightly, Zoe is on the ski patrol. Lilac was head of the group. But I can assure you my daughter knows nothing."

"Well, I'm glad you can answer for me, Mother," came from the doorway. A teenager stood with her hands on her hips. Everything about this young woman screamed rebellion. Despite the chill outside, she wore short shorts, her little fanny stuck out the back. She wore high heels that hookers loved because of the sex appeal they emitted. Her small bright red mouth was in a pout that I bet she had most of the time. Her eyes were heavily made up. She was the opposite of her classy mother.

"Really, Zoe," annoyance dripped from Hilary, "I don't think we need you here, please remove yourself, go listen to that obscene music of yours."

I just rudely interrupted giving my best *Chief of Police* voice, "I'd like to talk to Zoe. Ms. Doss, you can remain - after all she is a minor, being only fifteen."

"I'm almost sixteen," came from Zoe. "Mother, the Albanis are not obscene, their music is quite sophisticated."

To my surprise Fred spoke up, "I love the Albanis. Their newest album, *Star lite Killed* is excellent. Saw them perform last month, great guitar work."

Zoe lit up like a Yuletide tree, "Wow, really." The teenager went over and sat across from Fred making sure she didn't sit too close to her mother. "Have you ever heard of the Wildfires?"

"Oh, sure," Fred leaned toward her, almost conspiratorially whispering to her, "Ain't the lead singer, Alli Monstad, the best?"

"Oh, yeah!" the teenage brightened even more.

"Please Zoe, they are policemen. Gentlemen, ask your questions, we have a busy day."

Her daughter almost growled at her but mom just ignored. I took over, "Zoe what did you know of Lilac."

I got a shrug, "Not much, good skier, always had guys falling all over her. She was in her twenties, not in my crowd."

"Did you ever see her and Lawren Streng together?" I asked.

"Really, *Mr.* Brown! That is not an appropriate question to ask a teenage girl." I thought the socialite was going to explode, her face became bright red.

"Really Mother, stop being a prude." Zoe looked over at me, "No, but I saw her and Mrs. Streng together."

It took me aback. I lost my tongue. I was so surprised at the answer. Fred, however, did have something to say, "It is *Chief* Brown and *Senior Detective* Stoshingburg, ma'am." He looked over at Hilary Doss, he can be quite intimidating. Ms. Doss was going to retort, but Fred's big eyebrows went up. She closed her mouth.

Zoe giggled at her mom being put in her place. I found my voice, "How often did you see her with Mrs. Streng?"

"Oh, just a couple of times in the coffee shop, after all, Mr. Streng had put his wife in charge of organizing the ski patrol. I do remember that the last time I saw them, the conversation looked pretty serious as Mrs. Streng kept pointing her finger at Lilac. I remember she grabbed a pastry out of Lilac's hand and threw it away! Mrs. Streng looked pretty angry at her."

I saw Fred had his tabloid recording everything. When Hilary noticed I saw her frown, "Should I get my lawyer?"

"Not unless you want to," I pointed to the recorder, "it's the same as taking notes, we can't use it in court unless you give us permission." I didn't tell her we could, however, if we used the written transcripts.

She nodded that it was okay then. I continued, "Ms. Doss, you knew Lawren Streng well did you not, socially and as a business partner? He owns 49 percent of the Planetarians and you own the other 51 percent."

"I do know the Streng's. After all do you know who Mrs. Streng is?" Her eyes went wide, "She's the daughter of Calis McTenser. He's the big powerful XIL executive, dripping rich. My father was a friend of his when he also was an XIL executive. Her mother is from the Hafte family." When I looked blankly at her, she huffed, "They are the attonium barons! Hessina's lineage could not be better. Lawren was lucky to catch her, although she certainly is no beauty."

"Do you believe it was a marriage of convenience?" I asked.

It was Zoe who answered, "NO! He really loved her, she's a nice lady! I feel bad for her, she has that disease…"

Her mother interrupted, "Teenagers live in a fantasy world. What do YOU think?" It was obvious what Hilary thought.

"How did you get along with Lawren Streng, Ms. Doss?" I hurried on with my next question, "Why did he purchase half of your hockey team?"

"Lawren is, was a hockey fanatic. Hessina bought those shares as a wedding gift. I inherited the team from my father. I don't really care for hockey and since Lawren did, I let him take charge of it." She waved her hand in dismissal of the subject.

Zoe, however, spoke right up, "We had our first winning series, Kowel was named MVP last year "

"Yes, I know," I said with Fred nodding enthusiastically. "You almost won the final."

Zoe smiled, she was obviously a fan. She ran out of the room, quickly returning with four tickets. "Here, these are good tickets. The team is playing the Cosmostics tonight."

Before I could tell her no, Fred grabbed them up, "Thanks." He literally glowed with excitement.

We got up to leave, mama wasn't going to give us anymore answers as she stood up, dismissing us. "Angeliae, please show Mr. Brown and his assistant out."

Oh she had to get one last dig in. Fred, however, wasn't done. He dragged Zoe out to the corridor. The big guy had no trouble almost lifting the teenager. Ms. Doss went to chase after them but somehow I got in the way. By the time we emerged into the foyer, Fred was just finishing talking to Zoe. I saw her nod at him and race away.

"What did you say to her?" Hilary shouted at him.

"That's between this *assistant* and her," he laughed at the snobbish socialite and went out the door.

When we were in the back of the car I asked him what he had talked to Zoe about but I already thought I knew.

"The girl's on supfline. I could smell the drug on her. I told her that if she didn't give it up I'd put her in jail for her own good. I also told her if she wanted to tell me where she was getting the stuff,

I'd forget I knew she was on it as long as she followed up with rehab."

I had guessed right. Considering Fred's attitude toward drugs, I was surprised he'd not hauled her downtown. When I asked him why he didn't, he said, "I like her, she reminds me of myself. Her mom is a bitch. I would bet the kid gets in trouble just to get attention."

We got dropped off at the lodge. I went in to see if anyone had seen my rental equipment. Nothing, nada. Hill was in the lobby still asking the employees of this shift if they had any information. I gathered from her frown that she wasn't having much luck. She was also extremely upset as Nove Deck had served her with papers that prevented her from seeing Hessina.

"How dare he! That bastard. She's my friend. He can't keep me away." She moaned in frustration.

I looked at the document on her tabloid. It had been sent to her this morning. "Obviously, he can. We will have to get it rescinded but it'll take time. I'll see what Isaam can do." I put a call into him. My captain would get back as soon as he could. Hill was not happy.

I also called Artchie. His voice, which almost always held a smile, was chipper, "Hi Chief, all is well. Mrs. Hippnow is upstairs pet sitting. She is spoiling them all rotten, including Stanley." I heard Mrs. March in the background helping one of the tenants. All seemed well.

"I'm glad to hear that. Do you need to talk to Lt. Hill?" I was disconnecting my cell from my collar but stopped when he assured me he'd heard from *Judy* several times this morning. When I hung up I accosted *Judy,* "Don't bother Artchie too much. He's busy!"

"You're just jealous because he likes talking to me better!"

"He does not!" I half yelled.

"Yes, he does!" she yelled back.

"Stop it children," Fred sat down, eating half the bowl of snacks that the front desk had left out.

The three of us walked over to the chateau. It was just past noon and Julie had just returned from skiing as she was doing only half days, returning for the baby's feedings.   She walked out of her bedroom with a very quiet satisfied Jim. She gave him to Marty as Killa was making us java and feeding us fruit snacks. One look at Fred and the baby started screaming.

"Boy you have a way about you, Fred," Hill commented.

To my surprise Marty quickly gave the baby to Killa and within seconds little Jimmy was cooing and laughing. "There are some things she's better at," Marty conceded.

I didn't want to give Killa's secret away, so I quietly nodded. Ligithians are really psychic, although they claim not to be. They tend to emit a calmness that can diffuse an emotional situation. When they were slaves, their masters, the Laositians or Highbloods made them their nannies and brought them to hard negotiation meetings, knowing their calming powers.

The three of us went over everything we had. Hill had seen the doctor, who insisted on a court ordered writ for him to give out any information. Another thing for Issam to work on. When I mentioned to Hill about Zoe's claim that she saw Lilac with Hessina, my lieutenant got a strange look on her face.

"You know I heard that from some of the resort's employees. They saw the two together often. Now I'm completely baffled until I get to Hessina to ask why. I went over to the Floe's house. Nice little cottage. Lilac lived with them, said she couldn't afford to move out, although their daughter was optimistic about the future. They had no idea she was pregnant. I felt sorry for them, they took that news hard. Her mother, however, told us that Lilac had received a great deal of money lately." Hill took a deep breath and then continued, "We went to her bank and got an inexperienced bank clerk. The woman let slip that Ms. Floe has been getting deposits from Lawren Streng. The bank accountant assumed it was work related."

"Skip, we got this in our mailbox outside. It usually has announcements of what's on the agenda for the day but I think this is different." Julie handed me an envelope with my name written on it.

Inside was a plain piece of paper with "See me at the hockey game tonight" and two tickets. Not prime tickets like the teenage Doss had given us but upper tier level tickets. "I think someone has got some information he or she wants to share," I commented.

"Well, take Hill," Fred pointedly told me, "I'm using the good tickets. If you need me you can use your cell."

"That is fine Fred, except you and I both know cells don't work in arenas." I waved the tickets at him.

"Why is that?" my un-hockey Lieutenant Hill asked.

"Well, there have been scandals," I told her. "It is easy to hide a cellbutton in a hockey player's helmet. Then the coaches yell directions in them like "Look for the puck high, take the wing out, etc. So they made it that cellbuttons don't work, you have to step outside to use one."

"I don't mind sitting with you Chief." She took the two tickets, "You can teach me about hockey." Judith Hill smiled from ear to ear.

Lucky me.

Chapter Seven

I didn't want to bring attention to us so I turned down the squad hover that Chet offered. Instead we were all squished into a resort bus that was taking any quests that wanted to go to the Chester Hildan Sports Complex, named after the founder of the planet. The brightly lit complex was on the outskirts of Giles. It was a big rambling multifaceted compound that hosted many of the professional sports of Hilda such as hockey, basketball and even a futbol stadium, not to mention an indoor baseball field that housed the games of their Sector Champions, the Starmites.

Hilda, being a cold planet, had to build almost everything indoors or freeze, whereas Fulton Station built our stadiums and fields indoors for air conditioning. Hildaites had the snow and freezing temperatures to deal with, Fultonites had hot burning sun conditions. I couldn't help but be amused at both situations.

The hockey arena was the farthest building. It had a big white bubbly dome that cut the skyline like a lit up ice cream cone. The bus left the six of us - Marty, Hill, Fred, Julie, Ray and me off at the rink's front lobby. To my surprise, Marty was a big hockey fan, a big enough fan to actually leave the baby in Killa's grateful hands. Amazing! I would not have picked the severe looking woman as a hockey fan - wonders never cease. She was actually smiling, clinging to Julie's arm in anticipation of the game.

Even more amazing when we entered the lobby, Zoe Doss was waiting for us. Dressed in her short shorts, she ran up to Fred Stoshingburg grabbing his hand and pulled him along. "Come on I'll introduce you to the team!" she shouted.

Fred looked back at me, with the look of "help" on his face. We dutifully followed along with Marty almost running alongside Zoe in her eagerness of actually getting to meet the team.

A security guard just nodded at us as we loaded into a side elevator. Obviously Zoe was recognized. We passed by another security guard, who punched in an opening code for a door blocking our way. As it swung inward, we could hear a buzz of noise, human voices that sounded busy. We entered a reception area. The walls were outlined in cushiony chairs. A large telescreen was on the other side. It showed the ice rink, which I noticed was filling up with excited fans. A harried looking man stepped out of a side door. I recognized him as the general manager.

"Hi Zoe. Is your mother with you?" he asked eyeing all of us.

"Of course not, Caltun, you should know better!" she snickered. "You only see her when you're in bed with her."

"Zoe!" he looked horrified. "I, I…"

He was at a loss for words, stuttering profusely. I stuck my hand out, "Hello, Mr. Weler, I'm Skip Brown, I'd like you to meet my brother…"

He seemed to find his voice, "Aren't you the Chief of Police, didn't I see you on the newscasts?"

Now it was my turn-to-turn red, "Yeah, that was me. That female reporter caught me off guard. I usually wear shoes."

He laughed, "I've had that happen to me. I can never sneak out on them either."

To change the subject I introduced everyone. He looked at Ray and sputtered out, "Ray Brown - just like the racing champion?" he joked.

"Yes, I am the race car champion," Ray amusingly answered. "I don't have to pretend to be him."

"Then you're the famous racing brothers?" He looked at me, "but aren't you the Chief of Police for the sector?"

"It's a long story, and you have a game to play. It was nice just meeting you," I tried to tell him but he'd already opened the door he'd just come out of.

"Hey guys, guess who's here?" he yelled in as he waved for us to follow him, "It's Ray Brown, this year's Federation Race Car Champion and his also famous brother."

The room erupted in chaos as everyone, most half dressed in their hockey equipment, came over shaking our hands. Zoe was jumping around introducing Fred with Marty right by her side. Julie clung to Ray. They are all big guys and gals, rather intimidating. The players are all muscular and tall; many missing teeth and with scars on their faces. Only Fred could match their bulk.

I watched them dress, fascinated at the equipment they used. Hori Topplet, their star player, waved as he was snapping on his skates. I heard a "pop" and his skates laced right up. The most interesting person was their goalie. Heda Olfistene was a six foot six colossal lady. She was from the Sombrero Sector, planet Lorenzi. I'd met their ambassador on MOSS. Just like the ambassador, Heda had eyes that could look in different directions, and had a huge headful of fuzzy orangey-auburn hair. I couldn't imagine how she got her helmet on. The Lorenzis women were also known for their psychic ability to feel emotions. Some say they could read minds. I wondered if it helped her as a goalie?

Hill was talking to Heda. My lieutenant looked quite small next to the large woman. As I glanced around the locker room I noticed several even larger players, some women and some men. They all looked tough as they put on their protection gear which made them look even larger. Heda was showing Hill how her helmet had a proactive force field across the face part of the hood. She demonstrated by putting the helmet on my detective and then throwing the hard rubber disc puck at her. I saw Judy flinch but the puck just bounced off the force field.

Fred was trying Hori's stick. When he touched the stick, it started to glow green. I'd never seen one up close. It was amazing. It also set the puck glowing green. I knew they used the glowing sticks during penalties.

The head coach walked in. Silence. I knew it was time to go. We left quietly as the coach was giving last minute instructions. We went up an elevator to the main floor. Fred headed for the snack concession booths with Zoe tailing right behind. I said goodbye to Julie, Ray and Marty and grabbed Hill. Our seats were in the upper section.

We had to go up two escalators. I was quite used to the high tiers. In our home planet arena, Fred and I usually could only afford the higher sections when we went to watch Fulton's hockey team, the Nebulars. Hill and I were almost to the ceiling. Judy clung to me as we took our seats. The rink looked far below. The seats were almost vertical.

"Geesh, Chief," Hill sat down holding tight to the seat's armrests. "I hope there is enough oxygen up here."

I couldn't help but laugh, "You'll get used to it." I lowered my binoculars on my hat. I had stopped and got a *Planetarian* cap with the binoculars built in. I handed Hill the cap, "Look down there, near the team's benches, Fred and the rest are right above the player's bench." *Lucky sons of bitches,* I thought. Fred was smiling from ear to ear, eating his nachos with Zoe talking away to him. They all looked comfy in the big first class seats. I'd never gotten that close to the ice. Damn!

The lights went out. Hill grabbed onto my arm. "Ouch!" I yelled.

"Sorry," she yelled back as the music was loud. The players came out, their uniforms glowing brightly - Green for the Hilda Planetarians, Blue for the Solti Cosmostics from the Sol Sector. The crowd went nuts, everyone standing and screaming at the top of their lungs. Hill stood but still clutched onto my arm.

The lights came up and the players turned off the glowing of their uniforms. I looked around. Our informant, who had bought the tickets, had to be here somewhere. I looked to the right of us. An older couple with Hilda's team shirts, waving a Planetarian banner didn't seem good candidates. To our left was a kind of scruffy looking guy. He had an expensive camera with a lens vest full of costly optical equipment. He was kinda out of place up here.

"I hope it's a good game," I ventured and got only a nod. "Must be hard to get real good shots this far up?" I poked a little more but he didn't answer me. "Whose team are you for?" I pushed a little more.

"Hey, man I'm working here," he snapped at me as he clicked his camera. "They don't pay me to talk."

"Oh, sorry," I guessed it wasn't him.

Hill was full of questions. She had no idea what she was observing. I explained the ice rink, "It has three sections. Each side has their goal, which changes each period, and in the middle of the ice they battle it out. The goalies protect their caves - that's what we call the soft transparent goals that the other players are trying to get the puck into."

"Boy they all skate really fast!" she commented. "They skate as fast backwards as forward. Look how they use their sticks. It is like the field hockey that I used to play in school."

"Well, yeah but..." I didn't get to explain further as a Planetarian player slammed into a Cosmostics player, ramming her into the side boards.

"Is that legal?" Hill actually leaned forward, forgetting her fear of the sharp steep incline of the seats. "He could have hurt him!"

I knew the players, I'd seen them play our hockey team, the Nebulars, on Fulton, "*her*, he could have hurt *her*."

Hill looked at me like I was crazy as another body check, this time knocking the skater off his feet and down the ice. "This is normal. Hockey is a rough game," I told her as the players bumped and grinded down the ice. Heda stopped a lot of shots and I couldn't help but yell at each save, "Come on Olfestine, keep it up!"

Kowel ploughed into a Cosmostic, giving the player an elbow to the jaw, just under the electronic facemask. The referee put his hand up - penalty. I explained to Hill that a penalty against the Planetarians had been called.

"What made that any different than any of the other hits?" she sarcastically mused. "Do those hurt more?"

"Just go with it Hill," I remarked as I joined in with the crowd yelling obscenities at the referee.

The lights went out. The Planetarians and Cosmostics glowed green and blue. I explained to Hill, "during the two minute penalty, besides Kowel going to the penalty box, the Planetarians can not hit the puck or have possession of the puck when the puck glows blue. It is randomly set but it gives the Cosmostics the advantage.

The Cosmostics scored against Heda. The woman goalie bashed her stick against the ice in anger. The lights came on, the penalty was over but we were losing now.

I kept looking around, waiting for someone to show themselves. Nothing. The first period was over. Hill and I went down to the concession hallway. I got myself a large soda and headed back up. Hill joined me, still carefully climbing to our seats. She squeezed by me and I immediately smelled hotdogs! She had two hotdogs with her soda.

"Are we getting some bad habits, Ms. Healthnut?" I chimed in as she took her seat.

"Guess it's from hanging out with you!" she quipped. "I guess you don't want this cotton candy I got for you."

Ah, my weakness. I grabbed the pink cellophane container, ripping the top. It tasted so good.

"You know that's not good for you, young man," the old lady beside Hill lectured over my Lieutenant at me. Not a word to Hill about her hotdogs though! I saw Hill cover a smirk. "Your wife shouldn't let you have it!"

I went to correct her but Hill spoke up, "I only let him have it when we come here and he'll bring most of it back to the kids."

"Oh, that's nice." The old lady grinned at me.

I kicked Hill in the shin, saw her wince but still she smiled. Funny, funny- damn woman!

Why wasn't our informant contacting us? I looked around as the second period started. We got a goal the first minute. The crowd went wild. It was tied.

As the period went on, it got wilder. At one point the Planetarian goalie, Heda, tore off her helmet and charged a Cosmostic player who'd rammed into her. It was an unwritten rule that if one player took off his or her helmet, the opposing team player also took his or her helmet off.

Also, off came the big heavy gloves. Heda was at a slight disadvantage because her uniform as a goalie was bigger and more cumbersome but in reality she was so fierce that she was soon plummeting her opponent. To my surprise Hill was yelling, "Go Heda, Go! Get him."

Another Cosmostic came rushing at the goalie from the other side but Heda's roving eye saw him. She brought her big goal stick up and clobbered him. That brought both entire benches out; every hockey player was on the ice fighting with helmets off, gloves down, sticks flailing.

"Oh my goodness," Hill had jumped up out of her seat like all the rest of us, her fear of heights seemingly gone. The old couple was screaming obscenities that even made my ears burn. The lower crowd started throwing stuff on the ice. Even the higher tiers were throwing stuff. Hill, caught up with the moment took my cotton candy and heaved it.

"Hill," I screamed as I watched my delicious pink snack go floating downward. I looked down with my binoculars at Fred, he was pounding on the glass barrier, Zoe had climbed up on the glass and was shaking the glass. Marty was pounding on the inner glass with what looked like a cane of some sort. Ray and Julie just stood there, wide eyed. Julie had Ray's arm in a tight clasp. I suppose if you aren't used to the hockey atmosphere it could be rather intimidating.

It took the referees a while to calm everything down. The penalty boxes were full. Both goalies were in the punishment box so the caves were wide open for the next two minutes.

The Cosmostics had only four players left while the Planetarians had only three. The referee dropped the disc puck and the lights went out again. The Cosmotics got one minute of the puck being blue. So they had a minute of super power play. Could we hold them off? We could only check them when the puck was blue. No touching the puck!

I noticed Hill didn't throw her hotdog. I grabbed the box and took a bite of her remaining hotdog, "Chief!" she yelled at me. But it wasn't Hill that I noticed, it was a piece of paper that was at the bottom of her hotdog carrying box. I picked it out:

Meet me in the men's bathroom, top floor, third period when 10:00min left in game.

Do not come early or all is off!

Hill looked over at the paper, "Oh," Hill was big on words.

I hardly paid any attention to the game after that. I checked out the men's bathroom in-between the second and third periods. Then I just watched the game clock as the third period counted down. It seemed a long time to get from the twenty minute start.

When it got to ten and a half minutes, I got up excusing myself. To my chagrin Hill was right behind me. "I told you to stay put!" I should have known better.

She followed me all the way to the men's room. To my surprise the men's bathroom was blocked off with janitor barriers. An "Out of Order" sign blocked the way. I ducked around the wooden barrier. Hill was right behind me.

"Lieutenant, it is a *men's* bathroom." I turned to her.

"Yeah, is there something in there I can't see! Please, I'm a police detective!" She walked right past me. Damn woman!

It was a typical washroom with stalls on one side and urinals on the other with sinks on the back wall. A large mirror ran the entire length above the sinks with tile everywhere else. It seemed empty. I looked in the mirror and saw it wasn't quite empty. I could see the reflection of a pair of legs in one of the stalls. I turned to Hill, she'd seen them too. She had her gun out. I reminded myself to ask her later how she got that gun past security. Right now I was more concerned with the legs.

"Who's in here?" I asked the door but got nothing. I pushed the door but it was locked. Hill came from behind me and kicked the door open. I didn't have time to glare at her as the door swung open. Inside was a man, fully dressed, sitting on the toilet. In the middle of his forehead was a bullet wound, a gapping frigging bullet hole. Worse, I knew the guy.

"That's Reich Hisner," I told Hill.

"The stripper? Lilac's boyfriend?" She peered over my arm, "He's been shot!" Hill, always the observant cop! The guy had a hole in his forehead, pretty obvious!

"Looks like someone got to him first. There went our informer." I could see that he had been dragged and dumped on the toilet. He'd been shot by the sink, a little blood trail headed into the stall.

I turned and traced the blood back. Meanwhile, Hill was in searching the guy. "You are tampering with evidence," I pointed out.

"I'm just checking his pockets or do you want to wait until the coroner gives his report?" She had a point. "His pockets are completely empty, someone stripped him clean."

"I'm not surprised," I countered but then I saw her unzip his pants. "Hill!"

She paid no attention to me as she reached into his pants. "Aha, just like I thought, he's wearing stripper underwear. There is a front pocket in his briefs." She came out with a folded piece of paper. "Look, it's a note!"

Then we both froze. The note read, *Supfline shipment, Jump 33 23:05Fed time. Monday.*

"You'd better get hold of Chet. Either find an arena policeman or go outside and call Chet yourself," I told her. My head was trying to get itself wrapped around the note. This was a whole different ballgame. It was becoming an even more dangerous situation. Now I was glad Fred was here. Drugs complicated the already bad situation.

....

Fred joined us after Hill went down to his seat and got him. She had also put in a call to Chet from the lobby. Of course, Fred complained loudly as he came into the bathroom. "There are only two minutes to go!" The big guy stopped short, however, as he saw the sheet-covered body and shut up. He went over peeling back the sheet. "It's Reich Hisner, well I'll be!" We heard the final horn go off.

The hockey game was done. The crowds were filing out when Chet arrived.

"I told Julie to go home, that we'd be awhile," Hill told me. For once I was glad of her paying attention to details I normally forgot.

"How did he let someone get close enough to shoot him in the head?" Chet asked. "It had to be someone he knew, maybe even trusted."

"Yeah and it's a projectile gun. The killer is keeping to his signature method of murdering."

"The press will have a field day with this!" my Hilda superintendent of police moaned.

"Yup," Fred was so articulate. The big guy always hit it right on the nail.

The photographer was done, the body heading toward the morgue when I asked Chet if we could convene in his office or at my chateau. He chose the chateau because the press was hanging around the Giles station. So we all ended up in our kitchen with Killa feeding us java and snacks. It was after midnight and almost everyone else was in bed.

I showed Chet the paper with the note Hill had retrieved from Hisner's body. He found it amusing where the note had been hidden. He did not find the actual message amusing. "We have never had a drug problem here. Do you have any idea what that would do to our tourist industry? I'm going to have to contact the head of the Hilda's council, including our Dome representatives."

"Wait a little bit until we can confirm the information. We don't know exactly what Hisner meant by the note. He could have been misled, could have misunderstood. Let's check it out further. We'll watch that Jump and see what comes of it. As soon as we tell anyone at the Dome about the note, it'll be leaked to the press."

Chet nodded his agreement. We all sat in silence drinking our mugs of java, contemplating the chaos the press would cause. It was Fred that broke the silence. "Zoe had some interesting comments" Fred said as he grabbed another cookie. "She said her mother is broke. That her mom just sold off an expensive painting that had been in the family a long time. I think she said it was a *Vidmore*, as old as the Federation itself."

Hill went wide eyed, "Oh my god, how could she part with that!"

"Well, according to Zoe," Fred got himself another cookie, "she sold it for a pittance of what it was worth just to get out from her debtors. I gather Hilary Doss has a gambling problem. That is why she sold 49 percent of the team to Lawren Streng to begin with."

"Well that's why we saw so few servants while at her mansion. There wasn't even a guard at the entranceway. It explained a lot. Doss had to cut back on her lifestyle if money was in short supply."

"But does it tie into the murders, or is it a side issue?" Chet pondered out loud.

"It ties into at least one aspect," Hill pointed to the note. "If she is hurting for money, Hilary Doss would be open to a lot of corruption, even blackmail. We need to know where she's been and who's in her life." My lieutenant unfolded her arms, putting them on the table leaning forward to make her point, "Doss, being the socialite of Hilda can open a lot of doors - doors to illegal drug dealing."

"It fits with what Zoe told me," Fred conjectured. "A lot of strange people have been hanging around the Doss mansion. Not nice people either, the teenager hates them. Doss' daughter thinks they are rough and scary. That's Zoe's words, not mine."

"How about you do some tracking, both financially and travel related on our Hilda socialite," I told Fred. He had contacts throughout the sector. If Hilary had shady deals with any of the drug lords, Stoshingburg should be able to find out.

"Yup," he answered me, again a man of many words.

A knock on the door got all our attentions. "That would be Micky," Chet informed us, getting up from the table and opening the door. "I asked her to come over."

A stunning redheaded woman entered. "Hello, I'm Micky Nantelli." Her voice was a deep rich mellow. I'd bet she was a singer, she had the voice for jazz or blues. "I went to the wrong house, they told me at the desk that it was the one next door. No one answered and I saw lights on here."

"We changed chateaus. Damn front desk keeps getting it wrong!" I explained.

"Micky is my undercover gambling snitch," Chet joked and got a punch in the arm from the beautiful girl. "She performs at the casino and keeps me informed of anything that is unusual. I asked her to come over to your place after work. She worked with Reich Hisner. I wanted her input."

"Worked? As in past tense?" She took off her coat. She was dressed in a skimpy emerald low cut blouse and a short skirt. I noticed Fred was staring, really drooling and Hill had a big frown. I had trouble keeping my eyes off her until Hill kicked me under the table.

"He was murdered tonight at the Planetarian's hockey arena," Chet explained.

Micky abruptly sat down, shock was all over her face. "He was a nice guy, he was well liked at the strip club," she glared at us as if we'd shot him. "He got caught up with that Lilac woman and she got him in more trouble. I kept telling him, she was all about money but he wouldn't listen. He hasn't been to work since she died."

"Are you a stripper?" Hill blurted out.

"Yes," she looked at my lieutenant with a challenge to say more but Hill had the sense to shut up, but my lieutenant couldn't keep the shocked look off her face. "It pays well and I'm not ashamed of my body," Micky said defiantly to Hill. I smiled at her putting Hill in her place.

"Don't you say anything Hill, I've seen you in pasties!" I tried to break the tension in the room and it succeeded.

Fred let out a big guffaw, "Now I'd like to have seen that!"

"I was an undercover bartender at the Skantie Row casino, you asshole," Hill roughly told Stoshingburg, "And the Chief came over and broke Doug Blithie's wrist because he couldn't take the youngest Blithie son flirting with me. I was making headway too."

"You almost got yourself killed!" I reminded her, "And me too! Besides the young punk was dead that night from one of his security guards accidentally blowing his head away."

"Really?" Chet sounded astonished. "The Blithies are brutal, you are lucky you got out alive."

"With the evidence they brought back and my follow-up, we ended up putting most of the top family in jail, for a long time," Fred told him.

I got the conversation back on track, "Do you think Hisner's death is related to drugs?" I asked the female stripper.

"I don't know, although the male strippers dabble in drugs but nothing serious. I don't think any of them do Supfline. I've never smelled it and our area is pretty cramped with little air ventilation. If Reich was into drugs, it was through that Lilac girl."

"Fred, find out whatever you can," I told him. "Chet, you'll have to get a search warrant for the Floe's house and Reich's apartment." I saw my superintendent nod.

"We need to talk to the other strippers," Hill looked at me. When I nodded, she continued, "I'll go to the Chippy Chip Bar."

"They are a close knit group," Micky looked skeptical at Hill.

"I'm not going as a potential stripper but as a wealthy horny female tourist. See what I can get them to tell me if I pose no threat." She half smiled. Hill loved undercover work.

"I'll go with you," Julie said from the far corner of the kitchen.

"Neither one of you are going!" I nodded at my sister-in-law. "Did you forget this is a murder investigation and now drugs may be involved?"

"I think Hill should get her pasties out, it'll frighten the bejesus out of them!" Fred leaned back in his chair laughing.

"Fred!" we all yelled at him.

It was Micky, however, that spoke up as she stared at Julie, "You'd do well. You have an exotic beauty. They'd pay attention to you. The management would probably try to recruit you."

"No!" I guess I spoke rather loudly because Ray came jaunting into the kitchen. When he learned what Julie had offered to accompany Hill to the casino's Chippy Chip Strip Bar, he went crazy.

"No, no, no!" he plainly stated, as he shook his head at his wife.

"We'll go tomorrow night," Julie told Hill completely ignoring Ray's protest. Then she looked at her husband, "You and Skip can stay back here. We girls can take care of ourselves."

There was nothing more to be said!

Chapter Eight

The morning brought Marcus Nettlson and Bud Fachus, two experienced detectives that Issam sent to help with the investigation. Marcus was a computer specialist. He went right to work on both Lilac's and Reich's cell tabloids, while Bud gathered everything he could find that seemed relevant to the two victims. I was working hard trying to negate Nove Deck's restrictive court orders. Even Judge Button was running into problems circumventing his legal maneuvers. Karine was not pleased and very frustrated. Considering Button was not only a high level Parley judge, she also wielded a lot of power in Dome politics. She was beginning to realize how much influence the lawyer Deck had.

Bud Fachus worked a lot with Fred Stoshingburg back on Fulton. He took the gambling aspect that often went hand and hand with the drug industry, not to mention the prostitution angle. Fred along with Bud and Marcus, would tackle the casino's records, despite the lawyer's obstruction. If any of the mob families from Skantie Row had their fingers in the casino, they would find out.

Hill got word that Hessina's brother would be arriving that afternoon. She hoped he would help her get access to her friend Hessie. When she went to interview more of Sunrise's employees, she was told the manager Paul Bell had orders from their lawyer, Deck, not to talk to the police. Hill complained loudly but got nowhere.

My brother didn't ski all day, instead he argued with Julie about going to the strip club. I felt guilty and tried to convince my sister-in-law not to go. The more we pushed her the more she was determined to do it. Julie's independent streak was in full overdrive. I finally gave up but my brother didn't. Of course, Killa blamed me and wouldn't talk to me all day. Marty looked worried and spent the day just watching the telescreen in the den. It made for a very unhappy household.

I tried to get Hilary Doss to talk to me but again Nove Deck had done his work and she had refused to see me. That man was getting to me, enough that I had to take one of my blue pills.

Fred got the idea that we should ask the General Manager of the Planetarians more questions. According to Zoe, he was intimate with her mother. Since Stoshingburg was busy on the drug angle, I got a squad hover to take me to the sports complex. Caltun Weler was in his office, which was a large nicely decorated room close to the locker room that we had visited. He recognized me, he stood giving me his hand.

"What brings the police to my door?" he asked with a smile in his voice. Obviously he was not afraid of the long arm of the law.

"I just hoped I could get some info out of you," I quipped, making sure my police voice was totally absent.

"From me?" he sat down with a perplexed look on his face. "I hope one of my players isn't in any trouble. I took care of Heda's arrest warrant, I paid off the woman she assaulted. She dropped the charges."

"No, no," I waved my hand, "the team is fine. I'm here for your opinion of Hilary Doss."

His face took on a worried look, "I really don't know her well, Zoe exaggerated my involvement with her mother." I gave him my most skeptical look and he looked away.

"Mr. Weler, whatever you tell me will be kept between us, unless you've broken the law. Ms. Hilary Doss is not a minor, so I rather doubt you're guilty of anything."

"Look, she came on to me," he waved his hands to emphasize his point, "she's slept with half the team. I was just a passing fancy."

"Well, while you were *passing the fancy* did you notice anything unusual? For instance, did you notice if Mr. Streng was involved with her?"

"Lawren?" he shook his head. "He didn't even like her. Besides he was totally devoted to his wife. I like Mrs. Streng! I know, I know she's not a beauty but she's damn nice. It used to bug the hell out of me when Hilary would make fun of her. Doss has half the class Mrs. Streng has." I guess the surprise of his vehement vouching for Hessina must have shown on my face as he continued, "You are like all the rest, judging a book by its cover!"

"You're probably right and I apologize for it," I told him.

That seemed to placate him. "Well, I'll tell you this, Hilary has money problems. It is the reason she sold 49% of the team to Lawren and a good thing she did. Lawren saw to it that we got better equipment and better pay. You wouldn't believe the dregs that were coming around the team, trying to intimidate Hilary into selling. We were so afraid she was going to sell to those scumbags. They had liquidation all over their manner! Those were some scary guys."

"Who were they?" I asked as he had gotten my interest peaked.

"Well they dressed like mobsters and that damn lawyer was with them. Nove Deck was his name, rude as all hell. None of them had any interest in hockey. They actually treated the players like they considered them morons. Then Streng bought us, thank god."

"You never saw those guys again?" I asked.

"Not around here, but you see them at the casino. Don't get the wrong idea, I don't gamble but Hilary sure as hell does."

I left him but my interest was piqued. Once again the hair on the back of my neck stood up. Were mobsters from Skantie Row here?

When I got back to the resort, Hill needed a cop hover to go get Hessina's brother. I got us one. I wanted to talk to him so I went along. His Jump was arriving in less than an hour. I could see Hill was nervous. "I haven't seen Jarad McTenser since I was in college."

"Let me guess, he was more than a friend?" I semi asked.

"Yeah," was her reply and nothing more.

"Okay, who broke it off?" as if I didn't know. Hill was my presumption.

"I did, I gave him back his diamond," she sheepishly answered.

"You were engaged to this doufus?" I was acting like a jealous puppy. I mentally slapped myself and got more on a real track, "Is he talking to you?"

"Don't know," she shrugged.

"Honestly Hill, you try men's souls, literally," I snapped at her. "Good thing I came along."

"Oh, so you're going to play diplomat? That's hilarious," she snorted in disgust.

"Well, if you didn't leave male victims all over the place, I wouldn't have to keep cleaning up!" I replied snippily.

"Oh please!" she pointed her finger at my nose. "I suppose Judge Button is forever grateful to you for no reason!"

"Don't start!" I yelled at her, then noticed the police driver glancing in his rear view mirror and lowered my voice, "We will discuss this later!"

"Humpf, or not at all," was her only reply and she turned to look out the window ignoring me.

The Jump station was busy but Hessina's brother was on time. He was about my age and, of course, fit and trim. To our surprise, Judy's brother Matt was with him.

"What are you doing here?" she snapped at her sibling, "I told Dad I didn't need him."

"I'm not here for you. Hessina's father asked the General to please send someone to help with the investigation of his son-in-law. Have you forgotten how powerful Calis McTenser is?"

"Oh, well just don't interfere!" she angrily told her brother.

"I see we haven't changed any!" Jarad piped up. "Still proving you can handle everything yourself?"

Before Hill could reply I interjected myself between her and them, "Hello, Matt." He shook my hand. I had met Hill's brother when we were on MOSS, the medical space station.

"Hello, Chief Brown, this is Jarad McTenser, Hessina's brother." Hill's former fiancé shook my hand.

"I hear Judith works for you." He looked highly amused, which only got my hackles up.

"You have that correct. She's one of my homicide detectives and quite good at what she does!" I thought Hill would be glad I'd given her an up but I got a poke in my back instead.

"Stop patronizing" she quipped and then turned to Jarad, "I need to talk to your sister but Lawren Streng's lawyer, he's also the resort's lawyer, has an injunction against me doing so. Think you can help? Nove Deck is his name, he's slick and slimy but good at twisting the law in his favor."

"Why would he keep Hessina from talking to you? She's very fond of you, was devastated when we broke it off. Of course I'll help. The faster we get this suicide investigation done the better. The funeral is in a couple of days and then Hessina is coming home, period!"

"It's a little more complicated than that," I told him. "Let's go find a café and we'll explain further.

He looked surprised, but Hill's brother Matt nodded, "Let's go and have a cup of java. Consulate Assembly Governor General Pinote is lending his full support to the McTenser family. It will open a lot of doors, I assure you." He looked directly at his sister but Hill ignored him.

We had a corner table in the Jump Station Café. I explained, along with Hill interjecting her many comments, the whole case. Jarad looked shocked but it was Matt that really grasped what was going on. "Sounds like Skantie Row's mob families have their claws into Hilda's resorts and casinos. My father will not be pleased. He does not want that planet extending its influence beyond Skantie's own sphere."

"No one is pleased, Matt," I told him. "How deep or how far they've gotten is unknown but we'll find out. My top drug detectives are also here. We'll put an end to it. We have before. I just don't understand the murders - why bring attention to their plans?"

"I can't believe my sister or her husband could be involved. Despite her disease, Hessina is not easily fooled. Any problems, all she had to do is contact my father. He'd have helped them." Jarad sounded pained as if this reflected badly on the family. "My sister is not well," he continued. "We must protect her from too much stress. It will have a bad effect on her disease and will weaken her further. We thought her well settled with Lawren Streng. I can't believe he fooled us about his feelings for my sister."

"Let me talk to her." Seeing Jarad's distress, Hill put her hand on his, "Hessie needs to know she has friends and family nearby."

"Let me see what I can do," Hessina's brother smiled at Hill, an all too familiar smile, as he covered her hand with his other paw. I kicked her under the table. She withdrew her hand and frowned at me. Damn woman! Of course, she kicked me back, twice as hard as I had kicked her!

We headed back to the resort. Matt Pinote had rented one of the luxury chateaus, which I'd heard, were all booked up. I'm sure his father's influence had something to do with it. The condo was twice the size of our own and came fully staffed with servants. Hill refused to move in; preferring her room at the lodge. "Don't even hint I'm your sister, understand?" she told Matt quite strongly.

"If that is what you prefer but Dad gave me strict instructions I was to help Jarad. I will try and keep out of your way." He placed his hand on his sister's shoulder, "We use to help each other when we were kids. I'm there for you."

"Don't play diplomat with me, Matt," Hill pointed her finger right at his chest and then left, slamming the door behind her.

"Gee, that went well," Judy's brother grimaced. "Seriously, if you can use the influence of my father, please let me know."

Unlike Hill, I'd take any help I could get. "Just get that damn lawyer, Nove Deck corralled and I'll take it from there."

He nodded. I left and caught up with Hill on her way back to the lodge. I could see the steam coming off her head. I grabbed her arm and spun her around to face me. "Look, stop making this all about you! It's about the murder of three people and the influx of drugs into Hilda."

She was going to retort but stopped herself. "You're right," her eyes went sad, "why can't I get away from my family. Am I doomed to be attached at their hip?"

"Let's make a deal," I proposed. "I'll deal with your brother and Jarad. You leave yourself out of it. Okay?"

She just nodded and we headed into the lodge. Of course, I looked around for my skis but no dice. It didn't help that they looked like every other rental skis that were so numerous with the guests. Anyone could have them. There went a hefty sum of my savings. Geesh!

An excited Hill greeted me at the front desk. "I'm going up to see Hessina! I am going in with Jarad. Come on!" she motioned for me to follow her as she headed for the elevator.

"That was quick," I told her as she punched the fifth floor suite button. She was so excited that her hand shook.

The top floor was the Streng's apartment. It certainly was nicer than mine. Thick carpeting that our feet sank into, nice artwork by notable artists graced the walls. As soon as the elevator opened, Jarad came into the foyer through one of the doors, greeting us with a serious frown. "She's sleeping but come in. I'll wake her. She needs to know I'm here. My sister looks pale. The doctor says only that she's fragile."

We sat ourselves on a couch that faced a beautifully sculptured marble fireplace that was gas lit. The small blue flames flickered, almost mesmerizing us into thinking the logs were actually burning. Before sitting we had scrutinized the large room. One windowed wall faced Sunrise Mountain. The resort's large ski runs veined the entire side.

The sun was just starting to recede behind the tall peak, sending shadows across the valley. What a view of all the chateaus that graced the basin with the smaller mountains ringing the rest of the resort. I pulled myself away from the outdoor scene.

I could see a formal dining room to our left. They must have entertained a lot. The long wooden table, although appearing purposely rustic, was polished to a bright shine with a crystal chandelier hovering above. I would bet it was a "Chatlulae" constructed by the famous artist by that name. It must be worth a lot. Hill was staring at it too. "God, that's beautiful." There were twelve matching chairs. The whole setup fit nicely next to the huge windows showing Hilda's splendor and majestic appearance.

In the living room I noticed several tab books on a side table - all of them having to do with raising children. I cringed. This was not going to be easy, telling Hessina of her husband's infidelity and of Lilac's pregnancy. Obviously Streng's wife was planning on having a family.

As we sat on the couch waiting, I noticed Hill clutching her hands. I'd never seen her so nervous. "Do you want me to tell her?" I asked.

"No," was all she could get out. We sat in silence until Jarad came into the living room, helping Hessina to one of the chairs. The bird-like woman looked frail and her eyes looked dull and sleepy. I would bet she was heavily sedated. How would Hill handle that?

Jarad pulled another chair up to his sister's. She was wearing a bathrobe that had slipped open showing a frilly nightdress. Her long boney legs stuck out with her feet in big fluffy slippers. He motioned Judy to sit in the chair. My lieutenant sat and took Hessina's hand. Streng's wife looked up. Seeing Hill, she actually smiled, "Jude, I'm so glad to see you."

"I've wanted to come but had to wait for your brother. Your lawyer doesn't want me to talk to you." Hill's voice emotionally cracked. I realized my detective was covering all her bases, letting Hessina know everything so Deck couldn't accuse her of deception.

"For heaven's sake why not?" the bird woman seemed to perk up, "Jarad, tell him that Judy is welcomed here anytime!"

"I already have, don't worry yourself over it," he said giving Hill a frown and patting his sister's shoulder.

"Are you feeling well enough to talk to me?" Judy asked her friend.

"Yes, my nurse is standing right behind that doorway," Hessina's long skeletal hand pointed toward the dining room where a nurse stuck her head out.

"Please, Mrs. Streng, do not concern yourself, I'm only here as a precaution." The nurse looked like something out of the military, more likely a sergeant.

"Umpf," came from the thin mouth of Judy's friend. "The woman's a tyrant," she whispered over to Judy, making my lieutenant laugh.

"How are you feeling?" Hill asked.

"I'm okay, just a little tired. I'm mostly sad, but I will survive despite everyone fawning over me." She looked up at her brother and lifted her hand to his fingers that rested on the back of her chair. He lightly squeezed her hand. The affection in his face was unmistakable. Hessina was lucky to have such a devoted family. She was going to need it, I thought.

"Hessina, did you know Lilac Floe very well?" Judy softly asked, still holding on to her friend's hand.

Mrs. Streng pulled back her hand, looking rather angry. "Why? I knew her well enough!"

"Do you think Lawren knew her?" Hill was going cautiously, keeping any emotion out of her question.

"Jude, again why do you ask me? I'm not a child, out with it!" Hessina's voice was strong now as if calling upon some inner strength she possessed.

"Did you know that Lilac was pregnant?" Judy's voice was just above a whisper but it carried across to the bird-woman like a whip.

"Yes, of course I did!" Jarad's sister snapped. She pushed away her brother's hand that had come down to her shoulder.

"You did?" Judy now sounded totally confused, "Did you know it was Lawren's?"

"Yes, of course!" Hessina tried to get up but was too weak and fell back into the chair. "She was our surrogate!" the bird-like mouth managed to get out. Shock filled the room.

"Your surrogate?" Jarad was the first to get the words out.

"For god's sake, that's what I said," she half yelled, causing the nurse to come out.

"Please, Mrs. Streng, do not excite yourself, think of your condition!" The nurse grabbed Hessina's wrist checking her pulse.

"Please leave me be!" Hessina mumbled while trying to extricate her hand from the strong woman's grip.

"Leave her!" Jarad snapped and the nurse retreated.

"I'll not be held responsible for her relapse!" the medical sergeant snapped back.

"Go!" Jarad pointed to the dining room door and the woman slipped back behind it.

Hill took Hessina's hand again, "Lilac was your surrogate baby carrier?"

Mrs. Streng actually laughed, "Yes, that's putting it mildly different. She was impregnated with Lawren's sperm." Hessina cringed as she said it, tears filled her eyes.

We all sat in silence. This changed everything. It was again Jarad that finally recovered first, "Why this woman?"

"It was my mistake," Hessina lowered her head, looking at her hands that now rested in her lap. "I knew her from the ski patrol. Lawren made me in charge of organizing the patrol. I think he thought it would keep me busy and make me feel like I was part of helping him run the resort."

"So you chose her?" Hill asked.

"She was vibrant, beautiful, everything I'm not. I thought she would produce a child worthy of Lawren." Tears flowed down her sharply defined cheeks.

"Hessina, don't get upset," Jarad came around bending on his knee, taking his sister's hands in his. "Why did you think it was a mistake?"

Hessina looked up into his face, "She may have been beautiful but only on the outside. I tried to counsel her. I tried to be her friend. She wouldn't watch her diet. She even drank alcohol. She kept asking for more and more money. What could we do, she was carrying our child? She also hung around with all types of unsavory characters - including a male stripper!"

"What did Lawren think of all this?" Hill slipped the question in.

"He didn't know what to do. My husband left it up to me." Her eyes filled with tears again, "Now it doesn't much matter. She's dead, Lawren's dead!" she burst into tears bringing the nurse over again.

"Really, I must insist Mrs. Streng rest!" her voice was almost threatening. I'd had enough.

"Listen," I told the nurse and Hessina too in my *Chief of Police* voice. "You stay by her but my lieutenant needs to ask a few more questions. We have a slew of murders that need solving!" I left no doubt to any resistance and the nurse, wide-eyed, just took up standing behind Hessina's chair.

"Are you up to a few more questions?" Jarad asked his sister, who just nodded.

"Hessie, do you know who killed Lilac?" Hill's question was certainly direct.

"No," she shook her head definitively. "Of course we were devastated. Lawren was furious. He said, *The bastard chose the wrong woman.*"

"Chose the wrong woman?" I couldn't help but repeat the words. Hessina looked over at me.

"That's what he said. I have never seen him so angry but I was in such shock at her murder I didn't get to ask him why he said that. I figured he was talking about our doctor, who said Lilac was an excellent surrogate candidate." Her eyes started watering up again. It was hard seeing this already frail woman suffer even more. I averted my eyes to the glowing fireplace. Nothing made sense anymore.

"Hessie, where did Lawren go a couple of times a month?" Hill again slipped in another question.

"He'd go on business trips," her voice now had a cautious tone.

Hill picked right up on it. "Hessie, you know where he went. Please tell me, it could be important." My lieutenant was pushing and I saw Jarad's mouth tighten. He was going to interfere but his sister answered before he could object.

"He went to Skantie Row." Once she said it, her eyes widened in alarm as if she'd realized what it could mean. "It isn't what you think! He was checking out their casinos. The Hildan Company is thinking of opening more here. It was all he was doing!" She almost was pleading us to accept what she was saying.

I didn't accept it but I didn't say anything either. Hill just sat there, her eyes full of doubt. Even Jarad's expression was doubtful.

Hessina saw it too, "Please believe me. Ask Nove Deck or Paul Bell. They went with him sometimes. Ask Hilary Doss." Lawren's wife was pleading, trying to convince us her husband wasn't doing anything wrong. "Hilary was going to invest in the new casino. Ask her! It was all legit!"

Hill tried to calm her, "I'm sure it was, Hessie. Calm down. Maybe you should rest now."

"Yes," Hessina nodded, "I need my rest. I'm pregnant, I must rest for my baby."

The shock that filled the room was almost overwhelming. Jarad jumped up, Hill slumped back in her chair. I just stared, words failed me.

It was the nurse that broke the silence, "You are right, Mrs. Streng. You know what the doctor said. You are going to need all the rest you can get."

Jarad spoke, his voice cracking, "Hes, did Lawren know?"

"No," she sobbed, "I was just coming back from the doctor to tell him when it happened. She sobbed again, bringing the nurse, who helped the bird-woman to stand; leading her out.

Hessina, however, turned back, "It was so great seeing you Jude, please come again. I always hoped you'd get back with Jarad. I would love you as a sister-in-law."

"I'll be back and call me anytime you need me." Hill softly sent the words toward the retreating women.

For long moments we sat in silence absorbing what we had just learned. I finally couldn't sit still and walked over to the expansive windows. I looked at the snowy wonderland that lay before me. Hilda was a beautiful cold planet. I hated the thought of the scum that ruled Skantie Row getting its claws on this pristine place.

Nothing made sense anymore. Nothing. What Hessina had revealed was devastating to all our theories on Lilac. Was she an innocent victim? How about Reich Hisner? How did he fit in? How did Lawren Streng's business trips to Skantie Row fit in?

I saw Hill's reflection in the window as she came to stand next to me. Questions lurked in her face, the same questions I had. "Boy, that was a shocker. We need to get some answers. Chet needs to get his people into all phases of Lilac's life. I'll get some answers tonight at the strip club."

"I'm well aware of what needs to be done," I said with my frown echoing in the glass window. She saw it and shut up. Sometimes I wondered who was the *Chief*.

"I need to see Hessina's maternity doctor. I know my father will want to have her transferred to the medical space station. His company, XIL, has contacts on MOSS. That will be the best place for her to take her baby to term." Jarad joined us by the window. "This holiday planet will have nothing that can help her."

"Don't dismiss them so lightly," I ventured to tell him. "I imagine just being pregnant is a miracle that this doctor has brought on."

"And don't forget, Jarad," Hill was standing next to him, with her hand on his, "Hessie has trouble with the Jumps, she does not handle them well. So let's go talk to this doctor. Chief could you have my brother take care of the patient confidentiality that this maternity doctor was so concerned with when I last talked to him?"

"I'll see what Matt has to say. I'll see you back at the chateau before you and Julie leave for the club. Chet is bringing over Micky to brief you."

I left Hill with Jarad. She was going over to the doctor with her former fiancé. I called Matt and got him going on lifting the patient confidentiality on both Lilac and Hessina's pregnancy. He assured me it would be done. I walked over to our chateau, noticing the police tape was down from the chateau next to us. A pair of racing skis was perched on number 14's porch. When I got to number 15, Ray's and Julies's skis were there. It meant Ray had given up skiing to still try and change Julie's mind about the club. He was only making her more determined but I kept that thought to myself as I entered the kitchen.

Ray had the baby and was walking back and forth between the kitchen and living room, following Julie. "Come on Hon, think about the baby. It's unbecoming of you - you're a mother now!"

"Don't start Ray. I'm going with Judy. We aren't doing anything wrong. It is just a show!" She ran ahead of him, flopping down on a chair near the fireplace.

Marty was following right behind Ray, every once in a while putting her two cents in about how inappropriate going to a strip club was. Killa said nothing but kept her eyes on Ray and the baby as if he might drop the precious package.

I opened my book and ignored everything, including Killa's glaring looks in my direction. Finally the doorbell rang and my superintendent and Micky waltzed in. The redheaded stripper had two clothes bags with her. "I brought something for Julie and Judy to wear. They'll knock everyone's socks off."

I heard Ray groan.

Chapter Nine

"I'm not letting her go alone!" Ray followed me into the kitchen.

Chet, my Hilda superintendent, looked leery eyed at me. "You can't blame your brother, Chief. Micky Nantelli will see to it that no harm comes to the girls but Ray doesn't know my casino undercover agent from Adam."

"We will be there," I assured my brother.

"Julie will have a fit." He looked so troubled, in such a quandary that I actually felt sorry for him. My brother had such a great life, most of the time I envied him. His love for Julie and his wanting to protect her was fighting with his conscience that she was also her own person. Ray had always been proud of his independent thinking wife; he did not want to butt against this or jeopardize that part of their relationship. "If she sees me…"

"Perhaps we can somewhat rectify the situation," I assured him. "We are known quantities by a lot of the locals, so we will have to take precautions to disguise ourselves. Julie won't even know you are there unless she needs you." Ray headed into the den, moping with Marty who was watching the news since Julie had the baby with her. Killa was also moping about the absent baby, but in the kitchen providing drinks and snacks. Each to their own, I thought. Family relations were so complicated. Everyone handles the tension their own way. I took another blue pill.

Hill showed up, actually slumping through the front door. Killa gave her a hot cup of black tea and a hug. My little Ligithian hugged Hill more than she did me, for god's sake. My lieutenant did look haggard. "How did it go with the doctor?"

"He at first wouldn't tell us anything." Hill took a long sip of her tea before continuing, "I was ready to strangle him and he was showing us the door via the waiting room when his nurse told him he had someone very important that wanted to talk to him over his off-planet telecell."

"Ah, I think General Pinote was calling," I expounded, I couldn't keep the amusement from my voice.

"The General would really call him?" Chet looked astonished. "I'd shit my pants if he called me! That man could have anyone sent to farthest ends of the unknown universe if he wanted!" My Hilda superintendent had no idea that Pinote's daughter was sitting right next to him.

Hill actually laughed; perhaps she couldn't visualize how intimidating her father was. "Well the telecell conference did the trick. Jarad and I were given everything that Dr. Rogtheius had on both Lilac Floe and Hessina McTenser Streng's medical histories."

"Did you bring a copy back with you?" I asked, noticing the small tab she had put in front of her.

"Chet, can we use your Vorus tabloid? If I'm not mistaken, it looks like Dr. Rogtheius' files use the new tabs." I eyed his high tech tabloid with envy.

Chet Kodis disconnected his cell from his collar. He handed Hill his new high tech computer tabloid. She put the small tab in one of its data slots and up came the menu. She stretched the screen so we could all see it and up came Lilac Floe's medical file. It was so clear; the picture of her was intense. The naked shot showed the woman's beauty; her firm round breasts, her intense bright eyes, and beautiful white teeth behind full lips. According to the medical records, Floe had taken a birth control shot last year. The doctor had given her the counter shot and even shot her full of birth enhancing hormones. Then he had implanted Lawren Streng's sperm. She became pregnant three, almost four months ago. Everything was progressing nicely.

I noticed in his notes that Hessina had consulted him on Lilac's bad habits and the doctor had dully warned Lilac of her responsibilities toward the baby she was carrying. Unfortunately he had commented that it hadn't done much good - Lilac had told him to "bug off". I also noticed that the Strengs were paying big bucks for Lilac's medical treatment. This baby was costing them a lot.

Next on the doctor's file came Hessina's records. Her image was as realistic as Lilac's but it was anything but beautiful - the photo showed the tall bird-like structure of her body. She had long thin legs with bony knees; even her bare feet were almost talon like. She had very small breasts on a rib cage that poked out of her chest. Her face, although smiling, was craggy and her lips thin below a large beak of a nose. I almost felt embarrassed to be looking at her. I reminded myself that it was my job and became objectively scrutinizing. I was, however, glad that I had taken a blue pill.

Hessina had insisted that the doctor also try and inseminate her with Lawren's seed. Dr. Rogtheius' notes said they had tried placing Streng's semen in her womb for almost a year. They even tried impregnating Lawren's wife with one of her own externally fertilized eggs. Nothing they did had worked. The doctor had asked Hessina to give herself some time off, especially since Lilac was a success. Streng's wife had agreed that she was exhausted and agreed to stop her treatments for a while.

To the doctor's surprise Hessina had soon naturally become pregnant. He actually wrote that it was a miracle and of his doubts that she could carry it to term. So far, she is almost done with her first trimester and the baby seems fine. Dr. Rogtheius is still worried.

"The doctor explained to me that Hessina should be in the hospital under constant care. Jarad, of course, wanted her transported immediately to the Medical Operation Space Station. He even called his father to arrange special transport for her. Hessina, however, is insisting she will not leave until after Lawren's funeral, which is being held up until the coroner is done." Hill looked over at Chet.

"I haven't released the body until we are sure it was suicide, which we know it wasn't," he held up his hands in frustration.

"No, don't release Streng's body yet, I'll take responsibility," I assured Hilda's top cop.

"Jarad will give you a hard time," Hill interjected. "He wants Hessie at MOSS."

We were interrupted. I closed down the file as I nodded at Marcus and Fred who both had arrived at our chateau from their own investigations. Marcus showed us on his tab the computer files from Lilac's confiscated computer. She was indeed squeezing the Strengs for money. Her bank account was full of deposits from the "Sunrise Resort Inc." Given she still had six months to go before she delivered Lawren's baby, she was going to be one rich woman.

Marcus explained about Reich Hisner's lack of data. "He didn't even have a decent cell or any type of computer. From what I can tell he borrowed everyone's cell to make even simple calls. He was extremely short on funds but I found a bag full of actual money in his dresser draw. He hadn't taken it with him the night he was killed. Given his poor state, I think the money was recently obtained.

Bud, by the way, is still investigating the "Sunrise Casino" files. He's at the police station having a hell of a time getting everything. I'm heading over to Chet's office when I'm done here to help him. Once Judge Button finally got the rescinding court order, that lawyer, Nove Deck, must have loaded fifty tabs onto Marcus' tabloid. We are still awaiting the authorization for going into the Sunrise Resort's files. I think that prick lawyer is piling on the Casino files to make us too busy to do the actual resort's files."

"Well go ahead, do the best you can," I told him. "Call me if anything shows up to indicate any mob infiltration into their operations." I turned to Fred as Marcus left for the Giles' police station. "How are you doing? Anything on drug trafficking in the area?"

"I'm confused as hell." Fred grabbed several oatmeal cookies before continuing, "I haven't found anything that can be substantiated. Strange, very strange. Wish I knew what the Skantie mob families were up to here. A lot will depend on that alleged Supfline shipment tomorrow night. Chet, you have that monitored?"

"Yes, several of my officers, dressed in plain clothes, will be meeting that Jump. You are rather well known, so you and I can be close by, but out of sight."

"Good, I'll be there too," I told them. We were interrupted by Micky yelling for Hill. It was time for her to get dressed for the Strip Club venture. Hill disappeared into the bedroom. Ray just sat by the fireplace, holding little Jim. I took the seat opposite and Killa sat on the arm of my chair. Fred just kept eating all the cookies, while Chet had left for the office.

"Look Ray, stop worrying," I tried to smooth his fears. "Hill wouldn't let any harm come to Julie, it'll be a *girl's night out.* "

"I'm worried about Hill too," he said rather loudly causing the baby to wake up. Killa went and got her grandson, taking him into the den where to my surprise she handed him to Marty then came back. She placed herself on Ray's chair, putting her arm on his shoulder.

"I have faith in Julie," Killa expounded. It seemed to relax Ray, who just closed his eyes. "Remember, Julie worries about you all the time you are racing. It is good that you worry a little about her." Our old nursemaid leaned forward and kissed Ray on the cheek. "You both will survive this." Then she looked at me and frowned as if blaming this all on me. No kiss for me!

Judy and Julie both came out of the bedroom. Fred whistled loudly from the kitchen as each woman looked about as "hot" as a woman could look. Julie was dressed in a black velvet dress that tiered down to her knees in the back and was short-short in the front. The top of the dress was split down the middle giving a good view of her ample breasts without overly exposing them. A diamond choker was around her neck with matching looped jeweled earrings. Her feet had sequined black high heels that sparkled. Her slightly olive complexion only enhanced the exotic overall beauty of her deep dark brown eyes. Her silky black hair had one braid down the back, the rest of her hair cascaded down past her pale green bare arms and shoulders.

Ray just stared, mouth opened, eyes wide. He seemed to be at a loss for words.

Hill was just as stunning. I was at a loss for words. She was dressed in an emerald green silk sheer dress. The skirt was just plain short, emphasizing her long legs. The dress' top was slit on the sides. Just like Julie - the teasing openness showed off just enough of her breasts. The shirt was tied at the top of her shoulders with almost a promise of easy-off. Her tall high heels were strapped half way up her leg - sexy, promisingly sexy. Unlike Julie, her hair was piled on top, giving her height. Some of her curls seemed to tease her neck and ears, again promises, promises. Around Judy's neck was an emerald necklace with matching emerald teardrop earrings sparkling on her ears. She was breathtaking.

"Hill…" I started to say, but Micky came beaming out of the bedroom.

"Aren't they just perfect?" she excitedly pounced around the women. "They are exactly what I was trying for - rich sexy bitches!"

Ray was almost choking, "I think it's a little bit overdone." Marty, holding Jimmy so he couldn't see his mother, was right behind him shaking her head in agreement.

Killa took another view, "You look wonderful! Just what will get their attention."

We looked at our old nursemaid with astonishment. It was Ray that voiced both of our opinions, "Just remember who you are dealing with, and I would like you home before midnight."

Julie strode over to her husband, squeezing him tightly around the waist, "Don't worry Hon, I'll save it all for you when I get home."

Ray turned three shades of red and shut completely up.

I turned to Judy, "I'm not so sure this is a good idea."

"Cold feet? Really Chief!" she laughed. She was so gorgeous. It was my turn to turn three sheets of red. Her slight flowery perfume smell drifted over to my nose arousing my male hormones.

"I don't want anyone getting hurt!" I growled to hide my uneasiness. "Remember who you are dealing with. They have killed three times."

"I think he's jealous," Killa quipped.

"YOU ARE NOT FUNNY! This is serious business!" I exploded. Everyone cowered as my voice can be rather harsh. It usually sends a warning message not to play with me. My old nursemaid, however, was not one to be intimidated like the others.

Killa looked at me; all four feet two of her seemed to stretch higher, her eyes were dark purple, her hair flying and her ears were twitching so fast they were a blur. "I'm not being funny! Give these women credit and stop bullying them, both of you!" She looked over at Ray, who was standing stiffly silent. It certainly shut me up.

"Time to go!" Micky grabbed both Julie and Judy and headed them towards the door. She was giving them advice, "Remember, it is Luke Asit you want. He was Reich's best friend. Judy, try and get him alone. He will be wearing bright red jocks with a blue pocket in front. Wave a 100 credit chip at him and you'll get his attention."

I followed, grabbing Hill by the arm. "Really Hill, I'm serious, please be careful. I'll be nearby."

"Yes, I know," she softly said as she turned towards me, her big green eyes searching mine to emphasize her meaning. She knew me well. I just nodded and let go. I just let her go.

After the women had left, Fred got up from the table, "see ya there," he said with a wave as he closed the door. Fred is a man of few words but the ones that come out of his mouth are exactly needed. The big guy was letting me know he had my back.

As soon as the women were away in the cab, I headed towards my bedroom bringing a sputtering Ray with me. Once inside, I grabbed my suitcase bringing out my disguise kit. Yes, I know, it's pathetic, but I take it everywhere with me. The pouch has its permanent place in the pocket of my carry-on.

I gave my brother a ClaritAll yellow pill. "Swallow, you'll be a light blonde in ten minutes. Also put these contacts in, you're going brown eyed." Then I took a ClaritAll red pill, that turned my hair to a nice shade of red and contacts that turned my eyes dark olive green. I also added shades of gray around our eyes and mouths to make us look older.

I went into my closet giving my brother one of my drab gray suits. "This will be much too big on you, use one of your belts so it will stay up, but it will give you a look of a down and out of luck distressed gambler who's lost a lot of weight. Wear this white dress shirt, with this big tie and tuck it in loosely."

I took one of my suit jackets and turned it inside out. I had bought it at a theatre costume shop. The jacket was unique in that when I turned it inside out it was a green plaid sport jacket that made me look like a kind of geek bozo gambler. The good thing was I could turn it back to a regular suit jacket and blend right in when I got myself in trouble. It was perfect for the casino.

I rolled out my folded-up wrinkle free hat. It expanded to a wide brim fedora that gave my face extra masking.

"Gesh, Skip, I look ridiculous. How long does that pill last?" Ray frantically pulled me to him, "Julie will kill me."

"It will last for four hours. You'll turn back into a pumpkin before midnight," I assured him. "You could stay here."

He shook his head violently, "I'm in."

When we came out we tipped toed out into the kitchen carrying our shoes. Marty was in the den with the baby and didn't even look away from the telescreen news cast.

Killa was sitting at the kitchen table. It was almost like she was waiting for us. The little Ligithian had calmed down but her eyes were still dark, her ears barely twitched. She opened the door for us. I smiled and kissed her on the cheek. She grabbed my hand and squeezed. "Take care of them," she silently mouthed. I just nodded.

Chet was waiting for us near the lodge with his small hover. We jumped into the back. He looked askance at us, "Shit, good thing I knew you were coming. Good disguises. I'll drop you off at the side entrance. Most of the low rollers go in there. The Chippy Chip Stripper Club is in the back part of the Casino. It's located in the section that emphasizes *entertainment.* It's near the other night clubs and near their concert arena. Check out the times of the strip shows on the screens set up behind the bars. Good luck!"

Sure enough the side entrance was not like the front marquee which was all flashing lights and hyped-up blaring music. On the front street, sleigh after sleigh were dropping off resort guests. This side entrance that had a double glass door led us right into the casino proper, right near a huge bar. I suppose that's where not-so-lucky gamblers would first go.

This part of the casino was blaring with noise. We could hear a band to our left. The slot machines were dinging away reminding potential players of those that were winning. The poker and other tables were just buzzing. We could hear the roulette wheels spinning and the dealers were shouting out the numbers and pulling in all the chips toward themselves. We walked past the craps table, the shouting was almost overwhelming as winners shouted and losers moaned.

Micky Nantelli was right. The majority of women were decked out in jewels and skimpy dresses. All were in spiked high heels. Some of the men were in formal attire and some were like us, just playing the games and mostly losing.

Also dispersed in the crowd were skiers, dressed in their tight skiing outfits. Perhaps they were stopping by the playing tables after hitting the mountain. I found out later they had a skiing entrance right from the slopes. Gee, I should have worn my blue ski outfit, I'd really fit in. *Not!*

We wandered over to the high stakes tables. Here was the mix of formal attired people and casually dressed players but all had that serious intense gambler attitude. The tables started at 1,000 credits and went up to over 50,000 credits as a starting bet. The bar was an elaborate winter extravaganza with snow falling down to right above peoples' heads. At least it looked like big snowflakes raining down but it was obviously an expensive illusion.

I pulled Ray over to a bar stool that looked like a ski lift. I almost winced at the memories of my falling off them. The seat held the two of us, but at least it didn't swing. "This gives us a good view of the main floor." I checked out the screen behind the bar. "The men's strip show doesn't start for another hour," I explained to my brother, who was obviously out of his element. He looked so strangely comical in my oversized suit, gawking at all the noisy chaos.

"You think they'll come here first?" he asked scanning the large room.

"Most likely," I said as I looked over the whole casino motif. Winter Wonderland was the theme. High above snow was falling to about half way down, just like the bar but didn't go as low. The walls were simulated views of the mountains. Probably during the day they were big windows giving a panoramic mountain scene. Right now, because it was night, the walls just gave the illusion of the resort's beautiful day scenery. It still was breathtaking and rather tranquil if you could ignore the loud deafening gambling atmosphere, which did rather spoil it.

"This is impressive," Ray remarked. "I never went to any of the casinos at the race tracks. Never imagined something like this."

"This casino is much smaller than most of the gambling establishments in the other parts of the Crab Sector. That's why I'm so baffled. Compare this to the planet Amise's gaming houses, never mind their seaside resorts. Even their cruise ships have bigger casinos. Look at Fulton Station's casino. Ours is much bigger. You know, even on Nestor, the race track has a larger casino."

"Yep and your point is?" Ray looked at me, his dark brown eyes full of questions as he sipped his beer.

"The question is – *Why would Skantie Row's mob families be interested in this casino*? Hilda has limited capacity for tourism. They are a purposely small land mass planet. The planet is reaching the limit of people it can handle and most of the incoming tourists are more interested in skiing than in gambling. Skantie Row has a city full of casinos, bordellos and expensive shops and restaurants. Why bother with this small one? It's perplexing me."

I didn't say anymore as we both saw Hill and Julie enter the main floor. They stopped at the roulette table and were playing. Both were laughing and enjoying themselves. Of course, the men at the table perked up. I felt Ray tense. "Damn," was all he said.

"Easy," I touched his arm. At the same time I saw Hilary Doss over by the high roller table. She was dressed to the hilt with jewels on her fingers, on her neck, on her ears and even sprinkles in her hair. She was smiling right into the face of Paul Bell! To make matters worse, Nove Deck was holding onto her arm. Shit, what I wouldn't do to be able to hear what they were saying.

"Isn't that Paul Bell?" Ray asked. "What's he doing by that table? It is a 20,000 credit table! I didn't know front desk resort managers made that much!"

"Judgmental, aren't you?" I chided him. "Maybe he comes from a wealthy family."

"Yeah, sure he does." My brother's eyes went back to Julie. His deep frown creased his face making him look older.

"Hello, Chief," Hill was standing at the bar next to me.

"Funny Hill," I growled. "How did you know it was me?"

You wore the same hat on Skantie Row," she teased. "Hated it then, hate it now. It does nothing for you. Hello Ray, I see you let your brother dress you."

"You're not funny," Ray said. "Don't let Julie know I'm here."

"I won't, but she'd get a good laugh." Hill patted him on the back.

I took the hat off and shoved it in my pocket. "Look to your right. At the high roller craps table is Hilary Doss, the one that's wearing the expensive jewelry."

"What's Paul Bell doing there?" Hill turned back grabbing her drink from the smiling leering bartender. I glowered at him and he quickly went away.

"That's what I'd like to know," I snapped.

"Well, let me go find out," taking her drink with her and heading in that direction before I could stop her. I got as close as I could, pretending to be interested in the next craps table.

"Hello, Hilary," Judy went right up to the socialite. "I haven't seen you since the showing of the *Hissante Collection*, last year."

"Excuse me," Doss let go of Nove Deck's arm. "I don't believe I remember you."

"Oh, I'm Judith Pinote." Hill put as much disbelief in her voice as possible, "I'm surprised you don't remember me. I was with my father."

"Consulate Assembly General Govenor Pinote?" Hilary went wide eyed. "You're General Pinote's daughter!"

"He's dad to me," Hill laughed. "I'm surprised you don't remember me, we hit it off so well."

"Of course, I remember," Doss covered her tracks, "it just took me a moment. You look just like him. Why are you on Hilda?"

"My brother, Matt rented a ski lodge. We are all such lovers of skiing. Hilda is the place!"

"Oh, that's right," Paul Bell chimed in. "Your brother has one of our luxury villas. So happy to meet you."

"And you are?" Hill chimed with her most diplomatic voice.

"I'm the new General Manager of the Sunrise Resort," he almost burst with pride. I was worried that he'd recognize my Lieutenant but evidently, out of context, out of mind.

"The *new*?" Judy asked.

"Yes, unfortunately our old General Manager died suddenly," his voice was dripping with false grief. It made me cringe.

"I'm Nove Deck," the slick lawyer took Hill's hand and grandly placed a kiss on it.

I could have killed her, she beamed up at him, "Well, how do you do?"

"Perhaps I could show you around?" His voice was debonair; I wanted to punch his slimy face in.

"Well, thank you but I'm here with friends." Hill sounded genuinely sorry. I wanted to grab her away from him but she put him off nicely, "we are catching one of the shows, but maybe some other time. I'll be here a couple of days. Perhaps we could go skiing?"

"I don't ski but I do everything else," he purred. She giggled alluringly.

"You are taking me to the ballet!" Hilary Doss' voice dripped with anger.

"Oh right!" the lawyer took Hilary's arm, "my mind is everywhere, you must forgive me, my dear."

"Of course," the socialite smiled up at him.

"See you all later," Hill strove back over to the bar. The lawyer's eyes never left her until Hilary pulled him away.

When I joined her, Ray was nursing his second drink. "How did it go?" he asked.

"The Sunrise Resort has a new General Manager named Paul Bell."

"We will have to investigate him," Hill speculated without turning to look at us.

"Yup, better get back to Julie," I told her.

Hill went back to the roulette table. It seemed Julie was winning as her pile of chips had increased substantially. I heard Ray growl, "That's all I need, a wife addicted to gambling."

"I really don't think you need worry. Be happy she gambled on you. I'm really sorry I got you involved in this." It had bothered me all day that my family was knee deep in my work.

To my surprise Ray turned to me, his face was scrunched up in memory pain, "I owe you so much for getting me out of that blackmail deal, I could never repay you. I could have lost Julie on that one. You saved my ass, so don't apologize to me!"

"It was my pleasure," I softly slapped him on the back. "The girls are leaving. The men's strip show starts in ten minutes."

We slowly walked over to the entertainment section of the casino. It was housed on the far side. There was a long wide fancy tiled hallway with exclusive boutiques, everything from expensive designer clothes to classy antique shops to top of the line jewelry stores.

Half way down the hallway was a small wooden bridge with actual water going under it. Fish swam back and forth. Once guests crossed the bridge, posh restaurants of every type of cuisine graced each side. The smell was so enticing that I almost forgot where we were going. Of course, Ray was pulling me along, his nerves were stretched thin.

Finally we came to the night clubs. Each entranceway promised dancing, or good drinks, sports coverage and then came the Chippy Chip Club. Both men and women were dancing in the large windows. It goes without saying - *scantily clothed*. Wow, all the women were strongly built as were the men. Highly excited women, dressed to the hilt, were flooding in to see the show.

Ray and I joined the few men who also were walking in. The place smelled of perfume and cologne. There was also a deep sexual smell. I wondered how they managed that. Did they bottle it and spray it on the nightclub floor?

"Gee, what the hell," Ray scrunched up his nose.

"Just go with it," I reminded my brother, "remember what kind of place this is."

The room also had loud pulsating music. It was dark with strobe lights bouncing off the walls. Glittering ball lights rotated above what must be the dance floor.

I held onto my brother guiding him to the back of the room, where shadows would hide us from detection. We took one of the tables that hugged the wall. Immediately, a scantily clad waitress came and took our drink order. Both of us stuck with beer, a locally brewed beer. I thought the brew tasted rather good but Ray left it sitting on the table. He was looking for Julie.

In the front was a wide half bar, half stage setup. Julie and Judy were sitting on two of the stools. Four long poles graced the stage. Long ropes with handles hung down on either side. This part of the nightclub was brightly lit with rotating colored lights. An eerily looking and quite enticing woman, who only wore a G-string and two pasties, walked out onto the stage.

"Ladies!" she screamed. "Are we ready for some excitement?"

"Yeah," the crowd roared, all female high pitched voices, their hands clapping to the rhythm of the now thunderous beat.

One female yelled, "Come on, bring them on, we want to see some cocks!"

I saw my brother start to get up. I grabbed him and pushed him back into his seat.

This was going to be a long night!

Chapter Ten

"Think before you act," I told Ray as I grabbed him by his coattails, forcing him back into the nightclub's vinyl cushioned chair. "Take a deep breath, have a sip of your beer."

He looked over at me, his fake brown contact eyes staring angrily at me. "What is wrong with these women?" His hands went up in the air, "They are acting worse than men."

"Oh, just noticing are you?" I laughed. "Perhaps this is good for you. Women have just as much right to sexual prowess as men. You either trust Julie or you don't."

"It's not Julie…" he started to say.

I interrupted him, "Yes, it is. Trust or not trust? That's the underlining question. As worried as I am about Judy Hill, I can't let her take any less risks than my male detectives take, although sometimes my gut does somersaults." It shut Ray up as he slowly sipped his beer but his eyes never left the bar where Julie and Hill sat. Both women were whooping loudly and raising their arms toward the strippers.

The show was rousingly loud. More male dancers started coming onto the stage. Each new beat brought less and less clothes on their well-formed bodies. The crowd went crazy as each piece of clothing was thrown out.

"They must have a big budget for their getups," I conjectured, finally getting a laugh out of my brother.

"Since they all look alike they can probably buy in bulk," he sneered.

When they finally reached wearing only briefs, the women were stuffing chips in the front pocket of their skimpy underwear. The crowd must have been twenty deep as they reached over those sitting in front and stuffed in a multitude of casino chips.

I stood up on my chair. I saw one of the dancers reach over and touch Hill's nose and then dance provocatively in front of her. I swallowed hard, keeping my temper under control. I slipped a blue pill in my mouth, then gulped it down with my beer.

"What's going on?" Ray yelled over to me. "Can you see the girls?"

"Everything's fine," I lied to him. "It's just a show."

A new set of dancers replaced the first batch and it began all over again. The crowd of women and some men drew back trying to get the next batch of thrown clothes. It was then I noticed Hill wasn't in her seat, someone else was sitting there. Julie was still in her same seat sipping on her drink that I knew was a diet ColCola. She was nursing and definitely not touching alcohol.

"Where's Judy?" Ray asked.

"I don't know, I'll find her," I told him as I got up from my chair, carrying my beer as if I was just taking a walk.

The night club's room was filled with shadows and flashing lights. I circled the dance floor. No Hill there. I saw where one corner seemed set off. A circle of tall fern plants placed for privacy ringed the area which was even darker shadows. I headed in that direction. There were several booths, mostly filled with women sitting on men's laps. I heard Hill's voice in the booth nearest me. I leaned against the wall trying to get what she was saying but heard a man's voice instead.

"Hey babe thanks for the $100 credit chip. I can really use it. How about I earn some more? Just follow me up the back stairs. You won't regret it."

"How tempting, Luke," Hill was talking now. I felt my blood pressure rise but I didn't make a move. "Reich usually takes good care of me. Is he off tonight?"

"Yeah and every night. Someone offed him," Luke told her. He was sitting on the top side of the table, close to where Hill was sitting. He brushed his lips on her hair, his hand traced her neck down to her breasts as he slid in the seat opposite her.

"Do you mean that someone killed him?" Hill's voice dropped to almost a whisper. I had trouble hearing her.

"Yeah," was all that came from Luke.

"Do you know who did it?" she asked.

I peeked over from behind a fake bush that separated this room from the regular night club room. Hill had taken his hand in sympathy with him. He was just plain looking down her dress. Bastard!

"Well, kinda," he kissed her hand, "I'm just as good as he was. Let's go upstairs. I won't even charge you. Not often we get someone as enticingly beautiful like you. You could be one of my regular customers. Great discounts!"

I heard Hill chuckle softly, "Luke, you are a charmer. If you tell me more about Reich, I'll give you another 100 credit."

"What is it with Reich?" I heard the anger in his voice. "You a cop or something?"

"Or something," Hill reached down and pulled out her badge. She must have had it in her underwear.

"Craps, I'm outta here," he boldly announced and started to get up.

"I don't think so," I heard her say as she also reached down and pulled out her gun. "You are either going to talk to me or you'll be in jail as an accessory. Wouldn't the jail guys just love you?"

"I didn't do nothing!" he spat at her. "Reich was just a friend. He may have sold me a few joints but that's all!" He started to get up but I walked around. I had my badge out and shoved it in his face. "Talk to the lady, Luke. If she doesn't shoot you I will."

His face went pale as he sat back down. "This ain't legal," the pretty boy sputtered. "I don't know much."

"Tell us what you know and it had better be the whole truth. We know where to find you," I growled.

"Oh, he'll tell us," Hill crooned, "or I'll shoot his balls first. Even a small jolt will put him out of commission for a while."

"That would definitely cut his career short," I snorted. "Now talk!"

"I haven't even seen him since his girlfriend was killed." Luke's words flowed out now, "The guy was such a fool when it came to that damn

Lilac woman. She's the reason he's dead. She introduced him to all her *friends*. He was way out of his league."

"Were they dealing with drugs?" Judy asked.

"He never was into the heavy stuff but he said that girl had something good going and he was going to cash in on it too."

"You don't know what the *good thing* was?" I asked.

"He said they had the Sunrise Corporation by the balls," he slouched in his seat. "It had something to do with that Doss woman. Reich was spending a lot of time over in that mansion of hers. He also said Lilac was pregnant. Fool, getting her pregnant!" He spread his hands toward Hill pleading with her. "I know that whatever it was, Paul Bell was in on it. He told me Bell was going to be a big shot. They had some big plans together. He'd bring that pansy asshole here, showed him a good time. The guy tipped horribly. None of the guys really liked him!"

"He liked the guys?" I ventured and Luke nodded. Hill pointed her gun at him, aiming low. "What plans did they have?" she asked again.

"I don't know but whatever it was, he told me it had to do with Paul Bell getting revenge on Streng. That's all I know, honest!"

Hill tossed him another 100 credit chip and he slid out of the booth and bolted.

"Interesting," I commented as I slid into the booth. "What the hell is going on?"

"Well, Paul Bell is in the thick of it. We need to focus some of our investigation on him.

Evidently he wasn't just a *front desk manager*." She put her badge and gun back into her underwear.

"Isn't that rather uncomfortable?" I laughed at her.

"A woman does what she has to," she laughed with me. I think she actually blushed.

"No mention of Supfline, none." I was baffled. "Reich had that note in his underwear pocket. Why would he warn us of a shipment if the drug isn't the reason Reich was killed."

"There could be several reasons." Hill held up one finger, "He just didn't tell Luke that part of it. Reich just told him of vague blackmail plans." She held up another finger, "Maybe Lawren Streng or Paul Bell were really dealing with Skantie Row drug dealers." She held up a third finger, "Someone planted that on Reich to confuse us."

"What wonderful choices," I frowned at her perceptions. "Another reason could be that Paul Bell was just leading Lilac and Reich by the nose with promises of starting a Supfline dealership."

"I'm getting a headache," Hill complained.

We didn't get to expound on any other conjectures as shouting, threatening shouting, was coming from the nightclub's main floor. I jumped up heading toward our table. I saw immediately that Ray wasn't there. Shit!

I looked frantically around. The bar/stage area was in sheer chaos. Women and a few men were shoving each other. The bartender next to the stage was screaming for order. He was a big black dude with a deep bass voice. He reached down under the bar and came up with a huge bat which he pounded on the bar trying to get everyone's attention.

It worked for a few seconds as everyone stopped and looked at him. I saw a beer bottle fly into the air and come crashing down right near the big man. "Why you son of a bitch!" he yelled as the bottle shattered and covered him in beer and glass shards.

"Why you bitch!" the bartender yelled and jumped over the bar. Yeah, I kid you not, he jumped over the bar and in one hop!

A chubby short woman yelped when she saw he was coming after her. "Help me!" I wish she had thought of that before she threw her bottle of beer.

People scattered, some slipping on the floor causing others to fall over them.

"Security!" Another big black dude, dressed all in black, came running in. He actually had a whistle. He came running towards the crowd. "Get back, Jake," he actually pushed the bartender. "I can take care of the bitch."

"Bitch," yelled the chubby woman, "how dare you?"

"All you bitches stand back," he yelled but got no further as all the women standing around threw their drinks, glasses and all, at the two guys. Obscene curses reigned down.

As the two started towards the indignant female crowd, both the bartender and security guard slipped on the wet floor and landed on their backs. This set the crowd kicking them.

Meanwhile, I had forced my way through to the stage. Ray was there yelling at a female that was sitting next to Julie. "You touch my wife again and I'll shove your nose to the back of your skull," he yelled.

At least he was original in his threats. The nude, and yes I mean nude, stage male and female strip dancers were standing around the stage watching all the action below them. The whole scene was bizarre. They started yelling encouragements to my brother. Some were egging him on.

"Ray, let's just get out of here," I grabbed his arm. Julie was sitting behind him with a total look of horror on her face. She couldn't believe this blonde green eyed sloppily dressed shouting oaf was her husband. "You're not going to hit a woman," I reminded him.

"She's a fucking guy, Skip, a fucking guy!" Ray was so mad, he was choking as he talked to me.

I looked over at the person seated next to Julie. Sure enough, it was a man dressed in drag. Without scrutiny, it looked like an overweight woman with too much makeup. He smiled at me. He hadn't put on his lipstick real good making his teeth spotted red.

"Hey, leave him alone," one of the male strippers yelled over. "He's my father, he just wanted a good feel, nothing wrong with that." Pointing to Julie, he said, "Look how's she's dressed. She's asking for it!"

One of the female strippers came over and shoved the naked male stripper off the stage, "We are sick of your father, Tad. He causes trouble every night."

The pushed-off stripper landed on several people. "You're a whore, Candy." He yelled up.

Candy did not take it kindly. She jumped down and slugged him. The father also jumped up clobbering poor Candy. I tried to intercede but got shoved as more of the female strippers jumped down. Ray grabbed the cross-dressed guy and went to slug him but the guy hit Ray right in the eye causing a bloody nose.

Before I could react, Julie came over and slugged the overweight want-to-be woman in the jaw. The guy went down like a ton of bricks. Everyone began slugging everyone else. I ducked and tried grabbing a few of the female strippers but they were naked! Slippery, not to mention awkward.

Meanwhile the fight with the bartender and security guard was in full bloom. The floor was wet and slippery, so there were customers down everywhere!

Suddenly, the strippers were being thrown back on stage. Fred Stoshingburg came out of nowhere. He easily threw the fighting strippers back on stage and took the large fake woman and shook him in front of him. His wig came off and half his dress along with his high heels. "Get the hell out of here," Fred yelled in his face, slapping him once.

He threw the stripper's father half way to the exit door. The guy stumbled up and rushed past the bartender and out the door. The bartender looked like he'd been in combat. His eye was swollen and his nose was dripping. Fred picked him up and placed him behind the bar with a "Stay there." I saw the man slip out of site, probably out cold on the floor.

Then Fred picked up the security guard, setting him on his feet. Fred is so intimidating with his size, the crowd shrunk back from him. "Ok, folks, everyone calm down." To my astonishment they all did. The guard was leaning against the bar, trying to catch his breath.

It was then that Chet and his officers came rushing in the door. Everyone started to scatter as the sight of actual uniformed police would do that.

I saw Hill grab Julie and the bleeding Ray and head them toward the back exit. One police officer stopped them but my lieutenant shoved her badge in his face and he let them go. Chet came over, "Better get the hell out of here before the press shows up," he warned me. I took his advice and quickly left. Once I was out of the nightclub, I bumped into a huge crowd mulling around the outside of the Chippy Chip Club's doorway. I plowed my way through taking my sport coat off and reversing it. Then I headed towards an exit.

I ended up walking most of the way back to the lodge. The sleigh's hover crafts were all rushing toward the casino. Nothing like a brawl to scatter the patrons.

I was freezing, light snow was falling. My mind was racing, so I didn't notice too much. I touched my cell - *23:04 Federation Time, Sunrise Resort, Hilda.* I slapped it off. The mountain trails were all lit up for night skiing. I stood watching the mountains. I felt bad. I had ruined Ray and Julie's vacation. I had ruined our family time together.

The cell buzzed in my ear. I touched it, knowing it was Hill. "Where are you Chief?"

"Walking home, no sleighs available," I told her.

"We were all worried about you. I'll send a hover to pick you up." She sounded concerned.

"No, I need the walk," I told her. "Is everyone at the chateau?"

"Yes, all accounted for," she informed me. "See you soon."

I slapped it shut. I hated to think what awaited me at the chateau. Killa would kill me. Ray probably hated me, not to mention the animosity from Julie and Marty. Thank goodness Jim was too young to know how his uncle had screwed up.

The cold air bit at my cheeks. I hadn't worn my boots, so my feet were frozen. My suit coat was getting wet. Somehow I didn't mind. It seemed a good punishment for my family sins. I put my hand out watching the snowflakes melt as they hit my body heat. It didn't help that the investigation seemed more fucked up than ever.

Nothing made sense. What had Streng done to incur Paul Bell's wrath? What role was Skantie Row's corrupt families playing in all this? What had Lilac and Reich done to deserve being killed mob style? Why couldn't I see this clearly?

"Here put this on," Hill shoved my newly bought coat at me. "Your mittens are in the pockets."

"What are you doing here?" I growled.

"Don't take that tone with me," she half laughed. "Someone needs to protect you from yourself. You've done the same for me."

We walked in silence, the snow enveloping us in twirls of white. We passed the lodge. It was somewhat subdued with just small lights dotting the walkways up to it. We turned to look at the ring of chateaus, clearly visible from the entranceway. The villas looked like a wreath circling the bottom of the valley. The mountains with their lit ski trails loomed large behind the circle of buildings. The shopping mall and the casino were not visible but the line of sleighs bringing back the guests was a strong reminder of the chaotic evening.

Many of the vehicles were returning to the lodge bringing the patrons for one last nightcap. The excitement of what had happened at the casino was evident in the excited voices. "They need more security," one woman dressed in her white furs and trying not to slip in her high heels said. "Honestly, I was finally winning, what bad timing!"

"Honestly Miriam," her husband said as he grabbed her arm to keep her from falling, "a couple of margaritas and you'll forget all about it!"

Hill snickered, "I heard on our way out that it's not the first time the Chippy Chip Bar has had a brawl. It gives the place some excitement!"

"Not funny," I grumbled. "I just hope the reporters don't get the whole story. I never should have let Julie go with you."

"Listen, Chief," Hill put her arm through my coat sleeve, "I tried to talk Julie out of it but she wanted to come. She told me that being a racing car's mechanic was wonderful but she wanted to do something *feminine* and to do something exciting."

"That's crazy! She has Ray's racing, can't get much more exciting!"

"But it's Ray's. Everything is connected to her husband. She wanted to do this for herself." Judy shook her head as if exasperated with me.

I faced my Lieutenant, "Do you feel that way? I hate to admit it but my detective force is only 29% percent women. Do you need to prove your *feminine* side since you are with men most of the time, doing I hate to say it, grizzly unfeminine gore?"

"Of all the murders cases, only 12% are assigned to female detectives - but who is keeping count?" she countered.

"I'll bet Lara Null," I exasperatedly told Hill. "She's always busting my chops about the lack of women in major rolls on our fifth floor!"

"Well, she is right!" Hill grabbed my arm, heading me towards our chateau. "At least you try and be fair. I know what constraints they put on you."

I rolled my eyes, she had no idea how restrictive my boss, Laren Borger, could be and how often I had been pulled on the carpet for sending women into dangerous situations. Outdated views prevailed on Fulton. Just ask the women representatives at the Dome. It was a regular complaint from Judge Button, who claimed she had to come across as "tough" or no one took her seriously.

The lights were blaring at the number 15 chateau. Everyone was in the kitchen, all looked up as we walked in. Ray had an ice pack on his eye, his nose was still slightly dripping. Julie had an ice pack on her hand.

"I guess he had a hard jaw," she laughed, holding up the sore hand. Thank goodness she was laughing.

Killa just glared at me as she gave Ray a fresh ice pack. Marty was sitting next to Julie, almost in a daze watching her cousin. At least it had gotten their housekeeper away from the telescreen. I gathered the baby was sleeping.

"Here, have a cup of tea," Killa placed a mug in Hill's hand. "It is cold out there!"

I had to get myself a cup of java. No sympathy for me.

"No Fred yet?" I asked. Got "no" shakes from everyone so I placed a call to him on the cell.

"I'm coming up your steps now," he told me and then a few seconds later the door opened and both Chet and Fred walked in.

Killa handed both of them a large mug of java. Boy, talk about getting the cold shoulder. She also put a large mound of oatmeal cookies in front of Fred. I got my hand slapped when I went to get some. "They are for heroes," she told me and shoved them closer to Fred.

"I'm no hero," Fred lamented. "What a bunch of wild women!"

"You're an asshole!" Hill blurted at him, "all you know is brute force."

"And your complaint is?" he shouted back at her. "I wasn't in the back flirting with that stripper guy."

"Why you oaf!" Hill spat, "I was working. What were you doing? Being a peeping Tom?"

"No, I was leaving that to the Chief," he snorted.

"Okay, okay - enough!" I loudly growled bringing the room to silence. "Thanks to you Fred, you saved our asses. It was getting way out of hand. Hill needs to be praised - she got that Luke character to talk"

My Hilda superintendent leaned forward. "I'm all ears. What did you learn?"

Hill was tightly clutching her mug, I hadn't realized how wound up she was. My lieutenant also leaned forward, and said "Luke told me Lilac and Reich had some blackmail scheme going on with Paul Bell, the manager of the front desk who has just been promoted to General Manager. Luke knew that Lilac was pregnant but he thought it was Reich's baby. Which leads me to believe Reich didn't tell Luke very much. More likely Luke just heard things and came to some conclusions."

"That's why we have to sift through his answers and find what's concrete." I took a seat and grabbed my tabloid to write down what were facts. "For one, Luke is sure that Reich was hanging out at that Doss woman's mansion. He thinks Reich was also associating with Paul Bell. He said that Bell had a grudge against Lawren Streng and wanted revenge. Also Reich, although he dealt in small drugs, did not sell Supfline." I saw Fred take note.

"I can't find any Supfline deals," he confirmed. "I've checked all my sources, no leads whatsoever. Hilda is not on the drug radar screen. Zoe won't tell me where she gets her stuff, she's almost too scared to talk. *Talking* is her forte, so whoever it is, she's scared stiff of them. Don't worry I'll get her to tell me."

"Any idea what the revenge aspect was?" Chet asked.

"No, but I'm going to ask Paul Bell tomorrow," I said. "Before I do that I need some info on Bell's background. I will get Marcus on it first thing tomorrow. By the way, Chet, how are Bud and Marcus doing?"

"They are slowly going through all the casino's records. So far they are finding nothing illegal, all above board. As a matter of fact, Lawren Streng had a slew of accountants that kept strict correct records," Chet emphatically pointed out. "Lawren also had strict rules about gambling ethics. He ran a tight legal operation. Very baffling about Skantie coming in."

Ray spoke up, keeping his ice pack on his eye, "How bad was it at the bar after we left?"

"We straightened everything out and gave out a few strong warnings. The manager came and I gave him a written warning. They need more security on the floor. The guy actually agreed. The bartender and the one security guard had minor cuts and bruises." Chet looked over at Ray, "How did all this get started?"

"It was really all my fault," Ray moaned. "I saw the guy reach over and put his hand in Julie's blouse. I just saw red!" He pressed the ice pack hard against his face, "I'm sorry Julie."

"I'm not going to make anything of it Ray," Julie put her ice covered hand on top of Ray's shoulder, "I think you've suffered enough." She kissed him on his forehead.

"Nice punch, Julie, it stopped the chubby bastard in his tracks!" Fred said between bites of cookies. "Guess being a mechanic has its advantages."

"Yeah, you can't be a weakling and handle a wrench." Julie looked down at her injured knuckles, "Still, it hurts!"

Ray hugged her. Marty gave Julie a cup of hot cocoa. They all went into the living room, sitting around the fireplace. Julie sat next to Ray, leaning against him; he had his arm around her shoulders. I felt like crap, this was all my fault. Killa put a fresh cup of java in front of me and a big chocolate muffin. To my amazement she hugged me and left, heading toward her bedroom. I heard her say goodnight as she passed the living room. I think I was given a pardon.

"Well, I guess she's forgiven you," Fred said as he reached over and took part of my muffin.

"Tomorrow I speak to Bell," I told Chet.

"Let's speak to Hessie again," Hill informed me. "She has to know more than she's telling us. Let's try and go visit her when Jarad's not there. I don't want her intimidated by him."

"Fine. Tomorrow will be a busy day, let's call it a night." I was feeling exhausted and stumbled to my bedroom after Fred, Chet and Hill left. The living room was empty, they'd all hit the sack. I heard Julie and Ray talking in their bedroom but it was just an undistinguishable mumble. I felt another pang of guilt, imagining the conversation they must be having.

I noticed Ray had returned my suit, his eye contacts were on my night stand. I just threw my clothes on the floor, put my contacts in their case, and quickly scrubbed the makeup off my face. Then I fell on my bed, not even taking the bedcover off and sleep came almost immediately. I dreamt dark dreams. I lost every race using Ray's racing car and then ended up smashing the car just before I woke up. I was mumbling "I'm sorry, I'm sorry" to my brother.

I had a headache but I was so glad to be awake and not dreaming. I was drenched in sweat. I headed toward the shower, tripping over my discarded gambler clothes. One more reminder of how bad the night had gone!

Chapter Eleven

That morning, I admit it, I was rather a growling ugly bear. Even with three cups of java under my belt, I had a dull headache, a sore body and seeing Ray with a huge black eye and a swollen nose didn't help matters. Julie was just fine. She fed the baby, made sure Killa and Marty had plenty of bottles and then dragged Ray off to the slopes.

"Moping around, feeling sorry for yourself, won't make it any better," Julie had told her husband. "Let's get back to the slopes. I think Skip will do much better without us gumming up the works."

I had tried to protest but Julie just shook her head at me. So off they went. Ray, with his full shield helmet that hid his injured face, tried to smile but it hurt too much. My sister-in-law favored her right hand but assured me the injury was not bad enough to impede her skiing.

Killa knows me well and stayed out of my way, just handing me cups of java as I went over my substantial notes. The case's abundance of facts led me in circles. I was meeting Marcus and Bud for breakfast at the lodge. As I left, Killa was watching little Jimmy, rocking and singing to him. Marty was in the den. Her baby turn, I gather, was later in the morning. The family seemed back to normal. I breathed better, no blue pills for now.

I found both Marcus and Bud bleary eyed. They had been up most of the night going through the casino's records. Late last night I had called

Marcus about Paul Bell and he had found the time
to create an excellent dossier about the man.

"Wow, how did you do this so quickly?" I
asked him.

"I have my contacts and Fred helped me last
night," Marcus informed me between bites of his
pancakes.

"Fred?" The big guy, after leaving us, had
gone over to the Giles' Police station and had spent
the night with Bud and Marcus.

As if hearing his name, Fred came sauntering
in with Hill pushing him from behind to the table.
"Come on big guy, I promised Lara that I'd look
after you." My newest detective helped my
experienced detective slouch into a chair and
handed him two aspirins. She then ordered him two
breakfasts, which he gratefully ate.

"Look at this," I handed Hill my tab which
showed Paul Bell's files. Her eyes widened the
more she read. "So, he's been all over the Crab
Sector, mostly working at hotels. He worked on one
of Atlise's cruise ships that has a huge casino. He
worked on Abbis and Mody, again it was at the big
main hotels with casinos, but only for two years
each.   He's been to Nestor, worked at Strom's
Super Track." Hill was flipping through Bell's file
which started recently and headed back in time.

"Bell even spent time at the Dome. He was
one of Senator Zopte's assistants. How he got that
job with Skantie Row's top Dome representative
was an interesting mystery. He spent three years
with the senator," I pointed out. "Bell also did a
stint on Logan's Moon. He worked as a Jump

coordinator. That would come in handy in knowing how the sector works."

Hill had gotten all the way back to the report's beginning. I heard her gasp, "First sign of him is his leaving Skantie Row fifteen years ago! There is nothing more before that!"

Marcus spoke up, "We have traced him through the Jump records. Once we saw he had a ticket to somewhere we traced him further. But before he left Skantie Row there is nothing and I mean nothing!"

"So he's tied to that damn planet. I almost shit a brick last night when it came up," Fred said, his mouth full of scrambled eggs.

"Geesh Fred, close your mouth!" Hill smacked his arm.

"Why doesn't he show up more on Skantie?" I asked Fred who's an expert on the drug infested bordello and casino planet. He knew the three mob families like the back of his hand.

"I've got my contacts working on it," Fred assured me. "There is something shady here. The families sometime send out agents that become experts on the sector and help spread their drug trade but I can't be positive. It could be the link we've been looking for."

"Time to see Mr. Paul Bell," I said finishing my java. "I'll bring Fred. Hill, you need to find out a good time to see Mrs. Streng." I saw her nod. We left the three detectives in deep conversation over what to make of the records on the resort's casino. I saw Hill touch her cellbutton, probably trying to find a good time to visit her friend.

Fred and I went to the front desk. It was a quiet time as most of the quests were out skiing or doing some winter sport thing. I went up to one of the female clerks. She looked quite crisp in her yellow Sunrise uniform. She somewhat wilted when I showed her my badge and asked to see Mr. Paul Bell. I saw her glance behind her but no one was there. "I, I…" she stuttered.

"Who's the new front desk manager?" I asked her but that got her even more nervous and I saw her push her cellbutton and turn around whispering so I wouldn't hear her. When she turned back, she tried to smile but failed miserably. In a nervous voice I got, "I'm sorry but both men are out of the office. I will tell them you were here." She smiled the smile of a liar. I knew and so did Fred.

Fred took the steps up to Paul Bell's new office, Lawren Streng's old office. He opened it and yelled down over the baluster circling above, "He's in, come on up, Chief."

"No please, he's really busy," the front clerk almost yelled it.

I patted her hand which only irritated her. I was glad to see a spark of anger in her. She'd need it after we got through with Paul Bell. He was the type that would take it out on the lower echelons.

When I got up to the top of the stairs, Fred held the door open for me and waved me in. Paul Bell was standing at his desk, his face quite red, his hands balled into fists at his side. "I'm busy, don't you people understand!"

"Perhaps it is you that doesn't understand that there have been three untimely deaths on your resort!" I boomed much louder than he could ever manage. I saw the fear come into his gray slanted eyes. I noticed he was much older than I'd first thought. He dyed his hair a dark brown and I'd bet those eyes were colored by contacts. Now that I was looking at him close up, I saw fine lines of a face-lift with the skin stretched tight around his neck. He wore a large diamond in his left ear and had a couple of rings on each of his hands. Now that he was General Manager, he wore a nicely tailored gray suit which I bet cost him plenty. He had a nice brown snow tan, but that didn't help hide the lines around his eyes and mouth. As the front desk manager, he had slipped neatly under our radar, I'd bet on purpose. I had a feeling Mr. Bell was a chameleon. He was trained to be whatever was needed at the time.

"I beg your pardon, Chief Brown," his voice taking on a conciliatory note. "I'm new at this and I'm afraid I'm a little overwhelmed."

I wondered if perhaps he could also be trained as an assassin. Tread lightly, my brain warned. "I fully understand Mr. Bell, but you have to understand our position. We can't let another murder happen, surely you wouldn't want that? Think of the repercussions to the resort."

"Of course, I was not thinking straight. Please forgive my stupidity. What can I do for you? Please call me Paul. I still have to come to grips with Lawren being gone. It was a great blow to me. I can't tell you how much we miss him."

He was all slick now, playing the helpful grieving friend - he even teared up. "You must have been through Mr. Streng's records by now," I carefully said, not raising any alarms. I'd keep the questions general. See if I could lower his guard. "Is there anything that could be of use to us? Did he have any enemies, owe anybody money?"

"Oh no, Lawren Streng was an upstanding Federation citizen. He was very careful to be above board in all his dealings. Remember he was connected to the McTenser family through his wife. I'm sure they are very distressed over his suicide."

"So you liked Lawren Streng personally?" I asked as if it was just an off the cuff remark.

"Well, he was my boss, we did have just a few rub-ins," he carefully worded his remarks just in case the staff had mentioned their "rub-ins". "But," he continued, "nothing serious, I assure you."

I nodded at Fred, time to get serious. Fred took the cue, "Are you familiar with Skantie Row? Know the planet well, do you?"

I saw Paul Bell go pale right through his dark snow tan. He quickly recovered, if I hadn't been looking for it, I'd have missed his being taken aback. The man was good, a very good actor. "Everyone who went to geography class knows all the planets. I assure you Skantie Row is not one I've paid much attention to."

Fred pounced, "Then why did you leave the planet fifteen years ago. Our records show you had a Jump ticket for Atlise where you took a job on a cruise ship for about two years."

If looks could kill, Fred would have been dead on the spot. Paul Bell was now aware that we had looked him up. He slowly sat down on his comfy cushioned desk chair, giving himself time to come up with a credible answer. I could see him get himself together as he carefully composed his answer.

"Look, it's not the best place to be from. I rather like leaving that behind me. If you must know, my mother was a bordello prostitute. She did her best for me then sent me off planet to make my own way. I would appreciate if you did not spread that around, it could obviously hurt my career."

There was a knock at the door and the lawyer, Nove Deck, walked in. The interview was over. "Thank you, Mr. Bell." I stood up and with Fred following me; we walked out the door without even acknowledging the lawyer's presence.

We sauntered down the stairway. The desk clerk was staring at us all the way down with something akin to hatred. I wanted to ask her if anyone had turned in my rental skis but I didn't think now was the time. I did, however, wave to her and give her my best smile which again irritated the hell out of her. She looked away, ignoring me.

"That bastard," Fred grumbled.

"Which one?" I asked him and only got a shrug of his shoulders. I guess I could take my pick.

"I'm heading downtown," Fred told me. "I'm meeting Zoe. I want to ask her about the visitors to the Doss mansion. I'll see if I recognize any of them plus I want to ask if Reich spent a lot of time there. I can't imagine Hilary putting up with a stripper. He really wasn't in her social circle. There are some really strange goings-on, Chief."

I couldn't agree with him more. After he left, I pressed my cellbutton for Hill. "I'm in the Café with Jarad, Chief," she told me. "He's agreed that we should see Hessie alone, that perhaps she'll be more opened to me if he's not there. He's tried talking to her but she just gets upset.　Mr. McTenser, Hessina's father, wants some answers. Being an XIL company baron, he's used to getting responses quickly. Jarad is under a lot of pressure from his family to get Hessie to MOSS for medical treatment.

"Okay, when?" I asked.

"I'll see you by the Café, we can go right up," she informed me.

I headed toward the restaurant and caught them just coming out. Jarad had a hold of her hands and was bending down to kiss her. I yelled over interrupting the cozy scene, "Hill, let's get this over with. Come on!"

Hessina's brother let her go but deeply frowned at me. I guess I'm no one's favorite today. Hill sauntered over giving me the evil eye, "Was that necessary?"

"Yeah, I think it was." I turned and walked to the elevator. I looked back, Hill was still standing where she'd been, hands on her hips, looking annoyed.

"Come on," I waved to her. "Did you really want to kiss that chump? Isn't he old news?"

"None of your business," she said pushing the elevator button for the top floor. "It is none of your business - not unless you want to expound on Judge Button?"

I shut up. We rode up in silence.

There was a guard at the penthouse's entranceway but he waved us in. Obviously Jarad had called.

We were led into Hessina's bedroom. The drapes were drawn leaving the room darkened. Streng's wife was in bed with a dim light on the nightstand next to her. She was reading her cell. It was a book on child rearing. The bird-like woman beamed when she saw Hill. With the light spreading shadows across her face, Streng's wife looked drawn, her sharp pointed features prominently sticking out. I couldn't help but wince at the bizarre looking woman.

"Oh Jude, it is so good to see you," taking my lieutenant's hands as Hill dragged a chair next to her bed and sat. I stood back in the shadows; giving them some privacy.

"How are you feeling, Hessie?" Hill looked over at what she was reading, "Who gave you that?"

"Nurse Billow," the fowl-featured woman told her. "I have no idea how to raise a child."

"You'll have plenty of help. Your family will be right there with you." Hill squeezed her friend's hand as if to emphasize that the woman was not alone.

I looked around but I didn't see the sergeant nurse but she had to be somewhere nearby.

"The doctor was here this morning. He says all is well."

"That's good!" Judy tried to sound upbeat but I could hear the doubt in her voice and so could Hessie.

"Well, he said *as well as could be expected.* He was really shocked that I got pregnant, you know."

"Well, you can understand…" Hill started to say but Hessina interrupted her.

"I know, I know," Streng's wife let go of Judy and started waving her bony arms. "He called it a miracle."

"It doesn't matter what they call it," Judy tried to make light of it, "the baby will be a joy. You need to do everything the doctor tells you. Your family wants you at the medical space station. They have experts and will give you the best chance for the baby's survival."

"Yes, I know. I'm not leaving Lawren until after we bury him. He loved this place, you know. My father offered him several jobs but he turned them all down." Hessina seemed to be upset, her long skeletal hands fluttering in front of her.

"Don't go getting upset, Hessie!" Hill took the long tapered hands of her friend, placing them in her own hands and squeezing them. "You have to rest!"

Tears flowed down the avian woman's high cheek bones. "I know, I know," she sobbed. "I miss him. I know what everyone said," she looked at Hill, the tears freely flowing now. "He didn't marry me because of my family ties. He didn't!"

"Of course not," Hill tried to console her. "Everyone knows he really loved you."

"You know," Hessie half smiled, her lips were so thin it looked eerie. "The reason I got pregnant was that our baby was conceived in a very special place." The smile widened as if the memory was so noteworthy that it blocked out her grief.

"Where was that?" Hill asked.

Hessina lowered her voice, "Lawren has a special cabin at the top of the Astin Mountian," she lowered her voice to a whisper, I could hardly hear her. "It was so special. I made it up there only twice. It is usually only reachable by the big rescue snow cats. It took a lot out of me to go with him, but I did! It would have been a private place for our child to enjoy. It would have been our family's chance for privacy."

"That's wonderful, Hessie, wonderful," Hill was being careful but we needed more info so she pushed her friend to continue, "What was it like?"

"Well, he has a solar generator that gives us lights and it powers an old computer system that he can use to work from up there. It is a place that he can get away from it all." Hessie was talking as if her husband was still alive. "We spent an entire weekend up there. Cellbuttons don't work. It is all quiet and has complete solitude. We want to go back there, especially when the baby was born." Hessina was confusing her tenses but Hill kept quiet as Streng's wife continued, "Of course, that was Lilac's baby. I didn't get to tell him about our own." She sobbed loudly.

This brought Nurse Billow to come running into the room. "You are distressing her!" the medical sergeant sternly told us, "I must ask you to leave!"

"No, no, I'm fine," Hessina insisted.

Hill got one more question out, "Do you know why Lawren went to visit the planet Skantie Row so much?"

The nurse stuck her nose in again, "I'm insisting you leave or I'll call Mr. Deck."

Before I could kick Billow in the arse, Hessie answered Hill, "I don't know, really, but whenever he went, he came back in a terrible mood. He told me he hated the place."

"I'm calling Mr. Deck," the nurse exploded, touching her cellbutton.

Hill looked at me and nodded. As much as we wished for more, it was time to leave. "I'll come back soon," my lieutenant assured her friend, kissing her on the forehead.

"You know I wish you and Jarad would get back together," Hessina grabbed one last time onto Hill's arm. "We could be sisters, you'd be the baby's aunt!"

Hill just smiled. "I'll be your sister no matter what," Judy told her and got a big thin smile from Hessie.

We left the penthouse in silence. The elevator ride seemed to take forever, the dinging of floors seemed loud and accusing. I could tell Hill felt guilty for pushing her friend even if she'd done it compassionately.

When we hit the bottom floor, the sliders opened onto the lobby, both of us stood there as if hesitating to continue. I put my hand on Hill's back and gently pressed her out. "We do what we have to, we are cops, not angels."

"I feel like a traitor," my lieutenant hissed, "a goddamned traitor. She deserves better."

"She deserves to know who killed her husband," I commented. I saw my remark sink into my newest detective's brain.

"Then let's get on with it!" she growled. Judy stepped briskly toward the large map of the resort that dressed the far side of the lobby. Hill stood there studying it.

I pointed to the largest mountain labeled Astin. "It's the highest mountain they have!" I moaned trying to think of a way to get up there. "Even the ski trails don't go all the way up to the top!" I reached into my pocket getting out a blue pill, swallowing it dry.

"Come on," Hill observed, "we need a more detailed map." I followed her into the bar/café and slumped discouraged into a chair. Hill took the seat across from me. She immediately began fiddling with her tabloid. She focused a comprehensive topographical map of Astin Mountain onto the tabletop. I slid over to sit next to her. My eyes went wide as I realized how ragged the top of the mountain was.

"My god, Hill," I gasped, "how high do you think the cabin is?"

"*Cabins*," she expounded pointing to several places on the map. "There are several rescue cabins all the way up, four of them at the very top."

I moaned, "Do you think anyone would know which one Lawren used?"

"I would guess even Hessie couldn't point to which one it is." My lieutenant enlarged the very top of the mountain. Sure enough, four cabins appeared several miles apart just below the bare ragged top of Astin. "Pick one," she motioned to me.

I just put my finger on the lowest one. She enlarged the area. Nothing to indicate if it was the one Hessina had mentioned. I picked one after another; nothing to indicate anything different. "I guess we will have to just go and find it."

"We have to do it quietly," Hill pointed out. "We can't let anyone know of it. Of course, we could get up there and find nothing of importance. It could be Lawren just wanted a place to go for privacy."

"Let's hope not. Now how do we do this?" I asked her.

"How do we do what?" Fred had come up and plopped himself down on the other side of Hill. "What the hell is this?" he asked looking askance at the map.

We explained what Hessina had told us. "I'd get up there as soon as we can," he said. "If anyone finds out about it, they'll rush up there and destroy any evidence."

I moaned again. Mountain exploring, I put right up there with skiing.

"We're going to need some form of transportation," Hill pointed out the obvious.

Fred looked at her, "Really, Hill, you think?" His voice was dripping with sarcasm which only set my newest detective retaliating.

"Really, Fred, think we could find something big enough to haul your big ass up that mountain!"

Fred was about to retort but I interrupted, "Stop, both of you. Concentrate on our enemies instead of on fighting between the two of you!"

It shut them both up. "Let's do this quietly. I'll only tell Chet what we are doing. Fred, go check on transportation. Let's keep it to the three of us, any more and we'll be too obvious. Hill, go find out, without raising suspicions, what exactly is up there and do they have maps. You might start with the ski patrol. Let's try and meet in two hours. Dress warm!

We all went our separate ways. I went back to the chateau and called my police superintendent. He was not enthusiastic.

"That's rugged country up there," he pointed out. "Even with snow cats, it's rugged. We lost a skier once and it took five days to find her body."

"I wish I had a choice but we can't let any employee of the resort help. If it gets back to Paul Bell, we might as well kiss any evidence good bye and the aspect of surprise will be gone."

"I know what you're saying, Chief," Chet pointed out. "Just be careful. You'd better wait a day, as a storm is predicted tomorrow."

"We are leaving in just a few hours," I told Chet. "We still have half a day and there are lights on the trails at night."

"I hope you make it back for the night Jump coming in with the supposed Supfline shipment," my superintendent reminded me.

"If we don't, you are more than capable to handle it," I assured my top Hilda cop. "Although Fred will be sorely disappointed."

"Just be careful," Chet advised. "There is no cell coverage on top. Don't make me come looking for you! And don't freeze to death!"

How encouraging, I thought. I turned around to see Killa staring at me. Her whole body was stiff. Her hair was fizzing and her eyes dark purple. Her ears were trembling as were her hands. "Do not do this!" she managed to get out. Her throat was tightly strung making her voice crack. Her large ears had picked up my conversation with Chet.

"It's not as dangerous as it sounds. I'll probably be back for supper." I tried to make my words sound light in an unworried manner.

"Skipper, do not go up that mountain!" Her eyes rolled back, her arms pointed at me, her fingers extended in a prophetic type motion. "Death is up there. Do not do this!"

I went over grabbing her small body, pulling her to me. I felt her relax, the stiffness gone as she clung to me. Her small arms hardly went half way around my waist. Her face was against my lower chest and I could feel her sobbing.

"Killa, I'm a policeman. I'm their Chief. I can't shun my responsibility. It is what I do!" I pulled her away from me enough to look down at her. "You would not want me to do anything else. I will be careful. Fred will be with me. No one plays with the big guy!"

"You are bringing Judy also." It wasn't a question.

"Yes, but she's a policeman too. I wouldn't insult her by not bringing her." I kissed the top of the little Ligithian's head. My old nursemaid just nodded.

I took the time to call Artchie. He sounded his old chipper self and it made me homesick. He assured me that everything was running smoothly. He also assured me that the dogs were fine, the demon cat was fine. "Hey, tell Lieutenant Hill that she was right about old Mrs. Hippnow. She's been going to the OPD league meetings and she's a different person! The dogs love her! The cat sleeps on her lap."

I cringed. Mrs. Hippnow was a thorn in my daily existence. She was always reporting me to the Fulton Housing Authority, the city's dog catcher and the Noise Authority over my turbocycle. I couldn't imagine her not being a pain in the ass. I would have to make a donation to the **O**ld **P**erson's **D**epression League if they indeed had helped her. Hill will gloat, I thought. Damn woman. Killa just laughed when I told her.

"Judy can be very wise," she pointed her finger at me. "You could do worse."

I just shook my head. When Killa gets something in her head, it stays there.

Speaking of thorns in my side, my cellbutton rang. Hill's voice loudly resonated in my ear. "Meet us by the maintenance shed. Be careful not to be seen, come via the back of the sleigh shed. That's where they house those fancy hovercrafts."

"I know where they are located," I told her as I slipped my new boots and fur lined mittens on. I took my ear covering hat and slapped it on my head. "I'll be there as soon as I can."

Despite the fear in Killa's eyes, she didn't say a word as I left. It was early afternoon with no sun, just puffy clouds. The air smelled like snow. I remembered Chet's warning of a storm coming in tomorrow. We would have to hurry.

I carefully walked behind the chateaus and entered a small path which led around a clump of trees to a barnlike building. I went behind that and came to the sleigh shed. I walked around the back of that one, coming upon Hill and Stoshingburg.

They were standing near a large snowmobile-like vehicle. An enclosed cab sat on its platform body below which held huge tracks for plowing through the snow.

"Where did you get this thing?" I asked. It stood twice my height and was painted in green camouflage with a white and blue striped Hilda flag waving from its top.

"It is one of the ski patrol's rescue fleet. Climb up. Let's get going before anyone sees us. The patrol is out skiing and the sleigh elves are out driving guests. Get in!"

Getting in was not easy. I climbed up the huge steps into the cab. It was set for four people, but four "small" people. I sat in the back, just about taking up the entire area with Hill taking the front passenger side. Fred snugged his way into the driver's seat. Hill had to move as far right as she could to let him fit.

"Okay, here we go." He pressed a combination of numbers on the dash and the engine came to life. At first it sputtered but Fred made some kind of adjustment and the vehicle became steadier with a rhythmic rumble. He pressed another button and the huge tracks folded up and became a regular hovercraft.

"Aha," Fred cheered, "we are on our way!"

I was shocked into silence. Hill turned to me, "We don't have to use the big tracks until we hit heavy snow. Then we will lower them." She took out a map and pointed Fred towards a road that got us away from the barns.

I just nodded, as long as the damn thing got us where we wanted to go. It wasn't long before we were in a deeply forested road. I got glimpses of the billowy clouds overhead.

"Let's head over to Astin Mountain," Hill directed him. "Keep to this utility road and it will lead right to Astin Ridge Road." Obviously my lieutenant was going to be our navigator. I settled back into the rear seat, one tree looked like another to me.

It took us more than an hour to get up the rough dirt utility trail. The road had clearly been recently plowed. Hill was tracing the route on her map. The route became a less traveled looking road and became just a path. The terrain became much steeper with the snow becoming more prevalent and not groomed. The hover engines seemed to handle it just fine winding the vehicle above the snow easily.

"Follow the red markings up on the trees," Judy pointed to one of the marks. "This will lead us up the mountain. Every once in a while, we could see one of the skiing trails to our right with skiers zooming down the slopes. The higher we went the fewer skiers appeared as it became very steep and very rocky.

Suddenly I felt the tracks lower. The ride became much bumpier. "We are nearing the top third of the mountain. The snow is thicker here and the rocky outcrops are appearing," Stoshingburg remarked. "Yeah, it's a bitch to steer," Fred complained as he clutched the steering wheel.

"You can do it, big boy," Hill encouraged him. "Steady as she goes."

I was being knocked around in the back as we rolled over one bump after another. I could see why Hessina had trouble with the ride.

"Turn left up here," Hill instructed. "The first cabin should be coming up on your left."

Sure enough a log building with two small outbuildings came looming up. The trees had been cleared and a heavy stilt platform had been erected to keep the building level. Stoshingburg pulled up to the flat gravel driveway next to it. Climbing out of the large vehicle was a challenge and I ended up on my keister when I missed the last step.

We climbed the small stairs to the platform. Fred had to put his shoulder to the door. With a loud moaning creek it slowly opened. Inside the cabin, it was rustic with a fireplace and was built to be a shelter from the cold. This was definitely an emergency station. This was not the Streng's getaway cabin. We climbed back into the snowcat and backed down to the trail.

Fred steered our way for several miles and then we came to another cabin, similarly built. This time at least I didn't fall on my fanny. The air was sweetly scented with pine. We trucked up the set of stairs to find the exact same interior. Back again, up to the next one - again, no luck.

It was at the last cabin on the map that we hit the jackpot. We knew it as we climbed a well-made driveway trail to a leveled out landscape. No platform, just a nice level cabin with several outbuildings. The cabin itself had a garage building attached to it.

"I should have guessed it would have been the last one," I moaned as I climbed down the vehicle's ladder and stepped down into snow that reached to my knees. Hill was already ahead of me getting to the door.

"Oh, no," she bewailed loudly, "there is a padlock on the door. The windows are heavily shuttered and locked shut. We didn't think of this."

It was then that I felt the first snow drops hit my nose. I put my hand out. Huge snow flakes fell on my mittens. Great, just great!

Chapter Twelve

I stood next to Hill looking glumly at the large padlocked door. Both of us let out a big sigh. All this way for nothing? I heard Fred stomp up the porch steps; his heavy footsteps clumping across to stand next to us.

"Stand back," he yelled. We jumped back as he brought a big sturdy axe down on the padlock. The loud ringing of metal on metal hurt the ears. Fred had to swing several times and finally the lock broke apart with a loud clang.

Fred was smiling, the big guy looked like a tall cocky lumberman giant. "There is a whole bunch of rescue stuff inside the snow cat," he pronounced.

We opened the door. Unlike the other cabins it had a fancy wooden carved doorway. The door swung easily open, unlike the other shelters. The air that came flooding out wasn't musty either; it was rather sweet smelling. It was a smell that announced that humans had used this cabin recently.

I followed Hill inside. Fred had to duck his head to gain entrance. For several moments we all just stood gaping. The floor plan was one large room divided by rugs into several areas. One wall was a huge stone hearth with soft leather tan plush chairs facing the fire grate. A quilt covered queen sized bed, which was against the opposite side with end tables, designated the bedroom. The kitchen covered the far wall. It was more functional than mine at home and a lot more modern with a four-burner gas stove, a refrigerator with water/ice maker and a good-sized interior. It even had a "note taker". I went up to it and said, "*need bread*" and I'll be damned it started a grocery list. The stainless steel sinks had soap dispensers, rinse options and a digital clock just above with the time. The dishwasher was easily loaded as the shelves lifted up as high as the sink. Jiminy!

On the last wall was his office. It was the only part of the cabin that was rather old fashioned. He actually had a kind of lap top computer sitting right on the desk. Still when Hill touched it a voice came up and asked for an id and password. In the top left hand drawer there were several insert tabs, all labeled as to their function such as "casino ledger", "safety patrol records", "employee records", etc. In the right hand drawer were more insert tabs with his personal records such as "family photos", "financial records", and it even had one labeled "Hessina".

Heavy-duty shutters dressed each window. Hill found a control panel near the front door and opened most of them. The back of the cabin was all glass showing the mountain continuing upwards, with small pine trees dotting the landscape. The back must have been facing west as the afternoon sun was filtering in through the clouds. We could see that the deck made a complete circle of the house.

Fred examined the fireplace. "It's gas run," he said pressing a side button. Sure enough a nice warm fire sprung up giving the chilly cabin some needed warmth.

It was Hill that discovered the Profon solar generator in the corner near the fully functional bathroom.   "The generator keeps everything running and the temperature in the cabin up enough to keep the pipes from freezing," Judy told us as she also examined and gratefully used the lavatory facility. "This bathroom is better than my own on Fulton," Hill exclaimed.

I peeked into the bathroom. Hill was right, the bathroom was luxuriously done. It contained a spa tub, a multi-head shower, two sinks and a drying off cubicle. Streng had spent a lot on making the cabin ultra modern and extremely comfortable. The room was functional with sturdy but comfortable furniture with matching lamps and thick rugs. Had he done it for Hessina I wondered or for himself?

Fred was rumbling around the cabinets looking for something to fill his empty stomach. "There is nothing but junk," he complained as he held up one can after another of *Gumble's Healthy Meals.* "Who eats this junk?"

"People who want to eat healthy, you jerk!" Hill threw up her hands in disgust. "Don't worry, I brought sandwiches that I had made up at the resort's deli. I even brought a thermos but I think the cabin has drinks."

The look of relief on Fred's face was almost comical. I had to admit my stomach was churning from hunger. At least Streng had plenty of java and even Hill's black tea. Fred, of course, had to complain about powdered cream for his mug of java. I told him he should drink it black like I do.

Hill passed out the sandwiches and we ate them as we searched the cabin. I was nervous as snow was falling outside. It wasn't heavy but it still was making me nervous, we didn't get this on

Fulton Station. There was no cell service so I couldn't bring up a weather report.

"Let's pick it up," I reminded them, I wanna be out of here before nightfall!" I couldn't imagine the trek down in the dark.

"I'm having trouble with this computer," Hill complained. "It won't let me in, even using my police code, which is supposed to override any password."

Fred went over, shoving her aside and started typing. "Here you go!" He stood up, smirking at Judy, "All set, you're in."

"How the hell did you do that?" Hill demanded.

"I put in his password," Fred laughed at her. "I used good old fashioned police work, Hill! You might get off your high horse and try it sometime."

"I'm going to slug you," she yelled at him, "or worse I'll tell Lara!"

That threat did it, Fred spilled the beans, "I put in *Planetarians*."

"The hockey team?" Hill looked surprised. "You're right, Fred, I should have known. It was his obsession."

"Whatever," I told them, "see what you can get. I'm getting nervous, the snowflakes seem bigger."

While Hill searched his computer, Fred and I went into the garage. It contained several pairs of modern skis with helmets and poles neatly hung on the wall. It also contained snowshoes, sleds and right in the middle, two-snowmobile hovers.

Everything needed to enjoy the snow was in that garage.

"Wow!" Fred exclaimed at he sat on one of the snowmobiles. He took up most of the seat. "These are really heavy-duty, made to go through deep snow. They're fully charged. Let's take them for a spin." He looked expectantly at me while at the same time hitting a button on the vehicle and the double doors of the garage quickly lifted.

"Get off!" I growled as the doors exposed the snow coming down with more intensity. "We gotta get out of here, it's getting bad out!"

We went back into the cabin proper. Hill was deeply staring at the computer screen, it actually lit up her face. It made me realize how dark it was getting outside. I went and looked out one of the windows. The clouds were definitely darker and a lot more ominous.

"Find anything, Hill?" I nervously asked. "Can we bring that computer down with us?"

"I don't think so," she replied. "This is hard wired into the generator's output. We'd have to disconnect it and I'm not sure I could bring it up again. We could bring the insert tabs but they are bigger insert modules than our own tabs. Eventually someone on Fulton could get them working but we have the problem that if someone like Nove Deck learns of them, he could confiscate them as part of the equipment belonging to the resort."

"Crap," I spouted off, "what have you learned so far?""

"I'm learning that he kept detailed records and he was very hard working," she shook her head.

"I can tell by the hours he logged in, even when up here he put in long days."

"Well, he had time to impregnate his wife," Fred sniggered and got a very disapproving frown from Hill.

"You are a brute!" Judy sneered at him. "Can't you think beyond your small dirty mind?"

"Come on Hill, I was only kidding. You have no sense of humor. A cop needs a sense of humor. Lighten up!" He looked to me for some backing but I refused to get in the middle. The snow was really coming down now. I took a blue pill as my nerves were getting frayed. Criminals I could handle, weather threw me for a loop. Go figure. Oh well.

"How about his personal files?" I ventured.

"He wasn't rich but of course Hessina contributed to their funds. I found the files for the building of this cabin into a luxury home. It came from Hessina's funds and from what I gather she signed everything. Bringing everything up here cost a bundle. The generator alone cost more than my yearly salary."

"Well that's not saying much. Our pay wouldn't pay for the energy charge fee to get up here!" Fred laughed. I frowned, maybe because it was the truth.

"This is taking too long," I complained. "What did he do, write everything down when he went back?"

Hill looked up at me, "You are a genius, Chief. That's the rub, he had to have a way of transferring this data to bring back home." She began rumbling through his desk. "Aha, here it is, a data transferer." She put a small square box on the desk and pulled an antenna out of the top. "This is an old data transfer container. I've only seen them at the archives in Orbo's reference libraries. It let's you transfer from an old computer to your tabloid."

"Do you know how to make it work?" I anxiously asked as my eyes went to the windows. The snow was now blowing, actually blowing. The wind must have picked up.

"I just have to figure how to turn it on," Hill speculated as she poked the white box. Fred reached over and pushed a side button. "Don't touch it!" she screamed at him, "You could break it!"

Too late, the box sprung to life with red and yellow lights flashing. "Buttons are made to be pushed." Fred handed her back the now active data transferer.

"I'll remind you of that next time you diffuse a bomb, you lucky idiot!" Hill told him as she grabbed the gadget. She brought up her tabloid placing it next to the flashing box. "Okay, let's see if this works."

She put into his computer the tab marked "Casino records" and placed her own tabloid near the white box. "This is wireless, in the archives on Orbo some of the data has to be transferred using wires."

I just shook my head as she placed the next tab into Streng's old computer. The tabs were larger than the one's we now used. There were about ten business tabs and four personal tabs. She copied them all to her tabloid.

She put the tab labeled "Hessina" on the desk. "I think we should bring this one back and give it to

Hessie. It is really none of our business." She looked to me to agree with her.

I didn't get to agree or disagree. Fred grabbed it and shoved it in the old computer. "Don't be sentimental Hill, we can't afford it."

"You Oaf!" Judith cried but it was too late. Suddenly the old computer buzzed and from the side a hologram of Lawren Streng popped out. It was not really a good picture as it wavered and there was a slight tinge of green to the whole depiction.

"Oh, my god," we all said at once. Lawren stood there smiling. I had forgotten what a good looking man he was. He was dressed in casual mountain clothing. His hair was slightly amiss; it looked like he'd just gotten up. The hologram had obviously been made up here.

"Get him to talk," Fred poked her, "Come on, push some buttons!"

"I'm trying!" she half screamed at him. I guess Hill wasn't concerned about the privacy issue any longer. "Come on talk," she yelled at the hologram.

"Oh, that's helpful," Fred shook his head and reached over knocking the side of the old computer with his large paw.

"Eek!" Hill yelled at him but shut up as the figure of Lawren Streng began to speak. Even with the occasional static, his voice came out loud and clear.

Hess, if you are seeing this then something has happened to me. I'm sorry. I hope our baby is born without problems. Give Lilac all she needs and then sever all ties with her. I'm sorry we picked her.

Head home to your father, he'll keep you and the baby safe. He paused as if his emotions were overwhelming him. He looked back up.

Listen Hess, I know we've had arguments about me going to Skantie Row. I had to go, they threatened me. I tried, honestly, to change their minds. I met with Joala Blithie several times. I tried to talk him out of using the resort to get his revenge. He promised me if I'd help him revenge his family he would leave all of Hilda alone. Otherwise, he was going to expand into our casino and corrupt the planet with drugs. He's quite ruthless. He said he has the Hildan Corporation in his back pocket.

Again, Streng stopped. He was visibly shaken. He looked up again talking to his wife.

All they asked me to do is bring the Browns to the resort. I couldn't believe it, that Skip Brown is the sector police chief. He was one of the best racing drivers ever! They told me they would do the rest. I could keep my hands clean of it. They informed me that Paul was working for them so I had better keep to the plan. I think Paul is part of the Blithie family. Keep clear of him.

Streng seemed to get really upset. He put out his hands as if pleading with his wife.

I discovered, Hess... I found that they were planning to kill him and his family. Paul Bell bragged to me one day how they were going to give payback for something the Chief had done to the Blithie family. First they were going to frame him for a murder, then kill them all - his family and some of his colleagues who helped hurt the Blithie family. I can't let that happen. I'll figure out something or die trying... I love you.

We were all silent, stunned into silence. The puzzle pieces all started to fill in. What fools we were. It wasn't about the mob moving into Hilda, it was about us. Hill had the sense to make us cups of java. I sat at the table in a fog.

Why hadn't I pieced the puzzle together? Ray was given a great deal on a chateau to get us here. Then the murder of Lilac to get Fred and Hill here by having the Skantie Row and Hilda senators request them. They screwed up by putting Lilac's body in our old chateau, trying to frame me for the murder. Thank god for the front clerk's screw up. That must have panicked their plans. Killing Lilac probably was also why Lawren Streng stuck his nose into it and had gotten himself killed. They had killed his baby. He had told Hessina that they had gotten *the wrong girl.*

Reich Hisner must have gotten wind of something and they killed him. He had told his fellow stripper that Paul Bell wanted revenge. It wasn't on Lawren Streng, it was on us!

"What are we going to do?" Hill asked. I could tell it was just sinking into her brain as it was with me.

"I'm gonna kill the sons of bitches!" Fred sputtered out. "As slowly as I can!"

"If the bastards don't kill you first!" Hill reminded him.

Fred looked around, "Let's hope they don't know we are here."

"We've got to get out of here," I said a little too loudly as my nerves were frayed. I took another blue pill. The world was crashing down around me. I had to get back to Ray and my family. I had to protect them! "Why take the chance of killing us?" I asked Fred. "They can't hope to get away with it."

"You have to understand the mob families," Fred answered me. "They are completely loyal to the family members. It would be a dishonor to not get revenge. It would also signal weakness to the other families. We sent a good chunk of the Blithies to long-term jail sentences. You and Hill got the files. I followed up on the evidence. I have to admit though that I'm surprised at their audacity."

"If they get away with this," I told my senior detective, "there will be no stopping them. No cop, no informer will be safe. They would be sending a powerful message to law enforcement, especially if the law can't prove anything. They have been planning this for a long time. It's been a little over a year since we got those files."

We started getting our winter clothes back on and headed out to the snow cat. We had to plow through snow that was over our knees to reach the vehicle's steps. It was snowing so hard, the windshield wipers were having a hard time. Fred turned us around to head back down the driveway.

"We'll get stuck," Hill remarked. "We can't see where we are going!"

"She's right," Stoshingburg stopped the snow cat. "We have to wait until this stops. At least in the cabin we have protection. If we get stuck on the road, we could freeze to death." He turned the vehicle around, getting back to where we had parked it with some difficulty.

Inside the cabin we relit the fireplace and reopened some of the windows. Despite Fred's earlier remarks about the canned food, he ate four of them. Hill and I shared one. Our nerves were taut. I felt like we were sitting ducks, trapped animals.

We kept our boots on, just throwing our coats on the back of the chairs. We'd leave as soon as we could which would probably be morning when it would be easier to see our way.

I at least finally got to read my book. Hill fiddled with her tabloid, probably going over all the records she had downloaded. "You know, Chief, he wasn't a bad guy and he really did love Hessina." I just nodded, slouching further into the cushions, as I turned to the next chapter.

Fred paced. He was so angry. He went up one side of the large room, then back again. He was muttering to himself the whole time. I heard words like *hate, kill, strangle,* floating in the air. I let him rant; it was the big guy's way.

Darkness started to fall. The light from the fireplace sent waves of shadows filtering across the large room. Hill was still at her computer and Fred had finally worn himself out. He lay sleeping on the bed, his snores loud but somehow reassuring that life seemed normal even when it wasn't.

"I found a tab labeled *travel schedule*", Hill informed me. I looked up. She continued, "Lawren Streng went to Skantie several times in one six month period. He documented every meeting. If we can get to Capt. Issam, this should help pinpoint who was responsible for these murders back on that hell hole planet. It documents the new Blithie family leaders. It will help with keeping track of the drug trade."

"I am worried about my family, Hill," my voice cracked with emotion.

She came over sitting on my chair's arm, "Yes, I'm worried too. If they touch one hair on anyone I'll go to my father, I swear I will." She took my hand and squeezed.

"Now who is bringing up your family?" I laughed but it quickly dissipated as the thought of little Jimmy filled my head. "Let's hope you are alive to do that."

She looked around the darkening room, "They have no way of knowing we are here."

"I'm not so sure, they have been ahead of us the whole way," I said.

I must have looked so forlorn that Hill kneeled in front of me, reaching up taking my face exclaiming, "We have always beaten them, we will again!"

The fire flickered off her face. I realized how really beautiful she was. Despite being a pain in my ass, I was becoming entranced by this woman. She always seemed to be there when I needed her. Perhaps Killa was right. I touched her face.

Then I heard the sound of snowmobiles. Shit! "Fred," I yelled but he was already up and at the door. He had his gun out and was looking out the shutter slats. Hill had her gun out and mine was in my hand pointed at the door.

"Maybe it's Chet, come to rescue us," Hill said.

"It's the ski patrol," Fred looked over at us, relief in his eyes as he holstered his gun. I saw Hill lower hers.

"Are you in there?" filtered in a female voice, "are you guys okay?"

Fred opened the door before I could tell him not to. Standing in the doorway was a petite woman dressed in a ski patrol winter coveralls. She held a gun at Fred's chest.

"Good, Wendy," a man said from behind her.

"Mario?" Fred's voice held a note of disbelief as he stared at the figure behind her.

"Hi, Stoshingburg," his voice was a deep bass tone. "Put your guns on the floor or Fred dies real quick."

We both knew we had no choice and let our stun guns drop. The man stepped in and took off his winter protection mask. I gasped. Now I knew him! He had been in the bar but even more alarming was he had been our original busboy. He'd carried our luggage to Chateau 14 before we moved to 15. His rugged pock marked face now brought my memory back.

"Who is this, Fred?" I asked.

"One of Blithies' henchmen," Fred almost snarled it and got a slap from the woman of all things. She had to stand on her tiptoes just to reach Fred.

"Show some respect, Mr. Cop," she told him. Mario motioned for Fred to join us. The three of us stood by the fireplace. My mind was racing but I didn't see any escape.

"How did you know we were here?" I asked. Usually bully types like to brag and this one was no different. He wants us to know how smart he was and how dumb we were,

"Why nurse Billow of course," Mario motioned at the door. A bulky type man entered, he took off his head gear. *"Why Mrs. Streng, you should tell your friend about the cabin.*" He mimicked the sergeant nurse's voice.

I was shocked, *Nurse Billow* had been posing as a female medic. I looked over at him. Sure enough it was Billow's face. I heard Hill take a deep breath. She recognized the imposter also.

"Before we kill you, I wanted you to know, Chief Brown, how stupid you are!" Mario's voice was cold. He left no doubt of what a cold blooded killer he was. "We have led you by the nose since you arrived. Too bad I wasn't informed of your change in chateaus. It almost ruined our whole plan. I so wanted you disgraced before you died. But death will suit us fine."

"You killed Lilac, Lawren and Reich," I stated.

He laughed so hard and loud, it hurt my hearing. "Yes and Yes and Yes," he finally told me. "Stupid and stupid and stupid."

Fred growled. Hill took his arm calming him. She turned to Mario, "She was pregnant. It was Streng's baby."

"To tell the truth lady, I don't care," he smiled showing his yellow teeth. I cringed, this was a monster. "*Please don't kill me, please, I'm pregnant.* She was so pathetic." He actually laughed. "Then her stripper boyfriend tried to threaten us. Streng just couldn't keep his nose out of it. We warned him. He was the fool! Look at his wife, now there's one ugly chick."

I grabbed onto Hill as I felt her move forward in anger. "Don't," was all I said and pulled her back to me.

"Listen to the Chief, lady cop, after all he's gone and gotten you killed," Mario sneered. I wanted to exterminate the ogre so badly, my teeth hurt from clenching them.

"We have people coming," I tried to bluff my way, at least make him think of the consequences.

"No. Your superintendent is doing a stakeout with most of his police. They are waiting for a Jump. Waste of time. We set that up too, ha ha," He laughed again, swaying his hips in a mock dance. "We aren't the stupid ones."

"We were smart enough to get most of the Blithies and we will do it again!" I yelled at him.

He pointed his gun at me, "This whole house is going to burn along with all the evidence in it. Three bodies inside that just could not get out in time. Then we'll take care of your family, like you took care of ours. All accidents, another fire or perhaps a hover accident. Oh so bad. The press will play it up royally. The demise of the famous racing family. Boo hoo," he pretended to cry. "Hey, Chief, think babies burn faster?"

I lost it. I started to charge at him. He pointed his gun. I felt the blackness overtake me...

****

"Chief, Chief," I heard. It was coming from somewhere distant. "Wake up, come on wake up."

I must have had a seizure. My head ached and the smell of me throwing up hit my nose. I tried to focus. I opened my eyes. Hill was kneeling over me. I got a wave of nausouness that came flooding into my brain. I think I groaned.

"That's it, wake up," Hill was talking again, pushing my body with her head.

"Why aren't I dead?" I managed to get out. My mouth felt dry. I tried to sit up but I couldn't do it. "I need my pills," I don't think it came out right, but Hill understood.

"They've tied my hands behind my back, so I'll try and get the pills out of your pocket using my mouth," she was whispering. "They didn't kill you because they didn't want to get near you once you threw up."

I felt her bend down trying to get into my pocket with her mouth. "What the hell..." my dry mouth tried to form the words.

"They've tied me up. Just stay still, I'm trying to get your pills. I heard the cellophane wrapping that my pills were in. I opened my eyes, she was shaking the package. She bent down again. "Okay, open your mouth." I felt her lips and then a pill dropped into my mouth. I almost choked but managed to get it down. Ten minutes later I slowly sat up. I still felt like hell but at least I was awake. The pill was taking effect.

I looked down at my clothes. I had done it again. I wiped my mouth with the back of my sleeve. Hill was kneeling next to me. "Crap, Judy, that must have been a pleasant experience!"

"I've had better," she told me as I reached for my pills which were spilled all over my chest and got another one. This time I managed to get a little blue pill myself. I put the little blue tablets back into the plastic wrap and succeeded in getting them back into my pocket. It took several tries.

It took me another several minutes to focus. Hill had both her hands and feet tied with hemp rope. Easy to burn, leaving little evidence, came into my mind. Fred, with his arms and legs tied, was sitting with his back against the bottom of a chair. They had taped his mouth shut. His eyes were wild.

I could see why they didn't want to get near me. I know what my epileptic fits look like, smell like. They had left me, probably thinking I was dying. I noticed above the puke smell was a sulfur smell. The Blithie henchman, Mario, had stunned me. He hadn't wanted to kill me nor leave a burn mark so it was a low charge. Better I burn with no marks on me but he hadn't expected me to convulse.

I really fumbled with Judy's bonds. I couldn't quite stand yet and I couldn't reach anything to cut them. Finally, I used my teeth and pulled the ropes on her wrists free. She untied her feet herself.

When Judy went over to Fred, I heard her try to calm him, "Listen Stosh, you need to calm down before I'll let you loose." She was kneeling in front of him. I saw him nod and she cut his bonds with some scissors she had found in the kitchen. When she pulled off his mouth tape, he cringed. It must have hurt like the devil but he didn't yell out.

"Cripes, Chief, you stink. You scared the hell out of me! Didn't know what a seizure looked like." He was rubbing his mouth. He had a big red welt where the tape had been.

"Well, it wasn't pleasant for me either," I assured him. I took a towel and tried to wipe myself but it didn't do much good. It was then that I smelled the smoke.

"They are setting the fire," Hill informed me. "We gotta get out of here!"

"There are four of them with four snowmobiles. They took our guns," Fred barked at me. "Any ideas? If we try to escape they'll just shoot us. I'm sure that is why they aren't worried about us escaping."

"They haven't gotten all our guns," Hill reached into her hat which was next to the coats on the back of a chair. "I have this one."

I recognized her little pistol. "Is it charged?" I asked and got a frown.

"Of course," as if I was crazy for asking. Hill was always prepared.

"Oh that's going to do us a lot of good," Fred shook his head in despair at the small gun.

"It's better than nothing, asshole," my newest *inexperienced* lieutenant made it clear that we *experienced* detectives had nothing.

The smell of fire was getting more prevalent. Smoke was starting to fill the main room. "Come on, into the garage!"

Fred, who was peeking out the window told us, "Three of the thugs are watching the fire from the front. The fourth one must be out back. They aren't watching the house really closely. The thugs don't expect us to get out. And they called *us* stupid?"

We quickly put on our outer snow wear and headed towards the garage.

"Our only chance for escape is these snowmobiles. Let's hope the snow's not too deep."

"These babies can handle the snow Chief. The question is, *can these machines outrun those other snowmobiles*? The snow is really coming down so it should cover our escape but we are losing all the day's light."

"We'll do the best we can. I've never run one of these, give me a quick lesson," I told Fred.

"I know how," Hill announced. "You sit behind me. Here is the gun. Do what you can." Before Judy got on, she threw us three helmets that were hanging on the wall nearby.

"Don't bother, hurry up," Fred softly yelled over to her. "They may get curious and look in."

"I swear your brain is in your ass," Hill spat. "These are smart helmets. We'll be able to talk to each other and when we get close enough our cellbuttons will kick in."

Fred duly shut up.

We got on. Hill showed us the button that activated the helmets. We could actually hear each other. I could have kissed her. I had a feeling Fred felt the same way as he widely smiled when our voices came in.

To my surprise, the engines made a roaring noise. I was astonished as they were hover driven. Fred explained, "They are powerful hovers. Can't hide power, Chief, let's hope they are powerful enough. Ready? Keep close by, let's not lose each other. Hill nodded.

Fred pressed the garage door that opened on the back side of the cabin. "Here we go!"

Chapter Thirteen

We sped out the back of the garage. Fred led the way towards a marked trail that looked like it had been cleared by the wide lack of trees. As we passed beyond the garage, the woman yelled frantically as she realized we had escaped.

I looked back to see heavy smoke coming from the front of the cabin. We could smell the fire whose smoke seemed to hover above us. I didn't hear any pursuit. Perhaps we could not hear their snowmobiles above our own engines. I had to smile – what fools they must feel like discovering we had escaped.

The snow was falling in buckets. Hill was following Fred's taillights. We were also getting sprayed from his snowmobile. We dared not get far from him as the snow storm would blind us. I could see by the fading day's light that the tree tops were violently swaying with the wind gusts.

I saw Stoshingburg swerve left, leaving the trail. Hill followed him. I clung tight as our bodies leaned far over to the right. I heard, "Hold on Chief," in my ear. I made the mistake of peeking over her shoulder. Fred was right in front of us and I could see him dodging the trunks of trees. I wished I could reach my blue pills just to calm my heart. The trees swished by us, some rubbing against my coat.

After a good while, Fred stopped under a clump of trees that afforded a little relief from the snowfall. "I think we'll just have to try and head downwards," he came in loud and clear in our helmets.

"Okay, which way is down?" Hill asked as she got off the snowmobile. "I can't see anything!"

"Fred, where are your gloves?" I asked, noticing his bare hands.

"I must have left them in the cabin," he answered rather meekly for the big guy.

"Oh for god's sake," Hill yelled, it came over loudly in my ear.

"Please Judy, I'd like to keep my hearing!" I told her.

"Sorry, but sometimes he's just too much. What Lara sees in him…" she sounded so exasperated. She reached into her coat pocket, "Here put these on, I always carry an extra pair."

Fred looked at the small black pair of mittens, "I'm going to fit in those?"

"Try them," Hill threw up her hands, "at least they're something."

If it hadn't been so dire, I would have cracked up as Fred tugged and pulled them on. They at least covered most of his hands stopping before his wrist. I was glad we had dressed in rugged warm insulated clothes. The wind was whipping and I could feel it pounding on my coat and slipping cold shots up my sleeves. During the lulls, the forest was eerily quiet as if hiding the blizzard's deadly nature.

"Thank you, Hill," the big guy humbly sent the words her way. Hill just nodded. He continued, "I'm going to have to make an educated guess. We can go slowly, the snow is covering our tracks. They will have a hard time finding us."

Just as we were getting ready to leave, a wicked wind came tearing across our little sheltered area. The trees above us let loose all their pent up snow. We looked like human snowmen as wet snow covered us completely. I shook as much off as I could and got back behind Hill. I heard Fred swear as he gunned the snowmobile.

We followed as Fred led us to what he thought was a downward trek through the trees. Several times, we got hung up in the deep snow and had to push our way clear. I noticed the pines were getting bigger and closer together. The night began to descend and we couldn't see much beyond our lights. It also seemed to be getting colder as the lower temperature was reaching under our helmets touching our ears, threatening us with frostbite.

"We can't stay out here much longer. We have to find somewhere to get out of this wind," I urgently told them. "Fred, look for a rocky out crop that we can get under."

"Jeesh Chief, I can't see more than a few feet in front of me," Fred didn't sound well, he was shivering. I at least had Hill, who sheltered me from the worst of it.

"Hill, let me drive for a while and I'll take the lead," I told them, but only got grunts for a reply as if they didn't trust me to operate the vehicle. "I don't have to remind you I used to race cars for a living."

Another set of grunts. "You can't even manage to ski!" Hill reminded me. "You just don't handle snow well, Chief." It shut me up.

We went on, the night becoming complete, the darkness all-consuming. The only good thing was that the snow seemed to be letting up. The wind also seemed less intense. The frigid cold, however, was settling in.

"Whoa," Fred yelled and stopped. "Are my eyes deceiving me or is that the indent of the road ahead?" He slowly went forward. Sure enough a large cleared area came into view. "This is the road down," he sounded cheerful despite him stuttering from the cold.

"Yeah, it is," Hill remarked. "Look closely, there are snowmobile tracks - four of them!"

"So they came this way and not too long ago," I speculated. They must have assumed we followed the road down, instead of us going through the woods like we did. "I suggest caution, go slow Fred."

"If I go slow, I'll freeze to death," he commented.

"Do the best you can. High alert, keep our eyes and ears opened." I realized my voice was also shaking and Hill seemed to be shivering. I never thought I'd miss the heat of Fulton Station but I surely did.

It was easier going. The snowmobile wasn't bouncing as much; the engine didn't seem to be struggling as much either. "We've used up a lot of power, I don't think these will get us all the way down the mountain," Hill remarked. She sounded tired.

"If we can get a little lower on the mountain, the trails will be full of skiers. They'll get help. Plus our helmets should work as should our cellbuttons." I couldn't recognize my own shaking voice. Even my hands were feeling the cold and my toes were tingling.

Suddenly Fred stopped, we almost ran into him. "Fred!" Hill yelled as we slid sideways and almost tipped.

"Look!" Fred's shadowy silhouette pointed in our headlights. A black mass stood out to our left. "That's one of the cabins! Come on!" He gunned his snowmobile up to the clearing with Hill right on his heels.

Sure enough, it was one of the cabins. It's outline shown darkly against the cloudy sky. We would have missed it had it not been in a clearing with no trees behind it. We all jumped off, running up the steps and plowed into the inner hut's sanctuary. It actually seemed warm without any cold breeze hitting us. My face burned when I took off my helmet followed by my ears and fingers.

"I'll start the fire," Fred almost shouted with anticipation.

"No, don't," Hill interjected, "we can't let those assholes know we are here. We have to bring the snowmobiles around back - out of sight!"

Fred and I groaned, realizing she was right. "Shit!" Stoshinburg expressed our feelings exactly. He reluctantly said, "Okay, you and Hill bring the machines around back. I'm going to cover up our tracks."

"No, I'll do that," I offered.

"I'm tall enough to trudge through this snow. I've used snowshoes before. He grabbed a set that was hung over the fireplace. "It is not as easy as it looks."

"He's right, Chief," Hill just had to put her two cents in.

We went outside. I groaned as the coldness seeped into my clothes again. Hill and I moved the snow machines around the back. We stood on the porch as Fred took a large fir branch and swished it back and forth. I was amazed that the big guy hardly sank into the snow, as the laced shoes seemed to keep him afloat.

He went all the way to the road and then headed back to where we were standing. "Get in, I have to make this porch look abandoned. We stood in the doorway as he reached the lower limbs of an overhanging pine tree and shook it over the porch. Down fell a whole slew of snow. He then used his laced snow shoe to spread it to the stairs.

"With a little bit of luck, they won't notice our tracks on the road but will confuse it with their own. They probably went all the way down back to the resort, as they can't stay out here either."

"When they don't find us back at the resort, they'll be back up at first light," Hill caustically remarked.

We found some thick blankets that roughly tickled our skin. We didn't dare take off our clothes, just in case we had to make a quick getaway but Hill knew a trick. She set her pistol on its lowest setting and used the heat of the gun to somewhat dry our clothes. Only Hill, I thought, only Hill.

Although they were still sticky damp it was a hell of a lot better. When she had done the big guy and me, Fred went to grab the gun to dry her. She went wide eyed, "Are you kidding, you'd accidentally fry me." She handed me the pistol with a stern warning, "Be careful! Don't burn me."

I guess I was just a little more trustworthy than Fred. "Don't tempt me, Hill," I warned her, getting a deep frown from her mouth.

The cabin held a rugged hard cushioned couch. We sat on it bringing the long low homemade cocktail table close enough to put our feet on it. We ended up huddling together as our bodies helped temper the coldness. We wrapped ourselves with every blanket we could find.

The cabin was well built and sturdy. Of course, it was completely the opposite of Streng's luxury cabin but we were grateful just to be out of the elements. After groping around in the dark, Hill had found some canned food with easy pull off tops. It was mostly beans with small little sausages mixed in. Fred ate five of them and then finished off the few cans of fruit.

At first, I refused anything to eat. My stomach had not recovered from my epileptic seizure and I was still aching everywhere. The ride through the woods had done a number on every part of my body. Hill had insisted I eat, even calling me a blooming coward. I didn't get that comment, but it did make me swallow a few bites just to spite her.

Then we settled in for the night, our ears listening for any snowmobile sounds. Fred was talkative at first. "I've been meaning to tell you about what Zoe Doss told me,"

"Yeah, what did she have to say," I asked him - anything to keep our minds off the cold.

"Well, I found out who she's been getting her Supfline from," he snuggled closer. God we all smelled of musty wet clothes. I couldn't imagine how bad I smelled.

"Tell us, for god's sake," Hill reached over and hit him. "Come on, don't keep us in suspense."

"It's her mother," he spat it out with total disgust.

"Her mother?" Hill and I both exploded at the same time.

"Yep, her fucking mother," the big guy confirmed. "Her mother became addicted because of Paul Bell giving her a "recreational drug" as Zoe tells it. Reich Hisner brought it over. And before that, Lilac did. They were both making a bundle on it."

"Oh my god," Hill pounced on the implication. "Don't tell me Lilac took that drug while she was pregnant?"

"Yes, ma'am," Fred's voice was full of disgust. "Mrs. Streng didn't know she was getting a Sup baby as we call them."

"Oh, how horrible," Hill actually clutched herself, "what would Hessie ever have said."

"I think Lawren Streng had maybe gotten wind of it. That's why he warned his wife to take the baby and run." Fred snuggled closer to me as if it would keep the cold out. It didn't. "I also think that Lilac's doctor knew she was doing Supfline. Perhaps he was afraid to tell you. Remember, he talked about having to talk to Lilac about her bad habits. If we press him he'll tell you Lawren also had a talk with him."

"You know I had an inkling that there was more," Hill cocked her head as if thinking about her visit to Hess's gynecologist. "I couldn't follow it up as Jarad just wanted to get her to MOSS."

"Zoe says that is also why her mom is so broke. She is craving the Supfline and paying for it with her inheritance."

Of course, Fred had seen a lot of what Supfline could do but I just shuddered at the thought of the power of the drug.

"When we get back..." Fred continued. I was glad he said *when* and not *if.* "I'm getting Zoe and her mother some help. It won't help the teenager for her mom to go to jail. What I really want to know is how I didn't smell it on the mom. I'm getting feedback that they have some way of hiding the smell. That's not good."

Every small sound found us all tensing up. Hill kept her pistol close, Fred had found an old rusty axe that he was now sleeping with and I cradled a good-sized split log. Not much but it let us all fall sound asleep, exhaustion took precedence.

I woke up stiff, and I mean stiff but amazingly warm. Our combined body heat had actually warmed us up. Unfortunately, the minute we stood up the coldness seemed to stab right into us. The cabin had a raw bitter cold. The sky was just lighting up. Deep shadows filled the landscape around our cabin.

Hill took three flares out of one of the drawers near the outside cabinet. "If we can get near enough, we can signal where we are, but be careful with these. They can explode easily if mishandled. I saw a man once throw one that was not out completely into the snow and it exploded. Baboom!"

"We dressed up in our helmets and gloves. We had found several scarfs hanging on the wall, now that we could actually see the interior of our huddle. We couldn't open the back door of the room as snow was stacked high against it. We ended up trudging around to the back through the snow, then cleaning off the machines. To our relief, they both started right up.

"Let's go right down the road, until the ski slopes appear," Fred suggested and we agreed.

"How far down are we?" I asked.

"I think this is the lowest cabin," Hill conjectured by looking at the much taller surrounding forest. "If I remember right, we have only a few miles to the actual skiing slopes. It's early so we may not find many skiers out yet." She looked to the sky, it was light gray; the sun hadn't come over the mountain yet. "Our vehicles are at a quarter charge. Not much. Here, take my pistol," she offered me the small gun, "it also doesn't have much after drying our clothes but you'll be able to get a few shots out. Remember it only goes less than fifty yards. Put it on medium stun, it will last longer."

Down the road we went. Unlike the plowed road of yesterday, it was hardly visible. The tracks we'd seen the night before were covered up but the lack of trees led the way. We started seeing clearings but definitely not skiable yet. Large outcrops of rocks and deep ravines dotted the glades. The road was the only safe way down.

We heard them before we saw them. "Do you think it's Chet looking for us?" Hill asked but her voice couldn't hide her skepticism.

"Doubt it," Fred now had learned his lesson. "The ski patrol would have the snow cats, and those are smaller vehicles coming at us."

Stoshingburg veered to the left, taking us into the woods. We weaved in and out of the small clumps of trees now dotting the landscape. He came out on a clearing that was extremely steep. To tell you the truth, it took my breath away as I clung to Hill.

Fred swung to the right as he skirted a huge ravine. No one said a word as total concentration was needed. I could see the valley way below, way below.

Suddenly Fred grabbed his arm. A burn hole appeared in his ski jacket. He quickly clutched onto the steering grips as his snowmobile dangerously swerved.

"They are shooting at us but they are too far away to be lethal, keep going!" she yelled into her helmet's microphone. "Step on it!"

"We will kill ourselves," Fred shouted. "We will fall into a ravine if we're not careful!"

"Let me lead!" Hill suggested which only seemed to get Stoshingburg's pride in a snitch as he increased his speed to total insanity. I shut my eyes. I didn't want to know when we'd be careening over the side.

I heard the roaring of a snow vehicle. *It must be real close,* crossed my mind as I reopened my eyes. Running next to us was a small snowmobile. I'd bet it was the woman. She was trying to get close enough to ram us. Being the lightest of the thugs, she had the most speed. I aimed Hill's pistol and pressed down. I was aiming at her hands. I must have made contact as I saw her shake her glove. Then her snowmobile bowled over as she tried to save it. I saw her tumble down the slope.

"Good shot," Hill's voice was almost a whisper as she tried to concentrate on following Fred.

The clearing widened. The big guy swerved towards the middle but I saw another shot hit him in the back. "Ouch," came over into our helmets. "They must be closer, that one hurt."

Hill pulled up next to him. We ran side by side down the clearing; each of us waiting for the next shot. I tried to cover Hill by putting my arms straight down on either side of her. I felt a shot hit my helmet. It made a slight thud sound. I'm sure it must have melted the paint.

"They're gaining on us!" I shouted. "We have to do something!"

Hill seemed to shudder, "Okay, take one of the flares out of my pocket and throw it up the hill."

"What, do you think I'll hit them?" I asked incredulously. Was Hill losing her mind, or was she just panicking?

"DO IT!" she screamed.

It took me a little while to find her pocket. I dropped in her gun and brought out a flare. To my dismay, it slipped out of my hand.

I didn't tell her but reached in again, getting a second one. I pulled on the top, it took me two tries but I finally got it off. It started to light a small flame.

"THROW IT!" she again screamed in my ear. "Fred, head for that rocky outcrop. If we reach them, go right under them and stop!"

"Are you crazy, they'll catch us?" He exclaimed rather excitedly.

"JUST DO IT!" she screamed even louder. It was the last thing I heard as I threw the now completely lit flare. I heard it swish above me. Not even ten seconds later, a loud **_Boom_** filled the air.

A few seconds later it was followed by a huge overpowering rumble. The snowmobile actually lifted into the air. Hill struggled to keep it from tipping. I tried to hold on. I could actually see the rocks she had been steering to. I couldn't hold on, as the machine came down, I fell off.

Not long after I fell, I tried to stand up and run, but I was hit from the back. A wall of snow carried me head over heels downward. When it stopped, I was buried alive.

I tried to stay calm. As a matter of fact, I used my therapist's calming techniques. I tried to remember what we were taught during my skiing lessons about surviving an avalanche. I had a fleeting thought that I wished I'd paid more attention.

First I struggled to get one hand up and made a small hole in front of my face. It would be my air pocket but I knew it wouldn't last for long. I remember the instructor saying that it was a fifty/fifty chance I could dig myself out, or I could be digging upside down.

I'll admit it, I thought of Killa, Hill, Ray, Julie and little Jimmy. I'd probably never see them again. Still I edged my arm up, trying to dig upwards. Not easy, believe me. It seemed like an eternity but from what I was told later it was just minutes.

Water started dripping down. My mind grabbed on to the fact that water drips downward. Up was above my head as big drops hit my nose. I almost panicked in my frantic attempt to dig upward. Suddenly I could see light, a hole widened and a large hand grabbed onto my hand lifting me. It took several tries to pull me free. Hill kept widening the opening with her stun gun, melting the snow around me while Fred pulled me upwards.

I will admit it. I sat on the snow and cried. I kept gulping the air and rolling back and forth like a baby.

"Come on Chief, we have to find the others." Hill hugged me, kissing the top of my head once she'd gotten my helmet off.

"The others?" my mind couldn't focus.

"They all got caught in the avalanche", she explained. "We have to find their signals before they suffocate."

I stumbled after her and Fred as Hill had her cell tabloid opened. She went right to one spot and they started melting the snow with her gun. I just arrived at the spot when Fred lifted the woman up. She staggered falling face down on the snow, unconscious but still breathing.

Hill ran up the clearing, stopping again at a spot and again setting her gun to the snow. This time Fred pulled Mario out. He was unconscious, not breathing. I managed to stagger up and I started CPR on the guy. When I had him breathing, I noticed Fred and Hill had another two bodies on the snow. One of them Hill was working on. The other Fred was just staring at. I couldn't go any further. I had no strength left. I waited next to the leader of the gang, who was shallowly breathing but breathing nonetheless.

Hill joined me, looking disgustingly at Mario. "Nurse Billow didn't make it," she told me. "We've got to tie these guys up before they fully awake. Fred and Hill, together, ended up dragging them to our two snowmobiles that were sheltered under the rock outcrops. I had no strength left.

Hill, of course, had her handcuffs, always prepared. Of course, *we* didn't. She used the cuffs to secure Mario to one of the snowmobiles. For the two others, we found bungees and towing ropes in the back of our vehicles and wrapped them around the prisoners' wrist and legs until we were sure they couldn't get out of them.

The sun was now fully coming up. Below, we could see the resort including all the trails. We could even make out some skiers winding their way down the mountain.

"How did you find me?" I asked Hill.

"You have a smart helmet. It sends out a beep when it senses you're in trouble. The others had ski patrol outfits. They have built in beepers in their suits." She shrugged as if no big deal. It was to me, it was to me!

"What do we do now?" Fred asked. "I don't know if I have much of a charge left in our vehicles. It's reading empty."

"We just wait," Hill sat down on a large rock cliff that jutted out over the valley. "We just wait."

"Think they'll find us?" Fred looked at her as if she was crazy.

"Check your cellbutton. We have a low signal. Not enough to call out but our helmets, however, must be blasting our location."

We sat in the sun, letting the warmth sink in. Our tormentors woke up and screamed their bloody heads off that they were cold. I reminded them they were lucky to be alive; they could join Nurse Billow if they didn't shut up. They shut up.

Sure enough, we heard a copter's rotating blades approach in less than an hour's time. It circled where we were. I could see Ray waving from the cockpit. The hovercopter landed less than a quarter mile above us on the ledge.

My brother came running down with Julie right behind him. Two other guys joined us while Julie and Ray were hugging us all. My sister-in-law was crying and wouldn't let go of me. "Killa is crazy with worry," she told me. "We will call her as soon as our cells get a signal."

"It's gonna take two trips with all these people," the pilot informed me.

I let Hill, Ray and Julie head back first. Fred and I would go on the second trip bringing the prisoners. Hill could meanwhile call Chet and they could tell Killa we were all fine.

While waiting for the second trip, Fred just stood in the sun and shuddered. "You okay, big boy?" I asked him. He was pale and was rubbing his large legs.

"I'll admit, I'm shook up." He rarely confided his feelings to anyone. I think he felt it showed a manly weakness. I reflected we were probably very similar in that way. He looked up at the sun, as if finding strength from its warmth. "I couldn't help but think I never told Lara that I loved her. I thought I wouldn't get the chance. That was a close call, Chief."

"Yeah," I answered him, "but you know, I think our loved ones know we love them. Saying it is highly overrated."

"Is that why you don't tell Hill?" he looked over at me; the sunshine was hitting his wet hair causing a multitude of cascading colors. He looked like he was on fire.

I thought of denying it but instead just muttered, "Please don't tell her."

He roared with laughter, "No, don't worry, I won't if you keep the Lara info to yourself."

We heard the return of the copter. With the help of the two pilots we hauled the goon squad into the back of the rescue vehicle. They put the body of the fellow who'd played Nurse Billow in a basket underneath the belly of the copter and off we went.

Let me tell you, every muscle, every bone in my body hurt. My face felt hot as did the other extremities that belonged to me. I guessed I'd gotten frost bite. I saw everyone waiting for us on the landing pad near the casino, including Killa and Superintendent Chet Kodis.

When we disembarked, Killa came and just hugged me and clung to me. When she saw the dead body being lifted off the stretcher, she just stared, eyes darkening. I know what she was thinking; she'd seen death stalking us before I left for the mountain. I saw one large tear drop fall down her face and I heard the old Ligithian prayer leave her lips. It was one that we'd hear from her when things were dire.

Translated it went something like this:

Thank you Life for being here, for protecting those we love. Thank you for the breath of creation that sustains us daily. Thank you death for coming and leaving – taking only what you need. Move on to greener pastures, leave us in peace.

Ray looked over at me. He knew then that things must have been bad for our old nursemaid to be chanting her prayer. I saw the pain of it on his face. Last time he had heard the prayer had been when Uncle Jack had died, before that it was at our parent's death. Killa had foreseen each of those incidents. I went over and hugged Ray. "I'll tell you everything but first I have something I have to do."

"Do what you have to," he whispered to me and then turned and took Killa and Julie away.

Chet came over. "Hill filled me in, real bastards," was his only comment.

"I was the fool for not seeing it earlier. I underestimated the Blithies need for revenge. I'll never do that again."

"Even I got fooled," Fred chimed in, "I should have guessed but even I had no idea what lengths they would go to. We have some cleaning up to do at the Dome."

"Yeah, but first we have to some cleaning up to do *here*!" I looked over at Hill.

"Damn right!" she said and we started toward the lodge.

Chapter Fourteen

Hill was faster than both Fred and I. She crossed the middle of the resort where all the chateaus formed a large circular courtyard. My lieutenant didn't stop to look around her at the breathtaking mountains, nor heed her brother as he called out to her. Matt had his skiing gear on. I waved to him but he was busy watching his sister's march towards the lodge. He handed his skis to the guy standing with him and started after his sister. Great, another problem I didn't need.

It was still early morning, the lodge was full. Hill plowed right through the crowd up to the front desk. Matt was right behind her and Fred and I were right behind Matt. I saw her hold up her badge to the clerks. "Let me have your cells", she told them. When they were hesitant, she held up her pistol. It wasn't much of a threat considering the charge was dead. But they didn't know that, especially with the serious look on Hill's face. They all disconnected them from their collars and threw them at her and scattered.

"Hill, what the hell are you doing?" I yelled at her.

Matt pushed his way in front of me, "Judith, what's going on?"

"Stay clear, Matt," she told him and then turned to me. "I don't want them warning Bell that we are coming."

With that said she headed up the stairs, with Fred and I right at her heels. I have to admit that unlike the two of them, I was winded at the top. Hill went right to Bell's office door slamming it open. He was sitting at his desk with Nove Deck standing behind him, talking to someone who was sitting in the high back chair that faced the desk. The look on Paul Bell's face was one of astonishment. We were supposed to be dead.

"Get out!" he screamed. "I'm meeting with someone!"

"You are under arrest for the murder of Lilac Floe, Reich Hisner and Lawren Streng." I announced. "You are to come with us immediately!"

Nove chimed up, "You need a warrant."

"Look on your tabloid," I told the slimy lawyer, "I sent you a copy." I had Hill get one from Judge Button while I was waiting for the helicopter.

It was only then that Hessina's gasp brought our attention to the pale woman. She was the one sitting in the chair. She sat straight up, her hands clutching her small purse, her eyes were wide, her mouth opened in surprise.

"Hessina!" Hill inhaled sharply. "What are you doing here?"

Her friend said nothing, her large bird-like eyes didn't leave Paul Bell's face. She squeaked out, "What are they saying? Did you kill Lawren?" Her voice was high pitched, almost piercing our ear drums.

"Don't be silly, Hessina. Why would I do that?" he looked disdainfully at us. "They are crazy, just looking for an easy out. I'm an easy target."

"I wouldn't pay any attention to them," Nove spouted out. "Why don't you go back up to your suite. We'll discuss the settlement later. Be comforted that the Hildan Co. will take good care of you."

Hill was so angry. I have never seen her unfettered temper but it blossomed at Bell. She slammed her tabloid on the desk, pushing some buttons. Suddenly a small holograph of Lawren Streng stood above it. It was the same one we had witnessed up in the cabin; rather static filled and with a green tinge but it was clear enough.

Hess, if you are seeing this then something has happened to me. I'm sorry. I hope our baby is born without problems. The recording started. Hessina stood up. I noticed she had a small baby bump. Being so thin, she would show early. She leaned over the desk trying to see the hologram. Her eyes stared at her husband as he continued with his message to her. When it was done there was total silence. I hadn't noticed Matt enter the office but he stood next to his sister, astonishment filled his face.

It was Hessina that spoke first. "You took my life away from me. You killed my only chance of happiness…"

"Please Hessina, you are over reacting. It's a fake recording."

"I don't think so," Streng's wife sank back down into the chair clutching her purse so tight she indented the fabric.

"I, again, repeat, you are under arrest…"

"Shut up you pig," Bell spat at me. "You don't know who you are dealing with! My family will squish you until you squeal."

"You're a Blithie, aren't you?" Fred said. "I should have noticed the family likeness before…"

"Oh you're going to be dead too, Mr. Drug cop. And as for you," he pointed to Hill, you'll die a slow painful death. You're the one that snuck that file out! You conniving bitch!"

Matt stepped up putting his arm around Hill's shoulders, "If your family touches one hair on my sister's head, my father, General Pinote will personally see to your family's complete demise. DO YOU UNDERSTAND?" he shouted. Matt wasn't playing the calm diplomat; he was a full blown angry brother.

"Don't waste your breathe on him, he's not worth it." Hill turned to her brother squeezing his arm, affectionately.

Both Paul Bell and Nove Deck looked at Hill, suddenly realizing who she was. Nove spoke quickly, "Please do not think I had anything to do with this!"

"Why you bastard!" Bell spit at the lawyer.

No one had been paying attention to Hessina. She stood up; in her hand was a gun. She didn't say a word and before anyone could react she shot Paul Bell. The gun was on maximum charge and it was at close range. Paul Bell's head literally exploded. Nove Deck got sprayed with guts and gore. It actually looked good on him.

We stood in complete shock for a few seconds. It was Fred who was nearest Hessina. He grabbed the gun out of her hand. She looked at my big detective, craning her neck upward, "That was Lawren's. She collapsed back into her chair crying. "He ruined my life, how could he do that!"

Hill rushed over to her, taking her hand. I noticed we all had some blood on us. I was glad when Chet came rushing in with some of his police. He took charge, calling in his forensic guy. Jarad arrived, he took Hessina away. Chet gave him instructions not to take her off planet.

Before Jarad left, he reminded Nove Deck about who Hessina's father was. Nothing more needed to be said.

When the body had been finally removed and the office sealed off, we all went to change. I trudged up the steps of our chateau and entered the nice warm kitchen with a sense of relief. Ray and Julie were out skiing. Killa just looked at my clothes and shook her head. When I came back out of my bedroom, all cleaned up, my old nursemaid had a cup of java and a huge chocolate muffin for me. I really had no appetite and just picked at it. The effects of last night and the incident at Paul Bell's office had taken a toll on me. I had trouble even keeping my eyes open.

Hill and Fred, with Marcus and Bud trailing behind them, showed up near noon. Hill and Fred looked like hell. Dark rings were around each of their eyes. We filled in Marcus and Bud about the last couple of days. Killa fed us but none of us ate much lunch. For my detectives, it was time to go home. The closest Jump to Logan's Moon and then to Fulton Station was early the next day. We filled out our reports and then they all left. Sleep was on all their agendas.

I finally curled up with my book in front of a roaring fire but not before I called home. Artchie was bubbling up about the dogs and even the cat was behaving itself. I told him Lt. Hill would be on her way back. He laughed, he already knew, she had

called him earlier. Efficient Hill showed me up
again. Damn woman!

I also called my Captain Issam. He listened
quietly as was usual for the Castorian. I told him I
would have Chet send him all the files. Issam
signed off by saying, "How about you have a
relaxing time for the last part of your vacation."

I assured him, I was going to do just that.

"You still have three days to enjoy!" Killa
came over sitting in the chair opposite me. "You
could ski some more?" She was so tiny; her legs
didn't even touch the floor. Her head barely reached
the top of the armchair. She saw me smiling and
just shook her head.

Marty came over with the baby wrapped
tightly in his blankets. She took the last chair
around the fireplace. "Would you like to take him?"
she asked Killa.

"No, you can have him for a while. I have
plenty to do," my usually possessive Ligithian told
her. I was shocked. Had a truce been declared?

"Are we going shopping later?" Marty asked.

"Yes, we'll look for some new jumper sets,"
Killa told her supposed archrival.

I just looked at the two. Harmony actually
reigned in the Brown household. Ray and Julie
walked in, arm in arm. The warmth of it all, I
realized, meant a lot, a whole lot.

I took my book finally glad to relax and read.
I fell sound asleep immediately….

****

The sun was shining. The air was so crystal clear. My lungs couldn't get enough of it.

I was feeling pretty good. General Pinote and Hessina's father, Calis McTenser had brought a lot of pressure that no charges would be filed against Streng's wife. She was too fragile and they claimed the bird like woman was also too mentally ill to go to jail. Nove Deck agreed that it was self-defense. All charges were dropped. Fred was pursuing charging some of the Blithie family but I didn't hold out much hope for that.

"Hey, mister, you gonna add another floor?" I squinted at my helpers who were piling more snow on my masterpiece.

"Sure," I told the young kids who had joined me in my snow endeavor as I sculptured a round doorway into my ice castle.

"I think you could use a few more turrets," a voice came from behind me.

I looked up to see Judy Hill laughing her ass off at my creation. "Well, you try to build them! It's easy for you to criticize," I told her as I threw the perfect snowball in her direction. Of course, I missed.

"Okay," she said coming over to my immense white creation. "Do you want them Romanite style or Pullet style?"

"You know, only you would ask that," I told her.

She actually did a good job, getting my kid helpers to supply the snow. We stood back, looking at my well-sculptured masterpiece. It was good, really good.

"Why aren't you gone?" I asked her.

"I'm staying a couple of days to be with my brother and make sure Hessina gets off to MOSS."

"Seeing Jarad?" I asked her, trying to keep my voice even.

"No, I'm *here*, aren't I?" She had a half smile. "Besides, they are off skiing."

"Why aren't you with them?" I looked at her; the sun was highlighting her auburn hair. She looked quite fetching but I kept that to myself.

"I don't ski," she laughed full out now. "Never have, not my thing. By the way, Julie said to tell you that you will be getting a refund from the ski rental place since she returned your rental equipment early. The lodge returned them to your chateau a couple of days ago."

The relief on my face made my lieutenant smile. "You know Hill, I love you," I joked, knowing I was not really joking.

"I love you too," she joked back and then hit me with a snowball. She didn't miss. The kids picked up on the battle. An all-out snow fight ensued. My castle stood the onslaught. I hadn't lost my touch.

****

I dragged Killa's luggage up to her apartment. It had been an emotional goodbye as my little Ligithian had clung to her grandson. Marty had hugged Killa and assured her that Jimmy would be awaiting her visit soon. All was well.

"I'll be up to make you lunch," Killa informed me. "Judy was going to pick up some fresh vegetables and greens."

I moaned. Here we go again, I thought, healthy, no taste menus. I wondered if I claimed to have to check into the office, if I could sneak out for some pizza and beer.

When I came out of the elevator, Hoover and Bear couldn't stop jumping around. "Whoa, guys, let me come in." I got far enough in to hug them and scratch their ears as they put their paws on my shoulders. I was lucky I didn't tumble over.

I heard the elevator rising. It was too soon for Killa. The dogs knew who it was as they barked and jumped around in front of the elevator doors. Sure enough, Hill stepped out. She was carrying the black demon cat. Stanley meowed loudly.

The dogs just ignored Hill's feline female and just brushed against my Lieutenant. They were looking for their treat. Sure enough, Judy brought out two humongous bones out of her bag. They grabbed them, their jowls jetting out. They looked like they had balloons in their cheeks. They danced around the unfinished part of my apartment. Finally, they settled down, chewing loudly.

"It's going to take me months to get them back to normal," I growled at her.

"No, probably longer," Hill quipped as she let the demon cat down.

The damn black fur ball acted like it owned my apartment. The cat pranced around; rubbing against the dogs. I was shocked as they completely ignored the yellow eyed monster. Then the demon pounced up on my kitchen table and started cleaning herself. She completely seemed at home - on my kitchen table!

"I brought lunch," Hill held out her bag. I could see the vegetables. I frowned deeply. "Or," she continued, "we could go for a ride on your turbocycle and get pizza!" She had her head cocked, her eyes sparkling in a question, looking for my answer.

I bent over laughing. "I'm a bad influence on you, Hill," I chuckled, grabbing her to me. This time I wasn't joking. I kissed her lightly, "Sounds like a good idea. This time, you can call Killa!"

She did and we headed for the elevator. I looked over through my bedroom door. Both the dogs and the cat were sleeping on my bed!

"Hill!" I was trying to find the words as they were caught in my angry throat.

"Isn't that cute!" she chirped, "Come..." she dragged me into the elevator. Damn woman!

Thank you for taking time to read Murder on Hilda, the third book in the Space Detective - A Skip Brown Adventure series.

If you enjoyed it, please consider telling your friends or posting a short review. Word of mouth is any author's best friend and is much appreciated.

Also by Pj Belanger:

THE HOUSES OF STOREM – AN EPIC FANTASY

Vol 1 - The Thunderstone

Vol 2 - The Treachery

Vol 3 - The Triad

COLLECTION OF SHORT STORIES
Sci-Fi a-la-mode
Soldiers One – Warriors of Misfortune
Soldiers Two – Warriors of Courage

THE SKIP BROWN DETECTIVE ADVENTURES

Racing on Nestor – Race to Death

Murder on MOSS – Medical Mayhem

Murder on Hilda – Slippery Slopes

See more information at

www.pjbelanger.com